Double

Roger A. Price

There are different suggested provenances of the term 'Double Cross', but I particularly like the following one.

Before police forces were established, the duty of Constable was a civic role undertaken by various upstanding members of the parish. One of their first duties was to keep a ledger listing all the vagabonds, scoundrels and ne'er-do-wells.

If anyone gave the constable information, he placed a cross against their name, knowing he could speak to that individual again.

However, should such individual prove to be unreliable, the constable would place a second cross against their name to mark them as untrustworthy, and not to be used as a source of information again.

They were 'double crossed'. The meaning of the phrase through time has shifted slightly to its current usage, but amounts to the same thing. (Source unknown).

For Candace.

DOUBLE CROSS

Chapter One

Tommy Broadbent was not who everyone in Liverpool thought he was. He wore a sort of mask in many ways, behind which he was a scruffy man in his early forties riding his luck. Born and honed on the estates of this fine city it made him a natural chameleon. Many thought of Tommy Broadbent as the master criminal; the main man, a local raconteur and an all-round miscreant; including many of the city's police. Yet Tommy Broadbent was living a gross exaggeration; albeit one he was very good at. But he was sick of it and no amount of money would ease his nausea. He lived a double life, and it was wearing heavy on him. And as of five minutes ago, he was also a very frightened man. The text message read, 'RUN. THEY ARE AFTER YOU'. He didn't know who had sent it, and the number was probably that of a burner, but the content had been clear.

He'd known this day could come, even if he was not fully sure why. Though he could hazard a decent guess. It was another reason why he wanted out; he just wished he'd got his backside into gear earlier. He took the threat as real; it fitted in with various narratives he was aware of. He stopped dead when he'd read the message and instinctively looked all around him afterwards, but he couldn't see anyone. He dropped the phone down the nearest grid and took stock while his heartrate eased a little.

Across the road in the near distance under the slate grey sky, he could see the catholic Metropolitan Cathedral on Hope Street. It had a relatively modern circular design and was completely different to the Anglican one situated on the other end of Hope Street; which was a traditional looking cathedral and the largest in the country. Many thought the street was named Hope for spiritual reasons, but Tommy knew it was named after William Hope a local Merchant; probably one of Liverpool's early chancers. As this historical fact flashed through his mind he realised that the onset of sanctuary must be calming his nerves.

1

Although born a catholic, he'd not been a religious man but was turning to God now he was in trouble. The ultimate recruitment drive; once in the shit, they all come running. The same with most criminals; no one would ever talk to the police, until they had no choice. They were never born an informant, just fashioned out of necessity. But the building would provide refuge, somewhere to catch his breath and plan his next move.

Five minutes after the text he walked into the modernist designed catholic building after first ensuring that he had not been followed; he hadn't. He could spot a police foot surveillance unit at any distance, but he could spot a criminal tagging him with one eye shut. He took initial shelter at the rear of the church. The air was cold and smelled musty; it reminded him of attending mass as a child. Then he spied the confessional and headed towards it. He knew that most confessions were normally heard by priests in quiet parts of the vast open space, as opposed to the confessional itself. So that was probably the only private space in the place, it would be ideal for him to collect his thoughts unseen. As expected, it was empty, so he slid into one side and sat down to plan his next move, now that he didn't have to look over his shoulder continually.

Then he heard the sound of someone entering the priest's side. His heart nearly stopped. Had he been followed into the cathedral, after all.. He couldn't see through the divide, which was wooden with swirls and ornate carvings inset; though it let some light through, but not enough to clearly see the person on the other side. Tommy guessed it allowed for privacy while letting sounds pass easily. A few moments passed and he could see enough to realise that the person on the other side was facing forward, saying nothing. He was being paranoid, if the person meant him harm he'd have known by now. He chided himself. A priest must have seen him entering. It was the first time he had been inside one, and if he made proper use of his visit he'd keep the poor priest busy until this time next year. Nevertheless, now calmed, he felt obliged to go along with the charade in order to get rid of the priest, so he could then slip out unseen. He'd already started to hatch a plan of what he should do next, and

2

more importantly, where he should do it; and it wasn't here in Liverpool. He'd outgrown the city, and he knew once he left there was no coming back. He'd known too many criminals who had legged it for a variety of reasons, but for some strange purpose always ended up drifting back once they felt the heat had cooled. Only to live to regret it, or worse; not.

This would be his last day in his beloved Liverpool, but it would always be in his heart. 'You can take the boy out of the city, but you can't take the city out of the boy', or however the old saying went. But first, he'd have to play along with the priest; if he just upped and left he would mark himself in the priest's memory. Better to let things run their course, which would also buy him more time before he braved the streets once more. Plus, whatever was said in here was confidential.

'I'm sorry Father, for I have sinned,' Tommy said, keeping his face forward. He wasn't sure whether people really said that, or whether it was just like that on the telly. There was a pause, and he was about to repeat the comment when the priest replied, 'Yes my son, and confession is good for the soul.'

Tommy stumbled over his words, suddenly feeling nervous as the whole experience started to feel real. The priest reassured him that the Lord was a forgiving God and that confession helped to wash the soul of sin. He started to feel too drawn in and was considering ending it, irrespective of whether he would leave an imprint on the priest's memory.

Then the priest asked, 'And what sins have you committed?'

'Bit of thieving,' Tommy instinctively replied. He decided to ride it out. He'd be gone in a minute or so.

'Thou shall not steal.'

'Bit of extra-marital; but don't tell the bird.'

'Thou shall not commit adultery.'

'Told a few porkies along the way.'

'Thou shall not lie.' After a few seconds the priest continued. 'Is that it, my son?'

'It'll do for starters, Father, won't it?'

Another pause, after which Tommy was starting to feel uncomfortable, if confession was good for you, he wasn't feeling

3

it. He turned to face the divide to thank the priest and say goodbye but the father spoke first.

'You missed out your worst sin.'

'And what would that be?' Tommy said, caught off guard.

'Biting the hand that feeds you.'

Fear raced through Tommy as the realisation of his situation hit him. He impulsively turned to try to see through the small carved holes, but all he saw were the black eyes of the priest looking straight at him. Then he saw something else. The end of a gun barrel pointed at him through one of the holes. But before he could react he saw a flash of fire spit through the carving. He heard no noise, but as he saw the muzzle flash discharge he felt a white-hot searing pain lance its way into his arm, with a punch on its entry that sent him flying off his stool. He saw a second flash as his uninjured arm flayed about like a tendril in a vain attempt to grab support. But he fell out of the confessional and onto the cold hard floor.

He breathed in deeply and tried to look towards his attacker, but his eyelids were too heavy. All he saw was blackness, and then the pain was gone.

***

A man dressed in dark clothing exited the priest's side of the confessional and hurried out of the cathedral as he pulled a hoodie over his head. He was an athletically built man in his thirties, who kept his head down as he exited the building. He was always keen to keep his bald head covered when working due to the large scar across his skull. The result of a knife fight he lost years ago. He hadn't lost one since. He hailed a passing black cab and was gone.

Chapter Two

DS Martin Draker was on his way into their Preston satellite office when his boss DCI Colin Carstairs rang him on his hands-free. 'I'll be there in ten,' he answered with.

'That's why I'm ringing you, can you about-turn and head for the Liverpool Branch Office?'

'No problems. Job on?' Martin knew that as members of the North West Regional Organised Crime Unit (NWROCU) they covered the entire region, including Liverpool and Manchester. Often they would be called on to assist officers in another part of the region; especially when a fully staffed surveillance team was needed, which could number anything from six to sixty officers depending on what the job was.

'You could say that,' Colin replied.

'I take it we are just making up the numbers.'

'Not exactly, it's a strange one and they want officers from outside Liverpool, not sure why. I'll explain what little I know when I see you. I'm just leaving Preston now.'

'OK, see you there,' Martin ended the call and looked for a suitable spot to do a U-turn in the road. "A strange one"; now his interest was truly piqued. Usually, the NWROCU or Rock You as they were sometimes called, targeted active level 2 and 3 criminals proactively rather than investigating crimes after the fact. The latter was normally the preserve of CID, and units such as the Regional Homicide Unit and the Robbery Squad; all serious stuff, but after the crimes had been committed. Though to be fair to Robbery, they also actively targeted robbers that hadn't been caught yet, or against nominals they couldn't prove jobs against. He might try their unit at some time in the future; he quite enjoyed the mix of investigating jobs after they had been committed and catching them red-handed, too. But for now he was happy where he was and had a great working relationship with his boss, Colin. He was fifteen years younger than him and a couple of stone lighter; but they worked well together. Martin was more the tactician with current practical knowhow, whereas

Colin excelled in seeing the bigger picture, and therefore was good at seeing pitfalls before they became a problem. A lot of detectives would love to do a swap with Martin.

Fifty minutes later, he arrived at their Liverpool Office; it was a bland looking commercial unit situated on an industrial estate on the outskirts of the city. It had a fake company sign outside which he knew fooled no one on the estate. He had once called at the morning butty van, to grab an order of bacon barm cakes after an early morning raid, only to be told by the woman serving, "you must be from that secret police place"!

He parked his motor in the underground car park and entered the secure building, noting the time on the clock above the door linking the garage to the upper building. 10 a.m. exactly. He leaped up the stairs two at a time and used a fingerprint entry system to access the main building properly. He expected it to be busy and noisy, but the place sounded deserted. There were four syndicates each representing a separate office, each with their own workload. Often one or two might be out on investigations or surveillance, but there was usually one office at home; but not today.

Martin entered the main briefing room and was surprised to see Detective Chief Superintendent Paul Harding sat at the empty conference table. Harding was the head of Merseyside CID, and as such, nothing to do with ROCU, though his seniority would always hold sway with their operations, but they were never under his direct authority. This told Martin, whatever the job was; it was a top force-level one. Martin had met Harding a few times so there was no need for introductions, he said hello and received a gruff grunt in reply, so headed to the coffee machine. He held an empty cup up in the air, but Harding shook his head.

By the time Martin had made two brews, Colin came rushing in through the door.

'Morning boss,' Martin said, as he handed him a mug of coffee. Colin had a slight paunch which came courtesy of his mainly desk-ridden job of DCI. He thanked Martin and they both joined Harding at the table. Pleasantries passed between the two bosses, and then they got down to business.

6

'Yesterday afternoon there was a shooting in one of the city's cathedrals,' Harding started.

Martin had heard something on the evening news, but the report had given little details, so he just nodded, as did Colin.

'A strange place for a shooting.' Colin added.

'Indeed,' Harding replied.

'Who was shot?' Martin asked.

'I'll get to that,' Harding answered, and then continued. 'It was two rounds at point blank range.'

'Nasty job. But why in a cathedral?' Colin probed.

'Working hypothesis is that the aggrieved was being pursued.'

'So he or she took sanctuary in the church?' Colin asked.

'It's a he, and yes. He was shot in the confessional.'

Must have been some confession, Martin didn't say.

'I'm guessing that the Regional Homicide Unit needs some assistance from the darker arts?' Colin asked.

Martin knew that their unit often supplied the local forces with assistance when it came to covert operations. Merseyside Police had their own capabilities, but sometimes everyone became stretched for resources. The other reason they may need outside help would be for different reasons.

'It's not a homicide job, so the city centre CID has got it. The SIO is a local DI called Phil Devers.'

'Sorry?' Martin and Colin managed to say in unison.

'So he's not dead?' Colin added.

'Correct, but why he isn't is anyone's guess, the last update I received on my way here, was that he had stabilised during the night, and although still classed as critical, he is considered out of danger. Consequently, Homicide who were shadowing and preparing to take over has backed off and left it with the local DI, Phil Devers; who incidentally is one of my best DIs.'

Martin had come across Phil several times and he had always seemed a solid guy. The case would be in good hands with him, he was sure of that.

'So where does the NWROCU - or more specifically - us come in?' Colin asked.

'Phil has been tasked with investigating the shooting, but I want your expertise to run an investigation alongside his.'

Martin couldn't imagine what Harding was actually asking them, but said, 'I know Phil, loosely, so I'll bell him and set up a meet, once you've briefed us on what you want us to do.'

'That's the thing; I told Colin that I wanted you to run a parallel investigation for a reason.'

'Yes, why is that?' Colin asked.

'Because Phil Devers doesn't know, and mustn't know that you are working the same case, albeit from a slightly different perspective.'

Martin and Colin shared a longer look, this time full of incredulity. What Harding was asking would make things very tricky.

'Sorry boss, but you need to be open with us, now.' Colin said.

Harding shifted restlessly in his chair before he answered. 'As I said, Phil is one of my best, but there are certain sensitivities in this case.'

Neither Martin nor Colin said anything; they both left Harding to fill his own void.

After several moments passed, he did, 'OK gents. First up, the name of the shot guy is Tommy Broadbent.' Harding sat back in his chair as the name sank in. Tommy Broadbent needed no introduction, he had long been considered as one of Liverpool's top level criminals, he ran a club called Banging Sounds, and had been arrested a couple of times by Merseyside's Serious Crime detectives, but nothing had ever stuck enough to support a prosecution. He was suspected of dealing drugs, running protection and even on the cusp of getting into forced prostitution.

Martin had even been invited to a top level Tasking Group meeting to discuss whether their mob should target him, but there was not enough intelligence to confirm his supposed level of offending. Martin actually knew Tommy personally, it went back years, but it was not something he would share here today; it wasn't relevant to the matter in hand.

Colin broke the impasse, 'We know of Tommy, as must every senior detective in the area; many of whom will no doubt be arranging street parties. Is that why you want a parallel investigation?'

'You'd be forgiven for thinking so, but no, I know Phil Devers will put any personal feelings aside and do a fair and impartial job.'

'Well, what is it then?' Colin asked.

'To protect Phil, and his investigation into the shooting, which incidentally, we cannot allow to happen in this city; especially in a cathedral, for God's sake.'

Martin nearly smiled at the unintended pun by Harding, but suppressed it. Now was not the time for levity.

'He can never be allowed to know Tommy Broadbent's status.'

Martin could see where this was going, but glanced at Colin, who still looked nonplussed.

'Status. What do you mean by status?' Colin pushed.

'Tommy Broadbent has been, and still is, considered to be one of Merseyside's top informants,' Harding said, as he took a handkerchief from his pocket and mopped his brow as his words sank in. Martin knew historically Tommy had done a bit of grassing, most up-and-coming villains did. But having reached the higher echelons of his criminal empire, or so suspected of, it would be unheard of. It would be a death sentence, no matter how big he was. Now Martin was beginning to understand why there had never been any good intel on him.

'I'm guessing you think that's why he's been shot?' Martin asked.

'Well, it makes sense, and if it is, then his position has been compromised, and if that is true, we need to know how and by whom.'

'Which is why you want outsiders; in case you have an internal problem?' Colin probed.

'Exactly. I don't think we have, but the chief constable feels it is prudent to assume so until we know different.'

Martin and Colin both nodded their understanding. This *was* going to be a tricky one, that's for sure. But the next question was bothering Martin especially as he knew it would cause offence, but he had to ask, 'Sir,' he started obsequiously, which was a bit of a giveaway of the disrespect that was about to arrive, 'I have to ask: is the reason Tommy was never convicted of anything due to his "status"?'

Harding glared at Martin for a few seconds before his face softened and he answered, 'I suppose you have to ask; but no, we run an honest firm here, this is not the 70s or 80s.'

'It's just that if he is considered to be one of your top criminals: we need full disclosure.'

'I'm sure Martin means no offence,' Colin threw in.

Not taking his eyes from Martin, Harding answered, 'He may have been very active in the past, but we are sure for the last few years he has been living off his reputation.'

And his ill-gotten gains, Martin managed not to say.

'That made him a wonderful asset; not active but with all the knowledge accumulated from when he had been. Moral dilemma over.'

'Thanks for clearing that up,' Colin threw in, as the tension in the room started to lower.

'He's legit now,' Harding added. 'Just runs his club Banging Sounds.'

That was no doubt bought from misappropriated funds, Martin was sure of it.

Harding finished his briefing and left Colin and Martin to finish their coffees.

'I'll say it before you do: it's a ball-acher,' Colin said.

'It's the mother and father of all ball-achers.'

'Where do you think we should start?'

'I'm not convinced Tommy hasn't been running the game both ways. But I'll try to keep an open mind for now. Let's go and see if he's fit to speak with. I'm guessing not, but his doctor may have something for us.'

'Agreed,' Colin said, and they both rushed out of the meeting room and headed to the underground garage.

Chapter Three

Colin jumped into Martin's motor; he said he'd pick his up later. They drove to the Royal Liverpool University Hospital, which was a large infirmary next to the Liverpool University as its name suggested. Situated in the centre of the city it was a few hundred metres inland from the Albert Dock and the Liverpool One shopping mall. They were soon on the right floor for the critical care ward where Tommy was being tendered. The fact he had been moved out of Intensive Care was obviously a good sign. But Martin was surprised not to see an armed uniform guarding the room Tommy was in, and said so. Whoever had shot him may want to try and finish the job. He'd obviously upset some serious people.

'Possibly all down to lack of resources, plus, they probably have no live intel to suggest an attack is planned in the hospital,' Colin said.

'Shooting him twice already might be a clue,' Martin answered with.

'Not our call,' Colin said, shrugging his shoulders. 'Might even flag up where he is.'

Ever the diplomatic senior officer, Martin thought. He liked and admired Colin very much, but always knew that all senior officers were members of the imaginary "Ten Gallon Hat Club" where many had substantial egos and rarely criticised one another; well, not in front of junior ranks. He just hoped Harding's decision didn't backfire.

They soon found Tommy's room, it was a private one and they could see him in bed through the opened blinds from the ward corridor window. He looked fast asleep and was wired up to several monitors and drips.

'Can I help you?' a voice from behind said.

Martin and Colin turned to face a female doctor in her thirties.

'How is he doing?' Colin asked.

'Are you relatives?' the doctor asked.

'Not exactly,' Martin said, as he dug his warrant card out and showed it to the doctor who studied it. He noticed her name tag said "Doctor Jane Meadows". 'May I call you Jane?'

'Doctor Meadows will do.'

A bad start Martin thought, she looked irritated. Colin jumped in and gave it the old DCI bit, and Martin could see her demeanour ease slightly. Obviously rank conscious; he bet her nurses loved working with her.

'Okay,' she eventually said, and sighed before continuing: 'Shot twice, first round passed through his right bicep and shoulder, fairly cleanly. The second should have gone through his lungs and heart but hit his side and managed to leave through his abdominals missing anything vital. He is a very lucky man. I suspect he fell awkwardly after the first shot, which is why the second probably missed where the shooter intended.'

'But he was critical at first?' Colin asked.

'He'd lost a lot of blood which nearly killed him. We've replaced it and put him in an enforced coma while we assessed the damage. We thought the second bullet might have nicked his intestines, but when we operated, the damage was mostly limited to entry and exit wounds. Like I say, he's a very lucky man.'

'When could we speak with him?' Martin asked.

Doctor Meadows turned to face Martin and her face hardened again. 'I did tell the other detectives all this.'

'Please humour us; I'll explain more in a minute.'

Another sigh, followed by, 'A day, two at most. We will start to gently bring him out of the coma later, but he may then sleep on naturally for a while and I wouldn't want him disturbed until he's awake and we can assess his cognitive abilities.'

'We aren't going to interrogate him; he's the victim,' Martin said.

Doctor Meadows just glared at Martin. He'd upset her, again.

'Our interest is quite sensitive, and not directly linked to the actual investigation into the shooting,' Colin said.

'Sorry?'

'Well, it sort of is. I'm not explaining this very well; let's just say that there are sensitivities which mean we don't want the other detectives to be aware of our interest, or visits. I'm sorry I can't be any clearer, but it is of the upmost importance.'

'And I thought the NHS wasn't joined up; you lot are far worse.'

Martin knew to keep quiet now and gave Doctor Meadows his best smile to try and repair his previous blunders. It just seemed to bounce off her as she turned to face Colin once more.

'OK, Chief Inspector, your secret's safe with me. But any interviews with my patient will need my prior approval; no exceptions.'

'But of course,' Colin said, and then handed her his calling card.

She fished one out of her pocket and gave it to Colin before she turned and walked briskly away. Once she was out of earshot, Martin said, 'Well, I bet she's a top wheeze on a night out.' Colin just raised his eyebrows in response. 'Well, unless you are a detective chief inspector, that is. I think you've pulled there.'

'You certainly, haven't. You must be losing your touch, come on; let's get out of here before any of Phil Devers' team show up.

***

Lucy Pinder is a Nigerian national, currently residing in an Amsterdam Hotel bedroom. She is in her thirties, highly intelligent and hugely attractive supporting a buzz cut hairstyle cut close to her head, which actually added to her beauty in a way you'd not expect. The almost bald look accentuated her pretty face. She was on the phone. 'Don't give me this "it's not possible shit".'

'Well, damn near,' the caller with a Liverpool accent said.

'Listen, Jason, what do you think we pay you for?'

'I know, I know,' Jason Kinsella replied.

'It's not as if you don't know where he is!'

'I can't believe I messed up. It was point blank range. The first shot to move him, and the second to take out the bits that matter.'

'What happened?'

'He must have twisted and fell in an unnatural angle after the first slug hit him.'

'You're supposed to be the expert.'

'I know, but it's like a batter facing a spin bowler when the ball hits a hole and responds unnaturally.'

'You taking the piss?'

'No honest, just trying to explain. Maybe a cricket analogy wasn't the best to use.'

'Nothing to do with shooting through a lump of wood?'

'I thought I'd positioned the muzzle cleanly through a hole. I guess not.'

'I guess not, too.'

'Point taken.'

'Sort it.'

'I will, I promise.'

'You'd better, or you are in deep shit.'

'Does he know yet?'

'No, I've got that treat to do next.'

'Sorry again.'

Lucy ended the call without further comment.

'Who was that?' a male voice shouted from the bathroom.

'Jason,' Lucy replied.

'Good news I hope?'

Chapter Four

On the relatively short trip from the hospital back to the Liverpool Office, to collect Colin's car, Martin and Colin chatted about what they thought so far. One of the first things they agreed, was as soon as they got back to their satellite office in Preston, thirty miles away, they would get their field analyst working the case, too. Cath Moore was a recent addition to the team, having worked as an analyst for Lancashire Police. Her previous employment being a journalist, which had given her a "detective's nose" as Colin liked to call it. Martin often corrected him by saying that all females genetically had a "detective's nose", which was why he was glad that the gender balance in most CID units was becoming more even.

'I'm not happy at the background Harding has painted of Tommy; Cath is the obvious choice to dig into that and give us a more honest view,' Martin said.

'Agreed, but you do seem to be convinced that he is still actively a bad-un.'

'In my experience, most informants are; to a greater or lesser extent.'

Martin could feel Colin's gaze on him, as he kept his eyes on the road ahead.

'It's more than that, isn't it?'

'I knew him years ago, is all, and I don't trust him,' Martin said, which was true. He could have said more, but now was not the time. He just didn't want to lie to Colin. They had a great relationship, and like all good partnerships, they relied on trust. He just didn't fill in all the blanks; not yet. Colin had a great way of seeing the unseen, hearing the unsaid, and Martin expected supplementary questions, but he appeared to leave it alone, for now.

Cath was also Martin's new girlfriend. They had only been dating for a few months, and before they started seeing each other, Martin had been determined not to get involved again. He hadn't long come through a very traumatic divorce, and as distressing as these things were for all parties involved; Janice had had an extra team player on her side. It had hurt a lot, and still did if he let it. And as with all triangles when they eventually break apart, the innocent angle ended up blaming itself for it all. That's until he'd met Cath; not only had they got on straight away, there was a shared empathy between them. Their long chats had certainly straightened his guilt trips out. She'd been through a similar sort of break up a few years beforehand, so could speak with far more foresight.

They were still living in their separate addresses in Manchester – some of the time – and had both agreed to let nature take its natural course. Then something horrible, yet amazing, had occurred a couple of months ago. They had been involved in an operation where the suspects actively targeted them, intent on murdering them over a new drug called Space Haze, which was killing people. Martin shuddered as he remembered how close things had been. Seriously touch and go. But perversely, the aftermath had moved them closer together with a shared bond he hadn't expected. They really had each other's back, and it was a nice feeling.

Back to the here and now, he knew that Cath would unearth any dirt they needed on Tommy Broadbent. Then Colin broke his thoughts as he prepared to pull into the Liverpool Branch Office car park.

'Talking of Cath has popped a memory bubble from your past.'

'How so?' Martin asked, as he pulled up.

'Your ex, Janice.'

'You must be a mind reader; unfortunately, she crossed my mind just before.'

'Oh, how come?' Colin said, looking surprised.

'Not in a good way, just thinking about Cath and how she is everything Janice was not. How come you're thinking about her?'

'Is she still a nurse?'

'As far as I know, we don't actually communicate now you now.'

'She still work in Liverpool?'

Martin saw where this was going. 'As far as I'm aware, yes. But she could work for several different trusts, let alone the one

16

that the University Hospital is in, or the actual hospital ward matey boy is on…'

'It was just a thought; it would be good to have some eyes and ears on Tommy, that's all, just thinking out loud.'

'Be my guest, Colin, I'll give you her number, or the last one I have for her. No point me trying; I'm the last person she would want to speak to, let alone do a favour for.'

'Be good to know if she is working in the same hospital; then reassess.'

'"Over to you back up" as we say in surveillance terms.'

'I could ask Cath to—'

'Seriously?'

'Perhaps not on second thoughts. Just thinking out loud, again. Hopefully we can speak to Tommy properly tomorrow or the day after, anyway.'

Martin just nodded and Colin thanked him for the lift. They arranged to head back to Preston and bring Cath up-to-speed, but before Colin could alight from the car his phone rang. He looked at the screen and turned to face Martin and said, 'It's Paul Harding.'

Martin nodded and then listened to the one-sided conversation.

'Yes sir.'

Pause.

'No, just picking up my car from our Liverpool office.'

Pause.

'Can do, or will it wait until tomorrow?'

A pause followed and Colin glanced at Martin and then looked away as he continued, 'Understood, I'll be about forty minutes,' he ended the call, and turned to face Martin again.

Martin could feel his ears burning.

'He wants to see me at Merseyside HQ, ASAP.'

Martin restarted the car engine.

Colin unfastened his seat belt and said, 'He wants me to come alone,' and then he shrugged his shoulders before adding, 'It's probably nothing, doubtless just a boss and rank thing.'

Martin was almost relieved. He'd noted the way Harding had gruffly greeted him this morning, and accepted why he was being excluded. Colin would brief him later anyway. 'No probs, Colin,

17

the privileges of rank. I'll head back and brief Cath and catch you later.'

Colin nodded and got out the car.

Fifty minutes later Martin walked into their office inside Preston Central police station. NWROCU rented a small office from the local cops, which was supposed to be a satellite from the main offices in Liverpool and Manchester, but they seemed to be spending an increasing amount of time based there. Plus, the Lancashire chief constable, Don Rogers liked Colin, Martin and Cath and had called on their services specifically on a couple of occasions, which seemed to keep them rooted there.

'Hello stranger, haven't seen much of you over the last few days,' Cath greeted Martin with, as he slumped down behind his desk.

'I know, been stuck in Liverpool all day with Colin.'

'Sounds interesting; anything a top field analyst should know about?'

Martin hesitated, only for a moment as he took in Cath's beauty. It never ceased to amaze him how pretty she was, with her petite figure and strawberry blonde hair.

'What?' she said, as she started to straighten her hair with her fingers in a self-conscious way.

'Sorry, mate, I just still can't believe my luck,' he said, as he made a mock attempt to straighten his own hair, all seven stands of it.

'What have I told you about being so down on yourself. I can't believe how a senior detective, who eats pressure and deals with all sorts, can be so brittle when it comes to himself.'

'Sorry, I must seem like a wimp.' 'You are very good-looking, well, I think so.'

Cath was everything Janice was not. 'Right, you gonna brief me or what?'

'Yep, sure thing. We need to know all we can about a Liverpool nominal named Tommy Broadbent.'

Chapter Five

Martin briefed Cath with all he knew so far, which was limited. She said she'd start with the details of the shooting. As an analyst for the NWROCU she had access to databases from Manchester, Liverpool, Lancashire, Cheshire and Cumbria, which was a recent thing. She said she'd look for similarities with any other shootings across the region, although Martin doubted she'd find any. This was a targeted job, but her thoroughness would confirm or deny it. Colin texted to say he'd be late leaving Liverpool, so would head straight home and catch them tomorrow. His message gave no clues what Paul Harding had wanted, so Martin would have to wait until the morning to find out.

He was still reeling from the shock that Tommy Broadbent was an active top level source. The thought worried him. Martin had been a handler of informants and a source manager, and had spent a period as an acting controller; a role which was normally carried out by a substantive DI. So there wasn't too much he didn't know about running informants. They were like an old vinyl record. They could be the best providers of firm intelligence on the A-side, but pursuing their own agenda nonetheless on the B-side. Many handlers were never comfortable with the moral dilemmas involved. He'd known Tommy Broadbent from a couple of years ago, and what he remembered of him, was that he did nothing that wasn't in his own interests.

'Penny for them?' Cath asked, breaking Martin's thoughts.

'I was just musing whether the horse was pulling the cart or whether the cart was pushing the horse?'

'I've no idea what you are talking about.'

'Tommy Broadbent: if he was no longer the big hitter that a lot of people think he is, and has in fact gone legit—'

'That many do when they have made enough bent dosh,' Cath interjected with.

'Very true, I get that. But if he is making a good living from his club Banging Sounds—'

'And it appears, he is,' Cath interrupted with.

Martin welcomed her insights, but she did have a habit of interrupting; he conceded it was just her way when focused, and took a sip of his cold coffee before continuing. 'So why would he be a top informant if he'd gone legit?'

'Maybe he was just keeping the local CID happy?'

'Could be, but if he was no longer committing crime, how current would his intel be?'

Cath paused this time before she answered, and then said, 'I guess he must pick up bits and pieces in his club.'

'Granted, but it would surely be just tittle-tackle; nothing that he could run with.'

'I guess you'll find out once you can talk to him.'

'I guess.'

'Come on, let's get an early finish for a change and head back to Manchester and make a night of it. You can stop at my gaff if you are a very good boy. I've got a feeling that this job could kick on, and some, from tomorrow.'

'I think you could be right. I'll pick you up at yours at seven. Grab a bite in that Italian restaurant you like?'

'Deal.'

***

Colin closed the manila folder after reading the contents; there wasn't too much additional intel on Tommy Broadbent, but what there was, had included a surprise he hadn't expected. He reached across Paul Harding's desk and handed the file back to him. He now understood why Harding wanted to see him alone. 'I don't actually think this changes too much,' he said, as Harding took the file and fed it through a shredder next to his desk.

'Might add to the picture, but you obviously needed to know.'

'Yes sir.'

'That was the only paper copy, the original is locked away on the secure CHAMPS database.'

Colin knew the acronym stood for CHIS Handling and Management Police System, and CHIS itself was an acronym for

Covert Human Intelligence Source; God the cops did love their wordplay.

'Where to now, Colin?' Harding asked, as he glanced at his wristwatch. Colin guessed the meeting was over.

'I'm going to nip to the hospital on my way home.'

'Don't worry; to reduce your exposure, I'll be the first to know when Broadbent wakes so I can give you the heads up.'

Colin thanked him for that, but didn't want to go into detail about Martin's ex-wife; he knew there were risks involved. He'd had a discrete enquiry made, and not by Cath, only to come up smiling. By a fluke of chance Janice was still a nurse, and worked on the same floor as Broadbent's ward at the University Hospital. But instead, he told Harding that he was visiting a friend who just happened to be in hospital at the moment.

'Nothing serious, I hope?' Harding said, almost robotically.

'Gallstones, that's all.'

Harding said he was relieved to hear it, when of course he was not, and they parted company.

Twenty minutes later Colin hurried into the hospital. He was rushing because by another turn of luck, Janice together with other staff was to receive a commendation this evening at an open reception in a conference room. He planned to squeeze into the back and lose himself among the family and friends, and then try to catch a word with Janice as she left. He wasn't sure how she would receive him, being Martin's boss. He had only met her a couple of times so couldn't see why she would have an issue with him. In truth, he wasn't too sure whether he should approach her, and if he did, what should he actually ask her. Especially, now he knew Harding was able to give him the heads up when Broadbent woke, but Colin was interested to try and find out what other visitors he'd had. He could ask Dr. Meadows, but she probably wouldn't know. A ward nurse would have a better idea.

He decided to distance himself from Martin when he spoke to Janice, just make it sound as if he was keeping tabs on Broadbent; it would be in both their best interests. If she mentioned Martin he would lie and say that he didn't work with

21

him anymore. He was just there in an official capacity due to the shooting.

He tried to sneak in quietly as the ceremony was ongoing, but the bloody door hinge squeaked and several people turned to glare at him as he entered. He put his hand up to apologise and quickly hid behind someone standing at the back. The room was quite large but only the middle section was in play. There were several rows of chairs all front-facing towards a small rostrum, with a distinguished looking man in his sixties on it with a younger model of him stood by. Colin was just in time to watch the older man hand over an A4 sized framed certificate to a nurse who quickly left the stage and retook a seat at the front. It was then that Colin saw that the first row was full of nurses, presumably the award recipients. As he started to scan the back of heads in an effort to recognise Janice, whom Colin seemed to recall used to have a platinum blonde hairdo with purple stripes within, he heard the older man over a loudspeaker.

'And the last award of the evening for Sustained Excellence in Nursing Care in Support of the Trust's Goals…'

God the NHS loved their verbosity more than the cops, Colin thought…

'Goes to, Sister Janice Draker.'

The room applauded and Colin immediately recognised Janice as she walked onto the rostrum to receive her framed certificate. Her hair was just as he remembered. Then, as she was about walk off the stage, a pager-like device on her waist started glowing red and making an audible noise. She studied it before turning to the guy in his sixties and said something inaudible to anyone else. She then rushed off the stage and left the room via a door at the rear. Damn.

The guy on the stage leaned into a mike on a stand in front of him and said, 'Medical Emergency: the dedication of you all knows no end, nor the demands which are placed upon you. Well, that concludes the presentations; light refreshments will be served shortly for those of you who can stay. And it goes without saying that this invitation includes all family and friends at the back. Thank you.'

Colin left via the squeaky hinged door. It hadn't worked out as planned, and maybe that was for the best. It had only been a punt after all, and was probably too risky. Detective work often included taking chances, but this one was probably a step too far. Time to head home.

Chapter Six

Micky Mann or Micky the Man as he liked to be called was a brute for hire. A typical steroid enhanced doorman who worked various clubs throughout Liverpool, including Banging Sounds, which was where he'd met Jason Kinsella. He ran a lot of the security for various pubs and clubs and it was through Kinsella that he made a good living via two side-lines. One, knocking out Charlie to the punters, and two, using his physical skills to intimidate and hurt when required. Tonight's extra-curricular activities involved both. Kinsella had said it was urgent, and as a result, his boss would be paying double; happy days.

He was now sat in the lounge of an empty house in the Anfield district of Liverpool. No one was home, which he knew before he'd kicked the kitchen door in, apart from the black and white Collie he was currently fussing. He pulled a burner phone out of his pocket and sent a text message to the nurse telling her to ring him ASAP. He added that Rover was lonely. He didn't have to wait long before his phone vibrated to announce an incoming from a number with no caller ID, which he took to mean through a switchboard. That was a good sign.

'Yes, remember me, Nursey,' Mann started with.

'Yes, I'm afraid I do, look can't it wait, I'm still at work?' The caller said.

'That's the whole point.'

'What point? And who is Rover?'

'I'm sat in your very nice front room stroking your dog.'

'Oh my God. Don't hurt him, please.'

'Oh course not, just so long as you do as I ask.'

'Look, I'm off the gear now, and I'm saving hard to pay you what I owe, please just leave my dog alone.'

'It doesn't work like that. You owed the boss a lot of money, a lot of money.'

'I know I did.'

'And you also know that the loan was written off should we ever need a favour, you being a nurse and all.'

'Yes, but I thought if I could save up and—'

'Save it sister; you can't pay off the debt now; you agreed to the terms. So listen up; your whole life is on the line here, and I don't just mean your professional life.'

The caller didn't answer and several seconds passed.

'And I'll start with this miserable mutt here, just to warm up. Is that what you want?'

'Of course not. OK what is it I have to do?'

Micky then told her about the patient in her hospital, Tommy Broadbent, and that he was in an induced coma, but due to be brought around.

'What of him?' she asked.

'He must never wake up; something must go wrong, I don't care how you do it, but it must be done tonight.' More silence followed, for longer this time, so Micky added, 'It's you and your mutt, or him. And he's a scumbag that no one will miss; you'd be doing the community a favour.'

'I don't know if I can do it.'

Micky expected this and held his phone out as he kicked the dog. It wasn't a hard blow, just enough to make the dog yelp; probably more out of shock than pain.

'Stop, stop please.'

'Well?'

A further pause followed, and then the nurse whispered, 'Is he an evil man?'

'Oh, the worst, he makes me look like a boy scout,' Micky lied.

'Well, he is on a morphine drip, so a simple mistake could happen,' she whispered.

'I don't care how you do it, sister, and I don't need to know the details. Are you on all night?'

'Until 8 a.m.; I'm on a twelve hour shift due to shortages.'

'Perfect. Me and Rover here will get our heads down and await your call when it's done.'

'It may take a while as I'm on a different ward, so I'll need to engineer a reason to be there in the small hours when it's quiet. Oh my God, I can't believe I'm even saying this.'

'Remember what will happen if you don't.'

'I know.'

'And don't even think about ringing the filth, because if you do, your elderly mother in the next street will also get a visitor.'

The nurse screeched and then stifled it before she added, 'OK, OK, I'm not that stupid. But it might get towards the end of the night before I can swap stuff.'

'I'll be here waiting,' Micky said, and then ended the call.

***

'You need to be more adventurous,' Cath said to Martin as he finished his Hawaiian pizza.

'Now you're talking, sweetheart,' Martin answered, as he spat bread crumbs down his front.

'Not like that, you Wally, I mean your food,' Cath said, and then burst out laughing.

'But I like Hawaiian pizza.'

'I'm not sure the pizza aficionados would agree to pineapple on the hallowed bread.'

They laughed again, and Martin looked at his watch, and said, 'Shall I get the bill?'

'You're keen, lover boy.'

Martin smiled and said, 'For once it's not that, I was just about to tell you, while I was in the Gents I received a text from Colin. They have apparently brought Tommy out of his induced coma and he is now sleeping normally, but as it's evening time they expect he will sleep naturally through the night and then wake in the morning. Col wants us to be there from six-ish so we can have first dibs with him before DI Phil Devers' mob get there. They'll probably start work around eight and then get the word.'

'I can't wait to find out what he says to you, should make my research more directed, and hopefully, easier.'

'I'll kip at mine and catch up with you in the office later when we get back, if you like.'

'Steady on detective, a girl has needs; we don't have to have too early a night do we?'

Martin answered her with a smile a carthorse couldn't kick off, as he put his hand up to call for the bill.

Chapter Seven

Martin asked Colin if he should meet him at the hospital in Liverpool so thereafter they would each have a separate car. Manchester, Liverpool and Preston formed an effective equilateral triangle; each leg approximately thirty miles long, but Colin told him to pick him up en route. He could always nab a pool car later if he needed one. Martin thought nothing of the request and pulled up outside his Trafford address at ten past six. He could see a light on downstairs so knew he was up. And indeed Colin was soon out of the house and joined him in the car. Martin made some small talk as he headed for the A580 East Lancs. Road to take them to Liverpool. Normally he'd have headed for the M62, but he preferred the East Lancs. Road when it wasn't jammed with traffic. And currently things were moving quite nicely.

It didn't take long before Martin realised Colin had something on his mind, all his attempts at conversation had gone unanswered, or received short answers. He was going to leave it and let Colin open up in his own good time, but the atmosphere in the car was building, and to be honest, Colin's noncommittal attitude was beginning to bug him. So he asked, 'Is everything OK, Boss?' Choosing to use "Boss" rather than "Colin". He usually only called him Boss when in the company of other ranks.

'Yes, why do you ask?'

'You just seem a bit withdrawn, that's all.'

'Well, I do need to chat with you before we speak to Tommy.'

Martin knew they would have to agree a strategy before talking to him; if they were allowed to speak to him. 'To be honest, I'm still getting over the shock.'

'You and me both; but you first.'

Martin was unsure what Colin meant but carried on, 'Well, that he supposedly is now an active top level informant.'

'I'm surprised that you are shocked,' Colin said, as he turned to face Martin for the first time since he got in the motor.

27

'Sorry?' Martin said.

'That he is "*now an active top level informant*".'

'He must have been in the serious shit to go over to the dark side, as the villains call it.'

'You keep missing the point.'

'Sorry, Boss, you'll have to spell it out.'

'*Now*, I'm talking about the use of the word *now*.'

'Well, yeah, now as in, criminals at his alleged level don't grass.'

'When were you going to tell me?'

'Tell you what?'

'Tell me that you knew Tommy was a snout?'

Ah, so that was what this entire dance was about. 'How could I have known that he was *now* an informant.'

'Because you recruited him,' Colin said, as his voice rose to a crescendo.

Martin turned to face him and said, 'My God, that was years ago, before he rose to his present level.'

'Keep talking.'

'Look Colin, I would have told you as and when it became relevant; you know how need-to-know works. And back then he was just putting up some poor local level bollocks because he was facing a charge. The charge ended up being dropped anyway, and the stuff he was putting up was vague and dubious at best. Our relationship didn't last.'

'You still should have told me.'

'I'm sorry if I have offended you, but it really wasn't relevant. And anyway, how do you know?'

'That's what Harding wanted yesterday; he showed me the original paper "Recruited Informant File", before he shredded it.'

'Well, you'd have seen the last page then?'

'I'm not sure.' Colin said, suddenly starting to look less hostile.

'The bit where I marked him up as "Considered Dangerous – not to be used again", in bold red ink.'

'That was not there.'

'Then someone has removed it to open the door again.'

'If that's true, it was done for a reason.'

Martin nodded. It was why he was shocked to learn Tommy was an informant again. He could only assume he had been re-recruited recently, but would love to know why. Dangerous Informant markers were rarely, if ever, ignored.

'We'll have to ask him,' Colin said. 'When would you have told me?'

'Either when he recognised me, or during our chat when I would have mentioned it.'

'Fair enough,' Colin said. 'And I'll promise to look surprised. Help protect the integrity of the system.

'I appreciate that,' Martin said, and he did. It wasn't easy recruiting or running snouts, he was glad he was out of that game. 'Do we know who the current handlers are?'

'Yep, both call them themselves John, I put a quick call into one of them last night, we are meeting with them later at our Liverpool Branch Office.'

'Fair enough.'

'And who better than you to sit in and judge what they say and what they don't say.'

Martin nodded, as they pulled into the hospital car park.

Ten minutes later they exited the lift on Tommy Broadbent's ward and headed towards his room. It was just after 7 a.m. and Martin was starting to feel peckish. They were met by Dr. Jane Meadows who looked as friendly as the last time they'd seen her. Martin glanced at Colin who nodded; he'd leave it to him to do the talking.

'Morning Doctor, everything alright?' Colin asked, as they came to a halt just short of Tommy's room.

'It is now, but only just, you wouldn't believe it. What the hell do they teach them nowadays.'

'Sorry. Is our patient OK?'

'Yes.'

'What's happened?'

'A stupid nurse, that's what.'

Martin knew that nurses were far from stupid, and that this doctor was obviously a nightmare to work for, and as tempted as he was to jump in and argue with her; just for the sport of it, he kept his mouth shut and left it to Colin. But he was shocked at what she said next.

'That nurse could have killed him. I'll have to report her.'

Colin asked her what had happened, and Martin was feeling an impending sense of doom.

Dr. Meadows then gave them a lesson in morphine intravenous devices. Apparently, the older versions, which are no longer in use and haven't been for some years, had a self-administering button where the patient could technically push it to receive a booster dose of the painkiller. Same as the newer devices, only the newer ones had a timer attached to prevent a patient from overdosing.

'I take it that the older ones could be pressed repeatedly and each time a further dose of morphine would be released?' Colin asked.

'Exactly, though they were never intended to be administered by the patient, but theoretically they could be. That is why the newer timer failsafe devices were brought in to replace them.'

'How does this relate to Tommy?'

'His device was a newer one, but when he woke a short time ago, he complained of severe pain in his shoulder and the nurse said his device was broken so had changed it.'

Martin was relieved to hear that Tommy was awake, and OK-ish.

'But when I just happened by - and thank God I did - I saw that the replacement device was one of the old ones. I've no idea where she got it from and have sent the silly woman off with an order to stay away until I decide what to do. She claims it was just on the shelf in stores, but I can't see how she wouldn't have realised.'

'Thank God - as you say - that you "happened by",' Colin said. 'I take it that he's only had one extra dose?'

'She'd only just connected it when I walked by, so he'd not had any, thankfully.'

'Is there any more of the old stock?' Martin asked, deciding to join in.

'What do you take me for? Of course not, it was the first thing I checked.'

Martin put his hands up in an attempt to appease her, wishing he'd stayed out of it. Colin glanced at him to tell him to keep quiet.

'I know errors can easily be made, but thankfully, you were on duty, Doctor. That's all I can say,' Colin added.

This seemed to calm Dr. Meadows further, as she stopped to draw breath as Colin's words blew smoke up her derrière.

'I don't suppose we can have five minutes with him?'

She seemed to take an age to consider the request but eventually said, 'Five minutes; no more. I don't want you tiring him out.'

'That's very good of you, doctor, oh, and one last favour.'

'I know, don't tell the other detectives that you've been here,' she said, as she started to turn to walk away.

'Thanks, we appreciate it.'

'He must be very important,' she finished with, and then wandered off.

Colin's phone buzzed and he took it out and read a text message which he replied to, and then turned to face Martin.

'That was Paul Harding: the hospital has told DI Devers that Tommy's awake. He'd only just found out himself,' Colin said, as he raised his eyebrows.

'So much for the advance warning, it's a good job we are already here,' Martin answered with.

'Come on, we need to be quick, they are en route.'

Chapter Eight

Martin and Colin paused by the window to look into Tommy's room, Martin recognised him straight away now he no longer had an oxygen mask on. He still had a couple of drips attached to his arms, one of which Martin guessed was the new morphine one Dr. Meadows had been ranting about. But he was sat up, had some colour in his cheeks and more importantly was awake. Their eyes locked and Martin saw recognition on his face.

'Come on, we haven't got long,' Colin said, as he opened the door to the room.

Martin nodded and followed him in. They both came to a halt at the foot of his bed.

Tommy nodded at Martin and then said, 'DC Draker; it's been a while.'

'It has Tommy, and it's DS Draker now.'

Tommy shrugged and Martin quickly introduced Colin.

'You two investigating who shot me?'

'Not exactly, DI Devers from CID is on his way; he'll be doing that.'

'Ah. Still in that game are you?' he said, and then looked at Colin.

'It's OK, he knows of our prior relationship; you can trust him.'

'What do the two Johns say?'

'Your current handlers know we are here, we are meeting with them later.'

This seemed to relax Tommy, the fact they knew who the two Johns were.

'Look, we haven't got long,' Colin said.

'We just need to know whether the attack was anything to do with your status.'

'Your work with the two Johns?' Colin added.

'No idea. Never saw the bastard's face. And I've no idea what his problem is. Could have been a mistake.'

'So why were you hiding in a church confessional booth?' Martin asked.

'The answer's on the tin.'

'You never struck me as the religious type.'

Tommy just shrugged his shoulders.

'We both know that is bollocks.'

'Is it?'

'A witness saw you enter the church like your arse was on fire,' Martin lied. It was worth an educated punt.

'It was an urgent confession.'

The punt paid off. 'Alright, what were you fessing up to?'

'Nothing that would interest you.'

Martin looked at the wall clock above Tommy's bed; they'd been there nearly five minutes already.

'Is that what you are going to tell the investigating detectives?' Colin asked.

'Pretty much.'

That was something at least, Martin thought.

'How did you know you were in the shit? And don't bull me, we haven't got time,' Martin said, as he saw Colin check his wristwatch.

Tommy didn't answer straight away, but looked deep into Martin's eyes in clear contemplation.

'We got to go,' Colin said to Martin.

'Decision time, Tommy,' Martin said.

'Let's just say I received word.'

'From who?' Martin pushed, as Colin went to the window and scanned the corridor.

'No idea. Could have been from any number of people. Probably one of the doormen I use. I always treated them right. They have the best intel network in this city. Put your lot to shame,' Tommy said, and then laughed, but as he did he twisted and yelped and his hand shot up to his shoulder, he was in obvious discomfort. Martin quickly pulled a calling card from his pocket and handed it to Tommy, not knowing if he would take it or not, but he did, and quickly put it under his bed sheets.

'Martin,' Colin said, with urgency.

Martin kept his gaze on Tommy and said, 'Bell us when you are fit to leave and we will pick you up and take you home. Do a risk assessment of your safety.'

'Why would I need that?'

'Because we both know that this is some sort of feud, or related to your work with the two Johns; and until we know more we have to assume the latter.'

Tommy looked like he was about to argue having opened his mouth quickly, but he paused, said nothing, and then closed it slowly. Martin seized the initiative and added, 'Unless you want the gunman to have a clearer crack at you in a rematch.'

Tommy didn't answer again, and Martin could hear Colin's feet shuffling impatiently around the window. He heard him open the door. He knew time was getting short and said to Tommy, 'What were you working on? And I mean what have you not told the two Johns?'

'Times up,' Colin said.

'Times up,' Martin repeated, and started to turn to leave.

'OK,' Tommy said. 'But not here. I'm probably going to need your help. I'll blag off the other detectives, and not just to protect my little secret with you and the two Johns.'

Martin stopped and turned around, 'Give us a clue, but be quick.'

'I do want out, but it's not what you might think.'

'You always were a bit reluctant.'

'Not just out from you lot.'

'Out from what?'

Tommy looked very uncomfortable with the question, and Colin said, 'Martin we really have to move it.'

'Like I said, it's not what you think,' Tommy eventually said.

'OK, Tommy, just bell us as soon as you are ready to be discharged.'

'Will do.'

'Laters.'

'Laters,' Tommy replied, as Martin joined Colin at the doorway and they quickly slid out of the room and set off towards the lifts at the end of the corridor.

'That was interesting,' Colin said.

'Very,' Martin answered, as they reached a small concourse at the end of the ward corridor. 'It sounds like whatever he wants out from – apart from us, is big.'

'Agreed.'

There were two lifts at the end of the ward, one was on the ground floor, and the other was on its way up.

Martin turned around and located the fire door which led to a staircase. 'It's only three floors and it's downhill. Not worth pushing our luck any further,' he said, as he nodded towards the approaching lift.

Colin was ahead of him and pushed through the fire door and started down the stairs two at a time. Martin was right behind him, and could hear the lift jerking to a halt as the fire door closed shut. Moments later he was down the first steps and out of view from the level they had just left.

They cautiously left the hospital, both looking all around for CID detectives. Martin would recognise them if they saw any. There was just a certain look that CID had. The way they walked, the type of suits, or two pieces outfits they wore, their whole demeanour, male or female. But he saw no one. Colin commented that he would have expected Devers himself to come if he could, and if he did, he may well recognise Martin, even if his staff did not. As Crime Squad detectives, they rarely worse business suits themselves, but dressed mainly in smart casuals which helped them blend in, but Martin was only too aware that he had met Devers, so picked up his pace.

Several minutes later they made it back to the sanctuary of Martin's car. It would have proved tricky explaining what they were doing there, but in truth once they were off Tommy's ward it became easier. They had Colin's mate's gallstones story at the ready.

Martin slowly drove off the car park and Colin asked him what he reckoned to what Tommy had said.

'At least we got past the bullshit wall quite quickly.'

'This means he knows he is in deep shit, just for starters.'

'My thoughts, too,' Martin said. 'He was just sussing out whether he could trust us or not before he caved.'

'Probably worked in our favour that you had once handled him, after all.'

'Yep. Be interesting to hear what the two Johns have to say, or not say.'

'Very much.'

'How much do you want to reveal about this morning's chat with Tommy?' Martin asked.

'I think we should play it safe until we know more. Until we know who we can trust. Let's just say he's blanked us for now.'

'Fair enough, and to be honest he's not exactly told us anything.'

Colin nodded and added, 'I'll do the talking; I want you to study their every move and what they say. Then we'll we reassess.'

'Makes sense; you hungry?'

'Starving,' Colin answered, and rubbed his ample stomach.

'I'm glad you said that, I know a great greasy spoon near here.'

Chapter Nine

Suitably refreshed, Martin and Colin headed to the Liverpool Branch Office on its nondescript industrial estate, and parked in the underground carpark before they headed inside. It was a bit busier than the previous day, but one whole syndicate were out following a team of armed robbers as the intel suggested that today was the day the teddy bears had their picnic. They were in for one hell of a shock. Martin loved those types of jobs. There was no greater adrenalin buzz than taking out the targets before, just before, they committed a robbery. Even the most hardened criminal often shat themselves when the arrest went down. It was why he might consider a move to the robbery squad one day. But consequently, Number Two Syndicate office (no pun intended) would be empty for hours and had been placed at Colin and Martin's disposal.

While they awaited the arrival of Tommy's handlers, Colin logged on to a terminal to do some admin and Martin put a call into Cath at Preston. She answered straight away. 'You're keen,' he started with.

'I'd just ended a call when it went off in my hand,' she said.

'I beg your pardon.'

'Don't be smutty, your thirty whatever-you-are, not thirteen. Anyway, what is your exact age, you've never declared?'

'Does it matter?'

'Clearly, to you.'

'One year older than you.'

'I knew it, get in. Old man.'

Martin laughed and quickly brought her up to speed from the morning's events. And asked how she was getting on?

'Drawing blanks, so far, to be honest. Our Tommy seems to be a very cautious man who avoids leaving footprints at all costs. Historically suspected of drug dealing, and believed to have bought his club from the proceeds, so he may indeed have now gone legit.'

'He's hiding a big secret; we just don't know what.'

'He may be, but he could be a bystander rather than a participant,' Cath added.

Martin knew she was right. 'What's your next move?'

'Probably to get off my backside and do some sniffing around in the field.'

'OK, but be careful.'

'Yes Mother,' Cath said, and then ended the call.

Martin hadn't meant to come across as patronising. Apart from his obvious private concerns for Cath's welfare, he knew the role of Field Intelligence Analyst was new; first trialled by Lancashire, and now adopted by the NWROCU, among others. The police chiefs in their continuing battle to stretch the blue line as widely as possible had rightly come to the conclusion that the gatherers of intelligence don't need to be badged and warrant carrying officers. They didn't need police powers. So by allowing some analysts go out in the field, rather than waiting for others to feed them, it freed up a large number of detectives for other duties where their police powers were needed. It was still a new policy, but Martin could see it stretching to other areas, such as informant handlers, eventually. And as hard as it was to argue against the rationale, it meant the likes of Cath could be exposed to dangers they might not be equipped to handle. The jury was still out.

But he knew Cath was extremely capable and as savvy as anyone. His thoughts were interrupted by Colin's phone going off. He heard him say, 'Please show them through'. The two Johns must be here. He nodded his understanding to Colin as he ended his call.

The two Johns, if indeed that was their names were atypical grey men. Both in their thirties, average build, both with dark hair, but one slightly taller than the other. Greetings and introductions over, they both took a seat opposite with a desk between them. Martin did as per Colin's instructions and sat back in his chair to emphasis his observer status, so they would concentrate on Colin.

'The Authorising Officer for CHIS (Covert Human Intelligence Sources ((snouts))) Detective Chief Superintendent Paul

Harding, has showed me deactivated CHIS File: 2923, but not the current active one.'

Both Johns nodded.

'Only I and DS Draker are added to the need-to-know list.'

More nods.

The taller of the two Johns leant forward to speak as the smaller of the two eased back into his chair, observing; doing a Martin.

'Thanks, we've both been briefed by Mr. Harding.'

'Before we start, this is not a witch hunt into how you two have handled this source.'

Both Johns seem to relax a little.

'We are just after some background.'

'Appreciate that,' the taller John said, before he turned to face the smaller John who nodded his head ever so slightly. Taller John turned back to face Colin. 'OK, we have handled 2923 for two years. His Use and Conduct authorities are for organised crime.'

'Many believe he is one of the biggest organised criminals in the region.'

'If he was, we would have sacked him. He runs his club Banging Sounds and lives off a lot of bulled up reputation.'

'Been nicked a few times though.'

'But never charged. If he had been, then we wouldn't be having this conversation.'

'Fair enough. Good source?'

'He always came up with what sounded like good stuff, but never with any real evidence attached to it.'

'Just pointed you in the right general direction?'

'Pretty much. We were aware that he had been handled previously, but unlike you, we were never given access to that file. Though we understand it wasn't long before.'

Martin stiffened slightly on hearing this.

'And why weren't you shown the old file?' Colin probed.

'It's usual, to be honest. Supposed to prevent handlers from having their judgement clouded. Keeps you objective.'

'And your objective view is?'

'He did give us the names of two big hitters from London, called Danny and Joey, and as far as we are aware they are now firmly on the CID's radar, if not your lot's. So that was good stuff.'

'I feel a "but" coming.'

'But, that's probably it, or the best of it.'

'I've read an intel report about those two, without knowing where it came from, obviously, and they do sound like tasty villains.'

Two more nods.

'Any idea why Tommy was shot, or who by?'

'We were hoping you might tell us.'

'He wasn't very chatty in hospital, but to be fair he'd not been awake long. Said he didn't see the shooter and doesn't know why. Though he did ask after you two.'

'That's nice. No, we have no idea either. It certainly wasn't connected to anything we had ongoing with him.'

'How can you be so sure?'

'Because we had nothing on the go. Haven't had for a quite a while.'

It was Colin's turn to nod. Then he asked, 'What about a compromise over his status?'

'Our greatest fear, but as he wasn't exactly active, we can't see how that could have happened. Mr. Harding has already had a systems check done on CHAMPS and it's all good.'

'Please keep revisiting all that you know in case anything subsequently jumps out.'

'Will do.'

'Anything else?'

Both Johns rose, and the taller one, added, 'Only that he was hard work.'

'How do you mean?' Colin asked, as he stood.

'We had to push him all the time. It was like he didn't really want to be a source, but when we suggested parting company he always looked...'

'Looked what?'

The taller John didn't answer straight away; it looked to Martin as if he was searching for the right word.

And then he said, 'Frightened.'

'Frightened?' Colin repeated.

'Best way I can describe it, but he would always insist on staying a source, even if his face seemed to disagree.'

'OK gents, thanks for your time, we'll keep you updated of any developments.'

Yet more nods, so Martin joined in and offered his hand and said, 'Thanks.'

'No worries,' the taller John said, and they left.

Martin and Colin sat silently for several minutes until they were sure both Johns had gone.

Colin broke the impasse first, 'Well, what do you make of those two?'

'You mean Penn and Teller.'

Colin laughed and said, 'Yeah, the smaller one didn't say much.'

'He didn't say anything, but the unsaid spoke volumes.'

'What do you mean?'

'He was the lead handler, running the show. And it was all prepared.'

'They seemed a bit cagey.'

'Understandable.'

'I tried to put them at ease.'

'It seemed to work. I saw their body language ease.'

'But still guarded.'

'Yep. But so would I be in their position.'

'Granted.'

'The last bit was the most telling for me.'

Colin turned to face Martin.

'His reluctance to be a snout, but never wanting not to be one.'

'Aren't all informants conflicted?'

'Can be. And it may just be that, but their comments struck something with me. It dragged me back, it mirrored how I felt when I ran Tommy, albeit briefly. A gut reaction you won't find written down in any file.'

'Any conclusions?'

'Not yet; but I'm sure of one thing.'

'What's that?'

'Tommy's running a separate agenda, and perhaps has been for a long time. Irrespective of any shit he has currently got himself into.'

Colin added, 'I guess we'll have to wait until he's discharged.'

Chapter Ten

Micky Mann was back at his one-bedroomed apartment situated above a shop near the city centre, and was on his second coffee of the morning whilst awaiting a call back from Jason Kinsella. He really should give the place a clean but couldn't be bothered. He lived alone so only had himself to please. He'd tried the co-habituating thing a couple of times but it had never worked out well for him. The birds always started to assume what he called 'Wife's Rights' after a couple of weeks and started to take liberties. He liked things the way they were.

He'd given Jason the update thirty minutes ago and even he had been surprised by his reaction. Jason had ended the call saying that he would have to get further instructions from his boss, whoever that was. When Micky asked who, he was told it was better he didn't know; fair enough. Micky had gone out of his way to lessen the blow by explaining what Nursey had told him; bad luck and bad timing. He quite liked Nursey if he was being honest, and would love to give her one. He knew he'd come over very aggressively when he'd first spoken to her, but that was just a professional thing. What he found interesting, was that she had done as asked and had nearly got away with it. This told him she was complicit, and would do their bidding. He'd asked Jason to tell his boss that; it meant they could go again, and having a nurse on the payroll was no bad thing. Jason agreed and said that he'd stress the point; he reckoned all would be sweet, but they couldn't risk a further cock-up. He seemed calm, which had wrong footed him, but he knew from experience how Jason could blow hot and cold.

He went for a leak to make room for some more caffeine, and was admiring his naked torso in the bathroom mirror when his phone started to ring. He'd left it on the kitchen table so sprinted back to answer it. Jason never liked to be kept waiting. But it was Nursey again.

'Any news?' she asked.

'Look, I told you not to sweat it and I'd ring you as soon as I'd heard.'

'Yeah, but you're not the one in deep debt and deep shit.'

Micky figured it was time to dial it down a bit; it might even help if he 'threw her a line' about when all the business was taken care of. 'Look, there really shouldn't be a problem.'

'It's alright you saying that. You did stress that I was literally just about to press the blasted dose button when that twat of a doctor interrupted me?'

'Yeah, I did, and that with you being a nurse and all, you could come in very handy in the future, even if you don't get another chance to finish this job.'

'That's what's worrying me; he was already awake when I finished my shift. What if he's not there when I resume tonight?'

'There is always a plan B.'

'You seem very calm compared to last night.'

'Look, I'm sorry about being all heavy with you; I was under orders myself to ensure you did as you were told.'

'And now I have I'll probably never sleep again.'

'It proves your value.'

'I see.'

'And your dog was OK, it was only a tap I gave him to maximize the effect.'

'Well, it certainly worked; though, I had to go and find him when I got home.'

'Yeah, I couldn't be arsed waiting.'

'And what about kicking my back door in?'

A filthy thought flashed through Micky's mind and he realised he could utilise the situation to his advantage. 'Look, sorry about that, again it was for dramatic effect. Once we've sorted this, I'll fix it up for you if you like?'

Nursey didn't take the bait, but instead said, 'Please just ring me when your boss has rung you. I'll not rest until I know where I stand.'

'OK, but don't stress it, it'll be fine, I'm sure, just as long as you do whatever they ask.'

Nursey answered with a weak, 'OK,' and then he ended the call.

***

Cath Moore loved her new job; she had been one of the first analysts to be given free rein to go out into the field to collect intelligence and information that used to be the prerogative of the cops, though things nearly went seriously bad a couple of months ago when she'd been investigating the upsurge in drug deaths caused by an experimental drug, Space Haze. But she hadn't been put off by that. She'd worked as a journalist before, so was used to talking to people. Granted, it was a bit different nosing around into criminals' business, but that was where the real fun was. She checked her lippy in her compact mirror and admired her new bob haircut at the same time. She had planned to wait until Martin and Colin returned, but she'd taken a call from Martin, broadly outlining what they had learnt from Tommy and the two Johns, which turned out not to be much. Certainly, not worth hanging around for.

Cath jumped into her motor and set off down the A59 through Preston which would eventually take her to Liverpool. It would be a slower route than the motorway, but only if the M6 was drama-free, which was rare. Plus, she wanted to take in the area a bit more. If truth be known, as much as she loved living in Manchester, the daily - often two hour plus - commute was a bind. If the NWROCU was going to leave her at the Preston satellite office, she might consider relocating to the area, or perhaps, somewhere in the sticks halfway, just in case she ended back in Manchester. She passed Lancashire police HQ at Hutton on the outskirts of Preston, south of the river Ribble – which gave Preston its southern border - and quite liked the scenery. She knew there were several small villages in the area with old English names such as Walmer Bridge, and Much Hoole, which might be worth a closer look. She might even end up with company if things progressed with Martin. But it was early days. She switched off her mental meanderings to get back on task. She was headed to Liverpool, but had no idea where she should start looking.

The club Banging Sounds was one possibility, though it would be shut to the public at this time. She glanced at the clock on her dashboard - 12.30 p.m. - though there might be someone knocking about clearing up, or suchlike. It was worth a punt. She'd grab a sandwich, and then work out a cover story and go for a snoop around.

***

Micky Mann put the phone down from Jason and rang Nursey. She answered almost immediately, 'Yeah?'

'Told you it would be fine,' he said.

'Go on.'

'He has something he wants you to do for him, and it won't wait.'

'OK, but won't it look strange me coming into the hospital when I'm supposed to be sleeping?'

'We can work around that.'

'What does he want me to do?' she asked, her voice losing its tempo.

'Bit complicated to explain over the phone; we need a face-to-face, I'll text you the details, but need you to make a call first.'

'To whom?'

'Need you to find out when Tommy is likely to be released.'

'It might seem strange ringing in when I'm supposed to be sleeping after a twelve hour nightshift.'

'I need you to do it.

'I suppose I could say I'm concerned about the patient after I mistakenly set up the wrong drip. Ask if he'd accessed it before Dr. Meadows intervened. Say I was distracted when she turned up. I mean I know he hadn't, but she's not to know that.'

'Sounds like a Plan. I'll text you later with the rendezvous details,' Micky finished with, and hung up.

Chapter Eleven

Cath diverted to drive past Tommy Broadbent's home address, first, which was a semi-detached house on the outskirts of the city centre. There was no car on the drive, so she parked on the street and had a walk past. There was no one around and a side glance told her that the place looked unoccupied, which is what she'd expected to find. Emboldened, she decided to push her luck and have a closer look. She couldn't see any CCTV cameras at the front, but knew that there still could be some. A lot of homes had video doorbells, too nowadays so she had a cover story ready in case anyone was home. She nipped down the short path to the front. She couldn't see much through the frosted glass of the front door, but did notice a pile of mail and flyers on the floor behind the door. He clearly lived alone. She turned around in time to see a man in his forties walk down the driveway towards her. She tried to hide her shock and stuttered, 'Just looking for Mr. Broadbent, I'm from the insurance company, looks like he's gone away for a few days.'

The man was tall and well-built and came to a halt; he eyed her for a few seconds before replying. 'Yeah, I'm a neighbour, just coming to put his wheelie bin out, reckon he's gone away, too. Not seen him in a couple of days.'

The man didn't smile and Cath didn't want to hang about, so she wished the man goodbye and hurried past. She felt relieved to get back into her car, and she drove off quickly. She'd been dying to glance behind as she'd walked away, but was fearful in case the man was watching her; it might have looked suspicious if she had. But she was glad to get off the estate; there was something unfriendly about Tommy's neighbour. She checked her chest in the rear view mirror, she often coloured up when she was tense, it was one hell of a tell-tale sign, but she couldn't help it. But she had a crew neck top on today so any blushes were out of view. It amazed her how Martin always looked so calm. She'd been in a couple of stressful situations with him and he never looked ruffled. Though he always claimed afterwards that he was like the proverbial duck on a pond; all calm above the waterline while the feet were going mental below.

Next she drove to Tommy's club, Banging Sounds, which was located in the city centre. It was on a side street off Dale Street 500 metres inland from Strand Street, the main waterfront road. This was close to the Queensway Tunnel - one of the two tunnels that ran under the river Mersey. Parking was tricky so she pulled over on a yellow line and dug out her old press badge and stuck it on the dashboard; it had never let her down so far, and she didn't plan to be long. She noticed that although the place was not open to the public, the shutter covering the front doors was three quarters up, signifying that someone was in.

The shooting of an unnamed individual in a Liverpool cathedral had caused a media storm, so with her old reporter's head on she'd already decided to go in using that as her cover story. She pushed one of the doors open and gingerly walked inside the club, which she could see, was on two levels. Downstairs there was a long bar which seemed to run the length of the place on the right-hand side. Behind it was a scruffy looking man in his thirties busily restocking the mixers. He looked up as she entered, and ambient light from outside briefly added to the poor illumination.

'Sorry, love, as you can see we are not open,' the man said, speaking with a thick Scouse accent. Not one with the rounded vowels of someone born and bred in the suburbs of the city, but more guttural, honed from the inner streets. Rough. It matched the man's look.

'Press; could just do with a minute?'

The man stood up and looked tense. 'I've fuck all to say to the press.'

'But you don't know what the question is?'

'Doesn't matter, yous lot twist it how you like, anyway.'

'I'm just after a bit of background on your boss, Mr. Broadbent, that's all. It's terrible what happened to him.'

'How do you mean?'

'Well, getting shot in the cathedral.'

'Who says it was him?'

'Well, I've just come from the hospital where he is,' she lied. 'And he looked pretty shot to me.'

'Why didn't you ask him about his own background, then?'

'I er, didn't get the chance to speak with him directly,' Cath said, trying not to sound nervous.

'Well, you're not the first to come sniffing around here, and I can only tell you the same; "no comment".'

Cath knew people, especially criminals – if indeed this barman was one – were always cautious around the press. 'Well, I'm sure your boss will be pleased to see how concerned you are.'

On hearing this, the guy glared at her and she wondered if she had pushed him too hard. A long pause ensued before he spoke, 'Get out,' he said.

Cath started to turn to leave when he added, 'And he's not my fucking boss.' He spat the words out and looked as if he had immediately regretted saying it. She stopped and asked him what he meant.

'Well, he is my boss, sort of, but she's the top boss, really. Look, I'm busy and I can't help you add to your story, so I suggest you go and ask the cops what's going on. Though, those fuckers couldn't find their arses with a map.'

'I take it you two didn't get on, then?'

'Look, I wouldn't want him to get hurt; we just had our professional differences, that's all.'

Cath just nodded and thanked him for his time and left before she stamped herself too much on the man's memory. Quick in and out. It was one Martin's mantras. But she was well chuffed with what she had learnt, especially from the unsaid. The guy was obviously no great fan of Tommy's, or the police for that matter. She was glad she hadn't gone in all 'Police Intelligence Analyst'; though most people didn't know what that meant, even when you explained. And the mere mention of the word police here would have done her no favours with this guy. She realised that she hadn't even got his name, but what she had gleaned, was that Tommy was not alone running the club; there was another 'boss'. A 'she', and according to all the official records she'd accessed, there was no mention of anyone else. The trip had been worth it.

But her self-satisfied grin soon dropped from her face as she reached her car; there was a parking violation waiting for her under the windscreen wipers. Damn.

Chapter Twelve

Colin and Martin finished up at the Liverpool office, no reason to travel back to Preston only to then have to continue to Manchester; they might as well both head straight to Manchester from Liverpool. One leg of the triangle rather than two. Before they left, Colin put a quick call into Tommy's ward and a staff nurse confirmed there was no change, and any consideration of him being fit to leave would be deferred until Dr. Meadows had seen him the following morning. Whilst he did that, Martin said he'd called Cath, and had bought her up to date, before telling her to head home.

As they walked into the underground garage, Colin suggested they do another early start and try to speak to Dr. Meadows, and also see if they can get five minutes with Tommy. Anything extra they could garner from him would help Cath's background enquires.

Martin agreed, and then told him what Cath had said about Tommy living alone, the fearsome 'neighbour', and that the club has someone else co-running it.

'My God, she's good. Gets out and about and always comes back with good intel.'

'I guess that's the idea of allowing intelligence analysts out in the field. She just happens to be good at it,' Martin replied with.

'I still worry about her safety, and for all the new field analysts who will follow.'

'Me too; but when I mention it to her, she thinks I'm patronising her.'

'That's because you're too close. I'll have a word as the DCI; get her to have some elementary safety training from the Lancashire police recruitment department. The chief there owes us a few favours, big time.'

'Great idea, and better coming from you. Pity we can't allow her to have baton and CS spray training too.'

Colin thought about that as they came to halt next to Martin's motor, and then added, 'But if we could swear her in as a special constable – albeit in name only – she could then lawfully have access to those things.'

'What a brilliant idea.'

'I do have them occasionally, let me explore that, but don't mention anything until I have.'

'Sure thing.'

Martin then drove them both back to Manchester and dropped Colin off. It made a change to get home at a decent time. He'd been married to Stephanie for ten years and she never ever complained when he worked late, which made him feel all the more guilty when he did. She worked for the NHS in Manchester as an administrator, and had to work late occasionally, too, so part-understood. Nevertheless, a lot of his colleagues' relationships fractured due to the demands of the job. Martin was convinced that his ex-wife Janice had taken up someone else's arms because he couldn't put his around her often enough. And once distance between two people became an accepted norm, it could lead to trouble. Though, he had no such concerns with Stephanie, and he loved her all the more for it.

'You're home early, stranger,' she greeted him with, but with a wide smile on her face. She was in the kitchen pouring herself a glass of wine as he entered.

'Want one?'

'Do pigs defecate rurally,' he answered with, while admiring her as she reached up into the cupboard for an extra glass.

'It's bears, not pigs. You always get that wrong.'

'Well, OK, but don't pigs also do their business in the woods?'

'Well, I guess they do, but that's not the point,' she said, as she poured a second glass and handed it to him.

Colin took a sip of the Chardonnay, and could see that Stephanie had a quizzical look on her face, and that she was looking straight at him. 'What?' he asked.

'You've got five seconds, pig-lover, or the rest of that bottle goes over your head.

'Of course I've noticed. And I love it.'

'Is the right answer,' Stephanie said, as she rocked her head from side to side making her shoulder length hair swish to and fro.

She was a natural blonde and she had had coloured streaks, or highlights put in; or whatever it was they were called. It actually looked great on her, and took years off her age of forty-five, but he chose not to add that as he knew it would probably backfire on him. He often got his compliments wrong, but liked to think that he was learning.

'I thought it time to have a change.'

'Looks great on you, really does.'

'I've been thinking about it for some time but have only just summonsed up enough courage.'

Colin emptied his glass, and said, 'I'm glad you did.'

'It's easy to get in a rut when it's been the same style for so long. You don't think I'm too old, do you?'

Colin was immediately glad that he hadn't given her the 'years off' remark, and said, 'Not at all, you look hot.'

Stephanie smiled at him as she replenished their glasses. She still had that coy look in her armoury that always made his heart rate quicken. 'I'd better make this my last,' he said.

'Why's that, party pooper?'

'Need an early night.'

'Now you're talking.'

Perhaps he should have said that he'd got an early start in the morning instead, but then realised he'd said the right thing, after all.

'Dinner will be in ten minutes, and then you can complement me some more on my new hairdo,' Stephanie said, with glint in her slate grey/blue eyes, before turning to check the oven.

***

Martin walked into Cath's flat carrying a Chinese takeaway as per instructions. They both chatted as they ate, and he gave Cath a more detailed breakdown of his and Colin's conversation with the two Johns.

'Sounds like they were very cautious,' she said, in between mouthfuls of fried rice.

'They were, and I get why, though the shorter one of the two didn't say a word, he left the taller John to speak for both of them.'

'Any thoughts as to why?

'Not sure, to be honest,' he said. And he hadn't, though he did find something about the smaller John a little unsettling. 'But how about you? Every time you go out, you come back with something. Brilliant.'

'Why thank you, kind sir.'

Martin knew he had to be careful so as not to come across condescending. 'You just seem to have this natural ability to get people to talk to you.'

'Well, to be fair the guy in the club wasn't too communicative, and the so called neighbour gave me the creeps.'

'Do you think the "neighbour" had been watching Tommy's place?'

'It looked that way to me, though not sure why, as everyone must know he's in hospital.'

'Unless, they were on the same mission you were on; to see if he lives alone.'

'All they had to do was look through the front door to see the mail piled up on the mat.'

'Yeah, but they are not all as switched on as you,' Martin said, and hoped that came across as he'd intended it. He quickly added, 'You can ask Tommy yourself tomorrow, and about the co-owner at his club.'

Cath stopped eating and looked at him.

'I'd already suggested to Colin that as you are our analyst, it should be you and me who pick him up on release and take him home, or wherever for debrief. And in view of your findings today, that confirms the decision.'

'Excellent and Colin's OK with that?'

'Absolutely, you are doing the background and I've handled him in the past; makes sense.'

Martin then elaborated that they should all go to the hospital early doors. Colin was going to speak to Dr. Meadows while Cath and he tried to grab five minutes with Tommy. 'It will give me an opportunity to introduce you prior to his release,' he added.

'Any idea when that'll be?'

'Don't think it'll be long. I think we should both house ourselves at the Liverpool office from now on until we get the call.'

'Makes sense, in fact, I could do with access to a NWROCU terminal before we see him. I'll set off a bit earlier in the morning and then meet you and Colin in the hospital car park, if that's OK?'

'That's fine.'

'So I guess an early, early night is in order then.'

'Now you're talking,' Martin said, as he hurriedly finished off his Chow Mein.

'Stand down, lover boy, that'll keep. I need to shower and wash my hair before tomorrow if I'm up mega early. It'll mean I won't have to mess around with it too much in the morning, it'll save me time.'

Martin wasn't sure how time spent or saved now would be any different to time spent or saved in the morning, but smiled warmly as he hid his disappointment. Cath's hair always looked so nice, but he didn't envy her, or any woman. All he had to do with his was wet it, and run his fingers through it, job done.

She looked at him as she ran her fingers through her hair – which wasn't helpful in supressing his ardour.

'I'm actually thinking of changing my hair,' she said.

Martin knew he had to be very careful what he said next; he would be dammed whichever way he jumped. Since he had known Cath, she'd had her hair dark, light, with highlights, without highlights, and was currently back to her natural strawberry blonde. All her hairstyles had looked great, and he knew it was totally her choice that mattered. So he jumped on the fence and said, 'However you choose to have your hair will look stunning.'

She smiled back at him and said, 'I'm considering having purple streaks put it, it's totally on trend at the moment. She then bent down to pick up their empty food cartons and Martin smiled back at her while inwardly cringing.

Chapter Thirteen

It was just after seven when Colin rushed into the office they were using at Liverpool Branch Office. Martin and Cath were already there, and Cath was beavering away on one of the secure database terminals. 'Sorry I'm a bit late,' he said, as he thanked Cath as she passed him a cup of coffee.

'It'll be lukewarm at best I'm afraid,' she said.

Colin nodded and emptied the cup in two gulps; he was regretting the second bottle of Chardonnay that Stephanie had insisted on taking upstairs. And on a school night, too. She'd have to have her hair done more often.

Five minutes later, he and Martin left in one car, Martin volunteered to drive. Cath said she'd only be five or ten minutes behind them and would text them as she approached the ward. So in view of that, and the fact that it was still relatively early, Martin suggested that they had time to do a MacDonald's run. They were coming into the city close to Bootle Docks which were on the northern side of Liverpool, and he said that he knew of a 24 hour drive-though.

'Is it that obvious?' Colin asked.

Martin grinned back at him and said, 'Looks like someone had a good night.'

'Makes a change from you.'

'You're right as it happens; a hair related issue got in the way.'

'Actually, it was a hair related issue that did it for me,' Colin replied.

Both men laughed though neither could have understood exactly why.

'How is it that you know the location of every Maccy Ds or any other fast food outlet, anywhere?' Colin said, changing the subject.

'If you had spent as many years doing early morning surveillance as I have, you would too. Every time we had intelligence that a target criminal was going to do something really naughty, we had to plot up on him or her from early doors.

Just in case they broke the habit of a lifetime and got their arses out of bed before midday.'

'Better that than miss them, I guess.'

'Exactly, but the upshot was that you sat on plot around the target's address for bleeding hours before you got the "off", so you quickly learnt to keep up your food intake; never knowing when the next chance would come once you were up and running following the target.'

Colin knew this though he'd never done much surveillance, other than riding in the command car. He wasn't officially surveillance trained like Martin, and had nothing but respect for the artisans of the craft.

'In fact, sometimes we used to use a yellow highlighter pen on the operational order map of the target's home address. The map would show where all the teams were due to plot up around the address. The yellow highlighted rounded M would show the nearest MacDonald's outlet.'

Colin laughed, and Martin added, 'And it was rare that any of the targets didn't live close to one. Don't ask me why, but it was rare.'

Colin laughed again, as Martin headed into Bootle itself, the northern town/suburb that the docks were named after. He could see an illuminated yellow M sign in the distance, and was starting to salivate when their car's multi-channel set burst into life on the Merseyside Police's white channel - which was their overall channel, separate to their area ones.

'All patrols; we have report of a body on waste ground at the city centre side of Bootle Docks; attending call signs please,' the voice from their radio said. This was followed by a number of call signs shouting up. The nearest one being just minutes away from the scene, a uniformed patrol designated November Charlie Two.

Martin drove into the restaurant's 'drive thru' lane which was empty. It was still only 7.30 a.m. and Colin turned the radio set's volume down as Martin gave their order. Two minutes later they pulled out of the car park and Colin turned the set volume back up. He was aware they were not part of Merseyside Police, but they were still detectives and only a few minutes away from a potential crime scene.

Then the radio kicked back into life; *'CH to November Charlie Two, go ahead.'* Colin knew that 'CH' was the Merseyside Police's Force Control Room.

'November Charlie Two, to CH; I need an ambulance fast. There is a body here though I can't find a pulse and the body appears cold. I haven't attempted CPR as there seems little point.'

'CH received, paramedics are already en route and should be with you any second.'

'I think we need CID turning out,' November Charlie Two's voice added.

'CH received; the night DI is tied up with another body south of the river. I'll have to turn local CID out. Be with you as soon as we can muster them.'

'November Charlie Two received. Paramedics are here now. Standby.'

Colin looked at Martin and then at their two brown paper food bags. He knew it wasn't their jurisdiction but they were so close, the least they could do was to offer to protect the scene until local CID arrived. 'Looks like breakfast is off,' he said.

Martin nodded and threw his paper bag onto the back seat.

'November Charlie Two, to CH; paramedics confirm life extinct. And as they turned the body over, gunshot wounds were obvious. It's murder.'

Colin glanced at Martin as he threw his own bag of food onto the back seat and grabbed the radio handset. 'One CS Ten to CH; urgent.' He knew the use of the word 'urgent' would cut across the radio traffic, which was starting to increase dramatically as two further uniform patrols announced their arrival at the scene.

'One CS Ten, go ahead,' the control room operator said, with surprise in their voice.

'One CS Ten, we are on duty but not active and are only two minutes away; do you wish us to make and preserve until local CID arrive?'

'One CS Ten, much thanks, please make to the scene.'

'Roger, en route. One away.'

Martin accelerated hard and flicked a switch on the dashboard which Colin knew activated blue lights hidden in the car's front grill and in the rear indicator light housings. He could see the reflection bounce off parked cars as they whizzed past, confirming their operation.

As Martin concentrated on driving fast Colin sent a couple of instructions to the uniforms patrols on scene, via CH, to start a cordon, to keep outside of it, and commence a scene log.

They were soon screeching to a halt behind three parked livered vehicles on Derby Road close to Canada Dock, which was on the south side of the docks just two miles out from the city centre. One PC was stood guard with a clipboard by an unmade path which led onto waste ground on the city side of the huge wharf. Colin knew it had been built in the mid-1800s with a lot of timber from Canada, hence the name. But where they were now was not really part of the actual dock itself, but land adjacent. It looked as if it had been fenced and earmarked for renovation of some sort.

Two more PCs were busy with the scene tape and Colin could see a sergeant stood twenty or thirty metres in from the road. His bottom half was obscured suggesting that he was stood below road level.

He and Martin went to the boot of their vehicle where there were several packets of white paper over-suits and plastic overshoes. Colin was first to don his kit while Martin was still hopping around.

'I'll head in,' Colin said.

'I'll catch you up; this one is the wrong size.'

Two minutes later, Colin introduced himself to the sergeant as he took in the scene. There was a deep hollow set in the centre of the waste ground, which in turn was half-filled with water. At the water's edge was the body. It had been face down according to the sergeant's report until the paramedics turned it over and saw the gunshot wound; straight through the neck. That's when they'd left it and backed out to try and preserve as much of the scene as possible. The sergeant pointed to footmarks in the soft wet earth as the most likely egress taken by the killer or killers.

'Only one set of those footprints are ours. The paramedics jumped over the grass mound next to them,' the sergeant said.

Colin nodded his understanding and appreciation. He moved to one side, a neutral side as much as he could guess, and stepped forward a couple of spaces to get a better look. It was fairly light now, but cloudy, which didn't help. He intended to have a quick peep from where he was – about five metres away – before requesting a cover be put up ASAP. As if reading his mind the sergeant said, 'CSIs are five away; we'll get a tent up as soon as they arrive.'

Colin nodded as he took in the scene. The body was female, shot through the back of the neck, but at sufficient angle that the exit wound went through the mouth taking the jaw and the bottom half of the face with it. This was clearly murder. There is no way you could get the muzzle of a gun cleanly behind one's neck at that angle to commit suicide. Arms and wrists didn't go that far around. He guessed the female was in her thirties or forties, and knew it would take DNA to formally ID the body, which would take time. He wondered if that was in the killer's mind, too. Take out half the face and all the teeth and make ID difficult.

Though they hadn't got it quite right; the exit wound was through the mouth, and even though it had smashed all her teeth, or so it appeared from this distance, the mouth itself provided little in way of resistance to the exiting round. The face was part covered in blood and mud, but he reckoned a visual ID may still be possible once cleaned up.

The next thing he noticed made him even sadder, if that was possible; the female victim was wearing a NHS nurse's uniform. 'Who in their right mind would want to kill a nurse, for God's sake,' he said, to no one in particular.

The sergeant just shrugged at the obviously rhetorical question.

Then Colin risked a further step forward to try and get a clearer look. That's when he saw it. The hair, although covered in mud and blood, it was shoulder length, and blonde.

Blonde with striking purple streaks through it.

Chapter Fourteen

Micky Mann pulled up outside Liverpool Lime Street railway station in a borrowed blue Ford Mondeo. He glanced around to try and see which direction Jason Kinsella would arrive from. The guy was always a bit of an enigma and kept his own counsel. It wouldn't surprise him if he wasn't arriving by train, but just wanted Micky to think he was. But as he scanned all around he heard the passenger door open which made him jump. 'Where the fuck did you come from?'

'I'm hardly hard to miss, you should be more alert,' Kinsella said, as he heaved his chemically enhanced frame into the car next to Micky's steroid furthered body. If Micky had picked a smaller car they'd be rubbing shoulders.

'Come on before we get clocked,' Kinsella said, as he pulled a small black rucksack from his shoulder and stuck it into the passenger side foot well.

Micky nodded as he put the car into gear and drove away from the station's huge frontage.

'You still a bit nervous after last night?'

'A bit jumpy, yes.'

'Don't stress it, bro, it's natural. You done good, anyway. The boss is well-pleased. Should be a little extra for you.'

Micky smiled at the thought of a bumper pay day; though Kinsella hadn't actually told him what killing a nurse was worth.

'Also, good intel you managed to get from her before she went swimming,' Kinsella said, and then slapped Micky on his shoulder dragging the wheel slightly.

Micky righted the car and Kinsella asked him about the motor's provenance. 'It's all legit; from a scrapper, so will pass any checks but no one will miss it,' he answered.

'Excellent,' Kinsella said, and then heavy handed his shoulder again, but he was ready for it this time and gripped the wheel tighter to keep them going straight.

'Tell me again about the other issue,' Kinsella said.

'This tart turned up at Tommy's. Said she was from Insurance, but it was shit.'

'Why's that, bro?'

''cause before I approached her, I clocked her giving it nose through the front door.'

'Wondering why he wasn't in?'

'That was my take.'

'Let's hope you are wrong, the last thing we need is some bird to sort out, too. Who knows what Tommy might have told her?'

'On that, I don't know what Tommy has or hasn't done—'

'Better you don't.'

'Or what he might know that he could have shared with any bird—'

'Better you don't know.'

'But if that could be an issue, then we might have a problem.'

Kinsella turned to face Micky, who glanced at him. He didn't look happy.

'Go on,' Kinsella said.

'Well, like I said, I didn't buy the Insurance shit, so when she left, I followed her.'

'And?'

'She went straight to Banging Sounds. I parked so I could follow her when she left, but a bleeding meter maid showed up so I had to do one.'

'Fuck. We need to find out who she is.'

'Can't we just ask the guys at the club? The place wasn't open but someone was obviously inside.'

Kinsella didn't answer, and Micky glanced at him again. This time he was looking straight ahead in clear contemplation. Micky didn't know what was troubling him, but offered to take him straight to club if he wished.

'No,' Kinsella shouted, then lowered his voice and said, 'let's just drive past the dock, see if Nursey has been discovered yet.'

'OK,' Micky answered, who thought better than to question Kinsella as to why he wouldn't want to speak to whomever the woman had spoken to at the club. Probably better he didn't know that, too.

Five minutes later they headed up Derby Road away from the city, Micky could see several police cars parked up with their blue lights flashing, close to Canada Dock. 'Damn, I thought it would take longer than this. I put rocks in her pockets and pushed her out into a sort of manmade mini-lake. Thought she'd be there until the diggers found her, and that could be weeks away,' Micky said, sheepishly.

'Don't sweat it, they were always going to find her, probably some dog-walking wanker,' Kinsella said, in very calm way.

Micky relaxed, he'd have thought Kinsella would have been annoyed that he hadn't managed to sink the body properly, and wasn't sure why he was so ambivalent about it. But he knew better than to push his luck and ask why. They both kept their gazes to the front as they passed the scene, and as soon as they had, Micky asked where Kinsella wanted to go next. He told him, and Micky nodded, realising he'd have to find an alternative route back into the city centre.

***

Martin had tried two paper over-suits on before he realised that the remainder were all small or medium. Colin must have picked up the last large one, so he gave up and made do with just his legs in, and the top half - which he couldn't get anywhere near his shoulders - tied around his waist with the arms. He had his overshoes on, so at least his feet and lower legs were covered, which was the main thing really; especially as they were only going to have a quick look. They'd leave it all to the local DI when he arrived with his team.

Martin found it difficult to walk as he ambled down the path, the crotch of the paper suit hung low from his own groin making it difficult to move his legs easily - and some might call that fashion! He nearly gave up and left it to Colin, but he was curious. As he stumbled down the uneven mud path like a drunken Charlie Chaplain, he saw Colin stood facing his way, he looked shocked.

'It's the best I could do,' Martin said, as he pointed to his legs, but Colin didn't seem to hear him or notice him, until he was nearly on him. Then he suddenly sprang to life.

'Martin, stay where you are.'

'Sorry?'

'Stop,' Colin shouted, and he instinctively did.

Colin rushed up to Martin and stood directly in front of him, blocking the path. 'What is it?' he asked.

Colin just stared at Martin.

'What?'

'I don't know how to tell you this, but the body is female. A nurse.'

Martin didn't understand, 'OK it's a nurse; you just said, that wasn't too difficult was it,' Martin said, trying and failing not to sound sarcastic.

Colin put his hands on Martin's shoulders and said, 'Yes, a nurse. But this one has blonde hair with purple streaks in it.'

Martin noticed a uniformed sergeant looking on, perplexed. He wasn't the only one confused. 'So?' he asked.

'So who do you know who is a nurse and has hair like that?'

Martin was beginning to feel irritated and was about to ask Colin to spit it out when his last words took root. 'Oh my God, you're not suggesting…' he said, leaving his sentence unfinished.

'I'm afraid I am.'

'But how? Why?'

'Shot through the back of the neck. As to why, only God knows.'

Thoughts were now racing through Martin's mind, he had loved his ex once, and although they hadn't parted on the best of terms, he would always have a fond spot with her name on it, and would never wish her any harm. Then a naturally defensive reaction kicked in. 'Hang on, it's a pretty normal for women to have streaks in their hair, and you've not seen her for years.'

Colin didn't answer, but had that look on his face, the one where he looks like he is about to disagree with you, but for some reason is delaying doing so. Martin had seen it many times when they had debated issues. It was as if he was collecting his thoughts to make sure he blew you out the water with irrefutable argument. A sort of boss-type reaction, Martin had always thought. But today, Colin's grim facade said more. 'When?' he asked.

'The other night, I popped to the hospital and saw her, but not to speak to.'

'You never said.'

'That doesn't matter now, I'll explain later, but for now you just need to—'

Martin took his opportunity and sidestepped Colin and nearly fell flat on his face in doing so. In different circumstances it would have looked hilarious. He made it as far as a raised mound of grass when he came to a halt. The deceased body of a female nurse was now laid on its side; its face - what was left of it - was half-obscured, but he could see enough. It was Janice, he knew it, he was sure of it. Colin had been right. Utter shock flew through him in an icy torrent. He started to shake as he felt hands on his shoulders from behind.

'That's far enough, and that's an order.'

Martin knew that Colin never gave orders, just requests that you knew had to be followed. But he never used the word 'order' it wasn't his style, which added to the gravitas of it now.

He was spun around to face Colin, still speechless. 'Come on Martin, you've seen all you need to and this is now a crime scene.'

He knew his boss was right, and gave up the fight and let him put his arm around his shoulder and guide him back onto the path, and away from the grisly spectacle. Halfway back to the car Martin found his voice, 'Why the hell would anyone want to shoot a nurse dead?'

Colin didn't answer as they checked out with the cop with the clipboard. They then bagged and tagged their overalls and Colin attached exhibit labels to the two plastic bags and handed them to the cop with the scene log, as Martin climbed back into his car.

As the initial shockwave started to pass, Martin glanced up to see DI Phil Devers arrive on foot. He saw Colin approach and talk to him. By the time Colin turned to return to their motor, he was starting to get a grip of himself, he had to; it was the only way to deal with shock. Grip it, own it and get on top of it. The time for grief would have to wait.

'I've briefed Phil Devers,' Colin said, as he got back into the car. 'He's already sent a team to the hospital to do urgent background on all of Janice's workmates - if there is a motive, maybe they will find it there.'

'Random killings by passing nutters aren't usually done execution style with a handgun,' Martin said.

Colin didn't reply but then said, 'I'll run you home, you've had a huge shock.'

But before he could argue, Colin's phone burst into life, so he just listened as Colin took the call. Colin didn't say anything; he just listened until the end, and then said, 'Will do, sir.'

'Christ, talk about bad timing,' he said, as soon as he put his phone down.

'Paul Harding?'

'Yes, he's giving us the heads up, Tommy is about to be released, he says he can give us thirty minutes before he'll have to let Phil Devers know.'

'No time to waste, then.'

'Not you, me and Cath can do it. You're going home.'

Martin knew that Colin was only saying what he would have said, but also knew that sitting at home mulling over what had happened would drive him nuts. He needed to be doing, and to be doing something with purpose. But he needed an excuse, so said, 'Thanks, Colin but no disrespect, it has to be me and Cath.'

'Why's that?'

'Because I'm the only one out of us who is advanced driver and mobile surveillance trained.'

'Why is that important?'

'We have to get Tommy somewhere safe, and quickly and efficiently. Not that anyone else knows he's being discharged, they don't. But it makes sense to cover all possibilities.'

Colin gave Martin one of his 'about to vehemently disagree with you' looks, but this time relented. 'I guess it makes sense. We've had enough shocks for one morning.'

'Cheers,' Martin said, as Colin started the car engine. 'And you'd be doing me a great favour, I need to keep active.'

'OK, but I'll be keeping my eye on you.'

'For which I'm very grateful.'

'Alright, I'll put my nose around the ward before Phil's detectives turn up, see if I can't learn more about this awful event. Help you make some sense of it.'

'Thanks, thanks a lot.'

Chapter Fifteen

Twenty minutes later, Colin pulled over in a quiet corner of the university hospital cark park near to Cath's car. They swopped seats and Colin rang Cath to explain why they were late, and she was out of her car and into the back of theirs before Martin had turned the engine off.

'Martin, oh Martin, I'm so sorry,' she said, with genuine sympathy.

Martin looked at her via the rear view mirror and was conscious of not showing her too much emotion. He didn't want to sully Janice's memory, but was critically aware of getting his response proportionate; he didn't want Cath to think he was still in love with Janice, he was not. 'It was a hell of a shock, but thanks, Cath.'

'You sure you should be here?' she asked.

Martin glanced at Colin, and then answered, 'I'm fine, honest. It's Janice's partner who won't be.'

'OK,' Cath said. 'So what's the plan?'

'As discussed, you and Martin go and get Tommy. I'll try and have a word with Dr. Meadows and see if I can't pick anything up. The detectives en route, if not here already, will be those working on the attack on Janice,' Colin glanced at his watch, 'we have ten minutes before they are told Tommy is fit to discharge. Another team will no doubt be dispatched to collect him. We'd better get going.'

Colin then said he'd make his own way into the hospital and quickly got out of the car and walked across the car park towards the main entrance. Cath jumped into the front passenger seat and Martin drove to a space reserved for waiting ambulances close to the main doors. He asked Cath to stay with the vehicle to deal with any security attention and he would explain Cath's presence to Tommy as he led him out.

Once past reception, Martin ran up the staircase to save time and was quickly at Tommy's room. He was relieved to see that he was sat in the chair next to his bed, dressed and ready to go; as per Martin's texted instruction half an hour ago.

'I'm actually glad to see you,' Tommy said, as he entered the room. 'I don't know what's going on, but there are cops everywhere. I thought they had beaten you to it at first.'

'No, it's something else non-related, I'll fill you in as we leave, but we have only minutes before the CID investigating the attack on you know that you are fit to be released, and will be coming to collect you.'

'We'd better get a shift on then,' Tommy said, standing up.

Martin noticed his left arm was in a sling and he winched in discomfort as he stood. 'You fit to take the stairs?'

Tommy nodded his understanding and Martin led him out of the room. He glanced both ways to make sure they didn't run straight into DI Devers. Though he guessed he would be tied up at Canada Dock for some time. It would be someone else coming for Tommy on his behalf. Checking left, he just clocked the back of Colin as he entered Dr. Meadows' office, and checking right, the ward was clear to the end concourse where the lifts and stairs were.

Tommy was clearly walking as fast as he could, but it was no more than a quick amble and Martin's heartrate started to rise as they reached the end of the ward and an audible ding announced the arrival of an elevator. He managed to get Tommy through the fire door first, and didn't look back as he followed. He could hear the lift doors start to open as he did. Twice in a matter of days with seconds to spare.

'Where's your boss, Colin?' Tommy asked.

'He's tied up but I've brought a very nice analyst for you to meet instead.'

'Hold up, is there anyone you haven't told about me?'

Martin didn't have time for this; Tommy came to a halt on the stairway and turned to face him. 'She 100% trustworthy and no one else knows about you, absolutely no one. You have my word.'

This seemed to reassure Tommy as he nodded and turned forward again and resumed his decent down the stairs.

They were soon out of the hospital and into Martin's car; Tommy stretched out in the back and Martin took the wheel. Introductions over, he started the engine and looked at Tommy in the eyes via the driver's mirror. 'Can't wait to hear.'

'Hear what?' Tommy said.

'To hear what exactly you are running from?'

Tommy looked away without answering.

'Because you are running,' Martin said, as he started to wonder whether Tommy was going backwards since they'd first spoken.' He glanced at Cath as he turned to reverse the car out of the ambulance parking spot. He could see she got it, too.

'I'll be honest with you, Tommy, part of my job is to get all the background info I can on you,' Cath said.

'Well, good luck with that, you'll not find much there,' he said.

'I had to double check something this morning, but discovered that you do have a long lost brother, and that he is your only known family. Is that right?'

'He's dead to me. Not spoken in many, many years.'

Martin was impressed with Cath; it must have been the result of her early turn out. He smiled at her and she grinned an apology. None needed, it had been a hectic morning with little time to talk properly. 'I never knew you had a brother?' Martin said, while still reversing the car, and looking straight at Tommy.

He shrugged and said, 'Does it matter?'

'It does if we need to find somewhere safe for you to go to.'

'Trust me, that's not an option.'

'You do realise that you are in serious danger, don't you?'

'I'm coming round; you caught me at a low ebb the other day. Just need a lift and help to sort a couple of things out and I'll be fine.'

He was going backwards.

'You know about that nurse who cocked up your morphine tube the other day?' Cath said.

'Yeah, what of it?'

'Well, what if it wasn't a cock-up; what if she had more nefarious intentions?' Cath said, and then side-glanced at Martin.

He saw where she was going with this, good bullshit to scare the crap out of Tommy and get him back on side. He nodded.

'What a nurse? Who could get a nurse to do something that dodgy?' Tommy said.

Martin knew what was coming next and glanced at Cath as he drove along the car park road towards an exit. She mouthed "sorry" at him and he nodded for her to continue.

'The same nutter who shot a nurse dead last night.'

'Hence all the activity on the ward before,' Martin added, in support of Cath's remarks.

'Serious? Jesus, really?'

'Really,' Cath answered.

Tommy fell silent and Martin waited to let it sink in before he added, 'So you *are* in deep shit, and if you want our help, you need to level with us so we know what we are getting ourselves into.'

Another short pause, then Tommy said, 'OK, I'll stop trying to blag you. I am in deep shit and I do need your help, but it's big, man, fucking nuclear. Can we just swing by the club and then I'll direct you to my gaff to collect a couple of things, then you can take me where you want, and I'll tell you the whole sorry story.'

'Deal,' Martin said, and then winked at Cath who was smiling widely. It had been a can opener of a line she'd used on Tommy. Linking the unconnected death of Janice to an unconnected drip mistake, to Tommy's situation, letting his fear join the dots.

Then a sickening thought hit him; what if these events were actually connected? And if they were, what the hell had Janice become mixed up in? He shook the thought from his head. It was too farfetched to fathom.

Chapter Sixteen

Micky Mann had only been parked about half an hour or so, when Kinsella sat next to him broke the impasse, which had felt awkward. He'd no idea why, but since they'd arrived on the car park Kinsella had not been in a talkative mood. Until now.

'We may have to move around a bit if we start to draw any unwanted attention,' Kinsella suddenly said.

'Yeah, I realise that, I'm keeping watch for any security.'

'I hope it's a keener watch than when you picked me up.'

Micky was picking up a cooler vibe from Kinsella, 'You know you could have left this with me to sort. Save putting your face about,' he offered.

'Needs doing properly.'

Micky could feel his temper kicking in, boss or no boss, and said, 'We wouldn't be sat here now if I hadn't got Nursey to tell me when Tommy was due out; before she went for a swim.'

Kinsella's head spun around to face Micky, his face initially tight with temper, but then it seemed to soften almost straight away as he spoke, 'Fair enough, you did good there.'

Micky nodded and the mood in the car eased.

'Look there,' Kinsella suddenly shouted, and pointed towards the hospital's main entrance. 'Fuck me, it's him.'

Micky strained his eyesight and saw a man with his arm in a sling walking through the main entrance with another geezer. He'd no idea who the bloke was, but Kinsella was right, sling-man was Tommy Broadbent. He watched as both men got into a waiting brown/orange coloured BMW. Tommy in the back, and the geezer in the driving seat. Micky started their engine as he watched the BM pull out of its slot and head towards the exit. He drove down their tributary road towards the same exit. Moments later he put the brakes on to give way and overshot the lines by a foot or so, just as the BM passed. He saw the driver glance in their direction, and then the front seat passenger did too.

'For fucks sake, be careful, we don't want Tommy to clock us,' Kinsella barked, as Micky pulled in behind them and followed the BM through the exit barrier. His heart rate was off the chart as he quickly put his pay and display ticket into the machine followed by enough coins to raise the barrier.

'Don't lose them,' Kinsella said.

Micky ignored him as he sped after the BMW.

'And don't get too close, either.'

'I have done this before, you know.'

Kinsella didn't reply and the tension in the car was back, so Micky said, 'I don't know who the geezer driving is.'

'Nor me.'

'But I know who the woman is.'

Kinsella turned to face Micky, as he kept his eyes on the road and sped past a bus and then hit the brakes to slide back into his lane, a respectful thirty or forty metres behind the BM.

'Who?'

'It's the bird who pretended to be the Insurance person I saw at Tommy's house.'

'Fucking top stuff,' Kinsella said, and then slapped his heavy hand on Micky's left shoulder, nearly dragging the steering wheel sideways again. Micky looked at Kinsella who was smiling widely now. He'd done something right.

'This just gets better and better,' Kinsella said.

***

'Where to first, Tommy?' Martin asked, as he headed towards Toxtheth before he turned right onto the A562, which was a major thoroughfare that would lead them into Wapping, past the Albert Dock, and Liverpool's iconic Liver Building.

'I could do with nipping to my gaff but as we'll pass near the club on the way, can I just call in there, first?'

'No problems. But try and keep low down on the back seat, just to be on the safe side.'

'You're not expecting trouble are you?' Tommy asked.

'Trust me; we have no intel, just being cautious.'

'OK.'

Martin then drove up to a major traffic light controlled junction. There were two lanes going straight ahead and two lanes turning right. Martin chose the first of the turn right lanes, and came to a halt at the stop line with his right hand indicator on. This road would take them inland away from the waterfront, generally towards Banging Sounds. As the lights turned to green in his favour, Martin cancelled the right turn indicator and pulled to his left, back into the second of the straight-ahead lanes. He had to cut across the lead stationary vehicle to do so, whose driver hit his horn aggressively. The lights for straight on changed to green as Martin was manoeuvring, he put his foot down hard to clear the junction and pull away from the car he'd just karate chopped; whose driver was now suggesting via the medium of sign, that Martin was a self-abuser.

'Wow,' Tommy said, as Martin could see him rolling around on the back seat.

'Problem?' Cath asked.

'Relax everyone, I was just being careful. I saw a bus flash a blue Mondeo a bit back as he overtook it and then braked after pulling in front of it, and behind us. Then as I prepared to turn right at the lights, the same motor came up behind us with two unsavoury looking goons on board. So I thought I'd test the water. Sorry if I alarmed you.'

Martin saw Tommy, via his mirror; instinctively look out of the rear window. 'Keep your head down, Tommy, and worry not, we left the Mondeo at the lights. It hasn't come with us.'

'Better to be safe,' Cath said, and Martin saw a quizzical look on her face. He shook his head to reassure her that all was well. And then added, 'Just my anti-surveillance training kicking in.'

She smiled back and said, 'Shall we do Tommy's house first, then?'

'I was thinking that, as we've missed the turn offs for the club.'

Ten minutes later they turned into Tommy's street and Martin had given him strict instructions not to hang about. Cath said she would go in with him to help. Martin was relived to find that the street was empty of cars, and pulled in a couple of houses past Tommy's on purpose. He kept himself vigilant as he waited, and it wasn't long before they both returned, Cath carrying a holdall which she put in the boot. He noticed that Tommy was moving even more freely now, maybe his stunt in the city centre had focused his attention.

Martin pulled away as soon as the doors clicked shut, and said, 'Good stuff. I need you to be as quick at the club.'

'Don't worry, I will be,' he replied.

'And I can't come in with you this time, so you'll have to carry your own stuff,' Cath added.

'It's only some cash and documents, but why's that?'

Cath then told of her first visit to his club with her reporter's head on, but left out the co-owner bit, which Martin was glad of. Plenty of time to get into all that once they had Tommy housed safe.

Tommy laughed, and said, 'He's a top barman, Ted, but he is a bit grumpy towards nosy strangers. We used to clash sometimes, but got on well; not that anyone would have guessed. I did him a big favour once, so he owed me. That said, I think we are now probably straight. Though, I can't be sure.'

'Straight, how?' Martin asked.

'I think he may have given me the heads up of the shit-storm that was coming, though he wouldn't have known why; but I'll fill you in properly later. Anyway, where are you taking me after the club?'

'We'll start off at a hotel outside the city where we can catch our breath and have a proper chat, then we can sort out something more suitable, longer term; depending on what you tell us of course,' Martin said.

'Fair enough.'

'Come on Tommy, give us a taster; the suspense is killing me?' Cath said, as she glanced back at Tommy with that million dollar smile of hers which could open a clam. Martin was really hopeful that Colin got the green light to swear her in as a special constable. That disarming way of hers would be solid gold in a police interview room.

'Like I said, it's not what you think. It involves organised crime at a whole new level. And the most audacious plan your lot have ever, or will ever, come across.'

'Oh come on,' Martin said, 'you're torturing us here.'

'Look, I promise I'll be totally straight with you, but it's too complicated to go into in the back of a car. But I will need some serious guarantees. The people involved don't realise how much I know, but what they do realise, is enough to want rid of me.'

'What sort of guarantees?'

'New identity, relocation, and enough dosh to get me started in a new life.'

Martin whistled and said, 'That big?'

'That big.'

'Well if it is, we can do what you ask, but we will need enough from you, if not all of it, to get that agreement from my bosses in principle.'

'I understand, and Colin seems like a straight guy.'

'He is, but it'll be way above his paygrade,' Martin finished with, as he pulled up just past the club.

He turned to face Tommy, 'Be quick, be real quick. Like your arse is on fire.'

'I fully intend to,' he said, and quickly got out of the car.

As soon as the door shut, Cath said, 'I've studied the plans for this place, there is a fire door and yard at the back. I'll cover that in case he gets a change of heart.'

'Thanks, Cath, I'll keep my eyes on at the front. I'll text you a blank message when he comes back.'

'As will I if the slippery bugger appears at the rear.'

Chapter Seventeen

Micky was about to swing the steering wheel to the left when Kinsella's trademark lead-hand grabbed it and held it still. 'What?' Micky asked.

'Wait. He might have just changed his mind, or he might be checking for a tail; either way, if we go after him, we'll stick out like a Scouser's tax return.

'Does it really matter? Opposed to losing him?' Micky asked.

'What if the geezer is a cop?'

Micky had to admit he'd not considered that. The move at the traffic lights had been slick.

'We'll pick him up easy enough, but we can't show our hand until we are ready. If he is with the filth they'll have radios. We are so close to the club let's give that a quick spin and then try the house, he'll need clothes.'

Micky nodded and stepped on it. Minutes later they were outside the club and it was all locked up with the outer shutters down. Clearly unoccupied. He slowed down but didn't bother stopping. He glanced at Kinsella who nodded so he accelerated past. It didn't take long before they were outside Tommy's house, which looked no different than last time.

As soon as he pulled over, Kinsella told him to keep watch and hit the horn if anyone arrived. Micky watched Kinsella, who went to the front door and windows and peered through them, before then disappearing around the back. Two minutes later he was running back towards the car and as soon as he was back in, he said, 'We've missed him. Do the club again. He has to turn up there.'

'How do you know we've missed him?' Micky asked.

'Mail is all pushed to one side by the front door, so I kicked the back one in. Clothes pulled everywhere. He must have come here first. Now shut up and get your foot down.' Micky did, and ten minutes later they pulled into the side street off Dale Street in the city centre, just in time to see the tail lights on the BM as it

77

braked at the other end of the road, momentarily, before it turned left and disappeared from view.

'Don't lose it and don't let them clock you,' Kinsella said.

Micky had no idea how the hell he was supposed to manage both, so he just got them to the end of the road as quickly as he could.

Fortunately, the road was clear and he made the turn without stopping, and then immediately saw the BMW in the distance.

'Slow right down,' Kinsella ordered, and he did.

Seconds later two vans passed them and Kinsella told him to keep behind them and to keep his eyes on the offside. If the BMW threw a right he would see it. Kinsella said he'd keep watch down the left hand side. It seemed like a good strategy; they couldn't see the car, but they would if it deviated. Micky hadn't realised how much of a pro Kinsella was, he clearly knew his stuff.

'Next left,' Kinsella shouted, and Micky made the turn, relieved that one of the two vans in front of them did so, too. He realised they had gone round in a big circle as they passed the university hospital again, and were now headed towards the waterfront. The Queensway tunnel was dead ahead. Micky knew the tunnel was *the* original Mersey tunnel built in the 1930s, with its close neighbour, the Kingsway tunnel, following on in the 70's. The road they were currently on would lead straight into the Queensway one. He just hoped the BM continued going straight ahead, but he had no idea what Kinsella had planned next.

***

Martin had been relieved to see Tommy hobble out of the club a short time after he'd gone in. He'd quickly locked the shutters and re-joined them in the car, closely followed by Cath; whom Martin had texted as soon as he'd seen Tommy emerge. He was also relieved that as they'd pulled away there had been no cars in the street, and none entered as he turned left at the end of the road. 'Did you get what you were after?' he asked Tommy.

'Just some cash, unfortunately, but I can work around that when we sit down and chat.'

Martin wasn't too sure what he meant, but would remember to ask him later when they arrived at their destination.

He then did a wide circular route before passing the university hospital and heading towards the Queensway tunnel.

'So we are heading south of the river. I hope we aren't staying in Birkenhead?'

'No, you are going upmarket for a change; we've booked a couple of rooms in a nice hotel in Chester near to the Welsh border.'

'Must admit, I'll feel a lot calmer once we are through the tunnel,' Tommy said.

Martin kept checking his mirrors and was aware of the same large white van which had been behind them for a while, but there was nothing threatening about it. The Queensway road fed out of the tunnel's exit and round onto the New Chester Road, Martin saw the white van eventually turn off away from them. He then took a double take and scrutinised the rear view mirror.

'What is it?' Cath asked.

'Probably nothing, but the van that has been in my mirrors for ages has turned off to reveal a blue Mondeo behind us now, but it's a long way back.'

'Is it the one from earlier, with the bus thing?'

'I can't read its number plate from this distance, and to be honest, even if it was, it still probably means nothing. It can't have been behind us for long, and nothing followed us away from the house or the club; that, I'm certain of.' Martin knew that the road they were on was a major urban dual carriageway which led to other A roads and two motorways. The road was about as safe as it could be, busy and full of vehicles and people. He also knew there was a huge shipyard coming up on their left, and from that, a street ran parallel through an industrial area and then re-joined their A road a mile further down. It would be a great check route, so he indicated and turned left onto Campbeltown Road. He immediately wished he hadn't.' Shit.'

'What is it?' Cath asked.

'Might still be nothing, but the Mondeo has come with us. This road runs alongside the A41 and re-joins it just down the way. I won't get too excited unless he follows us back onto the main drag. But just to be on the safe side...' Martin said, leaving his own sentence unfinished as he reached under the centre console and pulled out a radio mike. 'One CS Ten, to CH.'

'The crime squad mobile calling CH, go ahead.'

'One CS Ten, we have a sensitive cargo on board and a following vehicle which might be nothing, but can your PNC check it please,' Martin asked.

The Merseyside police control room asked for details, their location, identity of the officers and the reason code for the Police National Computer check. Martin gave the details and within ten seconds a reply came back.

'No intelligence or reports on that vehicle, or on the registered owner who lives in Liverpool.'

Martin's attention was then drawn to the Mondeo which had closed the gap between them, and was now very close behind. He gasped, as he recognised the same two goons in the motor as he had seen earlier. He accelerated hard, keeping his gaze on his rear view. They were on a dead straight narrow road which was adjoined by a mixture of industrial and commercial units, the odd patch of scrub, the odd egress - most of which led nowhere - and little else. He glanced at the speedo, they were doing sixty - twice the legal limit - and the Mondeo was keeping pace. 'One CS Ten, urgent, this vehicle is chasing us, and its occupants may be armed.'

'One CS Ten, received....confirming, we have two ARVs en route to you now. ETAs please...'

'Romeo Three to CH, we are three minutes away.'

Martin could hear two-tone horns blaring out behind Romeo Three's transmission.

'Romeo Four, five away.'

'One CS Ten: armed intel, please?'

'One of the men chasing us is believed responsible for the shooting in the cathedral and we have the victim with us now, having just collected him from hospital.'

'CH understood: all Armed Response Vehicles making, authority to draw arms is granted.'

Martin could hardly keep his gaze from his driver's mirror as he accelerated further, and yelled at Tommy to keep low in his seat. As Tommy obeyed, Martin said, 'As we are risking our lives to protect your sorry butt, now would a good time to tell us why.'

'It's just…OK; I'm not what you think, she runs the—'

'MARTIN,' screamed Cath, interrupting Tommy.

Martin instinctively looked forward again and could see a HGV backing its trailer out from a nearside gateway up ahead. It had already blocked three-quarters of the road.

Martin stamped on the footbrake and an instant later his head was thrown backwards hard against his head restraint as the Mondeo collided with them full on from behind. The force of the impact propelled their car even farther forward, and his foot momentarily came off the brake pedal before he slammed it back on. The tyres were screeching and Martin could see that the Mondeo had moved to the opposite side of the road as its tyres also sounded the heavy fanfare from its vehicles locked up wheels.

Martin wasn't sure that they would be able to stop in time, but a surge of hope flashed through him as he realised the HGV had started moving forward again. Its driver must have heard their approach and was trying to clear the way. Martin was aware that the chasing vehicle was nearly alongside them.

As time almost stopped, they careered even closer and Martin could see that the HGV had cleared half the road. The Mondeo was clearly aiming for that gap. If he could just out-brake the Mondeo by a few metres, he could swing in behind, and they could both clear the end of the HGVs trailer on the offside of the road.

He pressed the footbrake even harder, not knowing where he found the extra strength in his right leg; he grabbed the handbrake up as hard and as far as he could, in an effort to add to their stopping ability.

Martin frantically looked to his right; the Mondeo was still side-by-side with them. Why wouldn't the driver come off his brakes and let them out? He must have known if he did, they would both be able to miss the trailer.

But of course they wouldn't, because keeping them penned in facing a certain head-on high speed collision, was what they no doubt wanted.

The solution came to him, just as Cath shouted it, 'Ram the bastards!'

Martin grabbed a handful of the steering wheel and glanced to his right a millisecond before he was to start his manoeuvre.

It was in that instance that he realised his efforts would be in vain.

The huge, front seat passenger, who was wearing a baseball cap pulled down low, had rolled down his window and was pointing a silenced handgun in their direction.

Then Martin saw a number of muzzle flashes spit from the end of the barrel, and in that same instance, heard Cath shout, 'Brace and duck,' as the rear passenger window exploded.

Chapter Eighteen

Martin copied Cath who was virtually in the foot well, but he couldn't get quite as low as her as he had the steering wheel to content with. He had a last glance through the windscreen before he dodged his head out of view. He'd managed to take forty miles per hour off their speed, but it wasn't enough. Impact at twenty miles per hour was imminent. As he hunkered down, his last forward glance told him that they were going under the HGV's trailer around its mid-section, if he could just miss the rear wheels. He pulled hard on the steering wheel towards the nearside, as he realised the bastards in the Mondeo were clear to pass and miss the end of the trailer.

In the following instant, the screeching sound of metal on metal was deafening. The roof of their car shot down to the top of the seat height. A second earlier it would have taken his head off. The airbags punched outwards in the next millisecond and pinned Martin and Cath fast, as their ruined car came to a grinding halt.

Its front half was securely stuck under the trailer, but the rear was clear and in the open air. At least Tommy would be safe, if he had got his head down in time, and would also be free to move.

Martin took a few seconds to catch his breath and realise that he was still in one piece. But it had been a close thing. 'Jesus, you OK?' he asked Cath, as he tried to turn his face towards her.

'I think so,' she replied.

'Thanks,' he said, as he could hear the sounds of the approaching sirens getting louder.

'For what?'

'The duck warning, I was too focused on the Mondeo.'

'It's a pleasure, I owed you one.'

'Becoming an unhealthy habit, this.'

Martin saw Cath offer a weak smile in reply; as he had a flashback to the time outside her house when he'd had to propel her through the air to get her out the way of a car aimed at them. That had been as close as ducking was here.

Time to check on their passenger, 'Tommy?' he shouted, up over his head.

'Tommy, you OK?' Cath joined in with.

After a few seconds of silence, Martin turned to glance at Cath, which was a far as he could turn his head. She looked back at him and then started to wriggle around in her seat to try and look through the car's centre console area. She'd more room to manoeuvre than Martin had. Then his attention was draw back to the front as he saw whom he took to be the HGV driver, stoop under his trailer and approach Martin's side of the car.

'You OK?' the HGV driver asked.

But before he could answer, he heard Cath scream; followed a second later by the HGV driver's wail as he looked beyond Martin.

***

Micky Mann came off the brakes as the car slew past the end of the HGV's trailer, and he steadied the steering. He looked in his rear view mirrors and could see the tangled and crushed front end of the other car rammed firmly under the lorry's trailer. There was no way the front seat passengers could have survived. The roof had flattened down to the top of the door level. 'The geezer and the bird are surely done for,' he said.

'I reckon so, and this little friend finished off what I started in the cathedral,' Kinsella said, as he held up his silenced handgun. Then added, 'Slow down a bit.'

'Why? Can't you hear those sirens getting louder?'

'Just do it.'

So he did, and watched as Kinsella threw his weapon out of his window, and saw the gun disappear over a rough grassy mound which bordered the tarmac. He then started to pull his leather gloves off and put them back into his rucksack.

'What are you waiting for, get us the fuck out of here,' Kinsella barked.

'Oh right, yeah, sorry,' Micky said, and put his foot back down. Kinsella wound his window up and Micky asked, 'Why did you throw the gun away?'

'That way they can't ever catch you with it and link you to the scene. Always leave the weapon behind. You just have to make sure that you are not linked to weapon, which I obviously did.'

'You must go through a lot of guns.'

Kinsella didn't answer; he was busy with some wipes and what looked like a bottle of bleach or detergent, wiping his arms and wrists. Removing any gunshot residue, Micky realised. When he'd finished he put everything back into his rucksack and then pulled out a gallon sized container.

'Once we are a couple of miles away, find a quite side street and we can fire the motor and do one. Then I can give the lovely Lucy the good news.'

'Who's Lucy?' Micky asked.

Kinsella didn't answer, but just turned to look at Micky. He took the hint and said, 'I get it; it's better I don't know.'

Kinsella laughed and gave Micky the heavy hand treatment and said, 'I'm actually warming to you.'

Five minutes later, they were still on a local road parallel to the main A41 in Hooten, south of Birkenhead, still among a mix of industrial units and wasteland, and Kinsella said, 'Over there, that'll do.'

Micky followed his gaze and could see a short cul-de-sac with nothing but grass all around it. It was one of those junctions they built when constructing a road so that the offshoots can be developed into a side street with its own industrial units, but one where no one has got around to it, yet. Roads to nowhere; an ideal place to dump the motor.

Chapter Nineteen

Martin was mightily relieved to see the Fire Brigade eventually cut the roof off their car so he and Cath could both sit up, stretch themselves, and climb out. That roof removal bit took no time at all, but first, the brigade had to jack up the trailer to free the car and then pull it free. It was the first time that Martin had been able to turn around properly and see what was left of poor Tommy. Several gunshot entry wounds were evident in his chest and Martin noticed that the grouping was tight. To do that from a moving car, into a moving car would require some skill. Hard to believe that the shooter had previously failed at nearly point blank range. That was assuming it was the same shooter; they could only speculate.

As soon as he and Cath were clear, officers quickly put a tent over the wrecked car leaving Tommy in situ for the time being; it was now a murder crime scene. They both stretched and complained of a few aches but Martin knew they had been very lucky indeed. They were both checked out by paramedics and they both turned down the offer of a trip to hospital, much against the prevailing medical advice. As they exited the ambulance Colin was waiting to greet them.

'Thank God, you two are OK,' he started with.

'But we've failed poor Tommy,' Martin said.

'It wasn't your fault, how could any of us know this would happen, and so soon after you picked him up.'

'Yeah, on that,' Cath said, joining in, 'how on earth did they know?' She then turned to face Martin, 'I'm not blaming you in the slightest, but they must have followed us from the hospital car park.'

Martin thought back to the bus flashing issue, and then remembered a glimpse of a car overshooting on the car park as they left. He hadn't seen it properly, they'd been past in a flash. It must have been the bloody Mondeo. He reminded Cath about the incident and said, 'I should have taken more notice.'

'Stop it, you. I glanced at that car, too, remember, but never saw it properly either, so I'm as much to blame,' Cath said.

'Stop it both of you, you are neither to blame,' Colin jumped in with.

'Back to the how, then?' Martin said.

'I'm sorry to voice this out loud,' Cath said, as she weakly smiled at Martin and then turned her head to one side. He knew what was coming next. 'It can only have come from the hospital, so...' Cath said, leaving her sentence unfinished.

'I know; I've already worked it out. Probably cost her, her life,' Martin said.

'Ah,' Colin said, re-joining the conversation, 'you are both thinking that it must have been Janice who passed the information to the criminals?'

'Well, it fits doesn't it? As unsavoury as the thought is. I can only assume that she had no idea what the crooks had planned to do with the information,' Martin said, and then turned to face Cath, and added, 'we didn't part on the best of terms, but she didn't hate me that much.'

'I'm sure she doesn't hate you, and I know it wasn't Janice who tipped off the killers,' Colin said.

Martin and Cath both turned to face Colin, who had made his last remark with some authority. 'How can you be so sure?' Martin asked.

'Don't take my word for it, you can ask her yourself if you wish.'

'What?' Martin and Cath manged to say together.

'As I was leaving Dr. Meadows' office - who incidentally, kept me waiting forever - I bumped slap bang into her. I was about to ring you when your chase started.'

'But, but...' Martin said.

'I know; had me fooled too, but it's apparently popular to have coloured streaks in your hair at the moment; it's just that both women chose purple.' Colin said.

'But I saw the side of her face, albeit it covered in shit. I was sure.'

'It's a friend of Janice's called Sarah; they look alike. Same height, build etc. In fact, Janice reckons she is a bit of a copycat friend. If Janice gets a new top, then Sarah turns up with a similar one a couple of weeks later. She says that although they were friends, in and out of work, it used to piss her off. Dr. Meadows referred to them both as "The Troublesome Duo".'

Martin fell speechless as he took in the shock.

Cath filled the void and asked, 'So was it this Sarah who meddled with Tommy's morphine drip?'

'Yep, according to Dr. Meadows, who caught her in the act without realising exactly what was going on,' Colin said.

'So Janice is not only alive and well, but she is nothing to do with any of this?' Martin said, finding his voice.

'Yes, a total red herring. Though she has given us some useful background on Sarah. Apparently, she had a bad cocaine habit last year, and owed a lot of money to some nasty people, but as far as Janice was aware, all that was in the past.'

'Well, the cocaine habit starts to explain this nurse Sarah's involvement,' Cath threw in.

'Oh here we go. Here comes trouble,' Colin said.

Martin and Cath turned around to see DI Phil Devers weaving his way through all the uniform cops and fire and ambulance staff, as he straightened up and made a beeline towards them with intent in his step.

'He certainly doesn't look very happy,' Martin noted.

***

After setting the car on fire using his rucksack and gloves as the seat, and with the help of a gallon of paraffin, Kinsella asked Micky to arrange a lift back into Liverpool. Micky knew many of the city's taxi drivers, as he had used a few to help transport his cocaine around, so it was a pickup with no questions asked. As they approached the Albert Dock, Kinsella suddenly told the driver to pull over. The guy offered to take him to his hotel but Kinsella said it was no problem. He was obviously being cautious, and Micky knew there were many hotels with walking distance, so it could be any. He'd obviously not come in by train this morning, that much was now clear. Micky thought he would get out with him and paid the driver fifty quid for his trouble, but Kinsella turned around once his feet were on the road blocking Micky's egress.

'I want to have a wander and cool my head, plus I've got to ring my boss. You carry on home. You've done good today; go home and relax.'

Micky was about to politely suggest that they go for a drink, and started to make towards the open cab door when Kinsella continued. 'The boss is coming in tonight on a non-related matter, so I'm going to be busy. Plus, I need to sort out what we owe you, and whatever bonus the boss sees fit.'

This stopped Micky and he sat back down on the cab's back seat, and smiled.

'You've done an excellent job and you'll be well recompensed, no problems on that score. I'll bell you tomorrow and sort out a meet.'

Micky nodded and Kinsella turned and walked away. He pulled the door shut and asked the driver to drop him off at his favourite brothel just up the road towards Toxtheth. Payday tomorrow means he could party tonight. He smiled to himself; he'd certainly earned some R & R.

'Fancy joining me?' he asked the driver.

'Tell you what, you're on. I'll drop you off, get rid of the cab and come and find you,' the driver answered.

'Excellent.' Things were looking up, he felt like he'd moved up a level, and Kinsella's boss was obviously a serious player – especially, if he had the balls to have Tommy Broadbent taken out – and if they were happy with him, then he might even get taken on as staff. He'd done his apprenticeship on the doors, time to expand.

Then a thought hit him: he'd hurt people before, men and women, sometimes seriously, but he'd never actually killed anyone; not that he was aware of. And in the last twenty-four hours he'd one confirmed kill to his name, and was part responsible for another three. There was no going back now. Then he shrugged his shoulders, fuck it, why should he care.

Chapter Twenty

Lucy Pinder was in her Amsterdam hotel room doing a crossword while she awaited Kinsella's call. Her bag was packed ready, and she was wearing her trademark white T shirt and blue jeans. She was just about to give Kinsella a ring when her phone started to vibrate and dance around the glass coffee table. She picked it up; Kinsella. She answered it with, 'Well? Better be good news?'

'It is; told you I'd sort it.'

'Are we sure this time?'

'I put four rounds into his chest and watched the body bag being carried into the mortuary. Not in doubt. The police have reported it to the media as a fatal car accident, at the moment.'

'Excellent, his nibs will be pleased. Who else was in the car?'

'A couple, not sure who they were.'

'Both dead, I hope?'

'They were both in the front, and I saw the roof collapse on them as they crashed under a wagon's trailer,' Kinsella said, and then he went into detail to explain the chase.

'What are the press saying?'

'They've only confirmed one dead, at this time, but I can't image they survived the crash. I'll send you a photo of the wrecked car and you can see for yourself.'

A second later, Lucy's phone pinged and she looked at the photo taken by a local press photographer; it certainly looked a mess. 'How long were they with Tommy?' she asked.

'Only a matter of minutes before we took their attention. Probably just mates collecting him, so he wouldn't be chatting about business, plus, they didn't have time. I'm sure everything is cool.'

'It better be; we can't afford any more cock-ups.'

'I realise that.'

'Keep monitoring things in case they were just injured?'

'Will do, though we've lost our nurse contact now, of course.'

'A shame, but a lose end that needed sorting.'

'And re the other lose end, before you ask, it'll be sorted.'

'Let me know as soon as.'

'Will do, and let me know if you need anything else whilst you are over here.'

'I will,' she said, and then ended the call.

As soon as she had put the phone down on the table, her partner in love and crime walked over and handed her a drink.

'I take it that the mighty Tommy Broadbent is officially, no more?'

'Jason's done a proper job this time; they'll be a bit more noise around it, but that shouldn't be a worry,' she said.

'Excellent, he'd served his purpose, but all things have to end, and we don't, or shortly won't, need what he gave us.'

'As someone once said, "The King is dead, long live the King".'

'Didn't know you were into French middle age history?'

'Neither did I.'

They both laughed and Lucy stood up to clank her glass against his before emptying it. 'I've promoted Ted to manager at the club, and will have a quick check in while I'm there.'

'How long do you expect to be?'

'A few days, maybe less, but I can't see why you can't come across in a day or so and join me. Just keep a low profile.'

'Will do.'

'I've got something else in the pipeline, so hopefully, will have that sorted by the time you join me.'

'Sounds intriguing?'

'Can't say too much until I've proved it works, but trust me, if it does, we are going supersonic.'

'I don't know what I'd do without you.'

'Nor do I, but for now, you do what you do best and wish me bon voyage properly; I've got thirty minutes to spare.'

'What, you want it twice?'

'You can still manage thirty minutes in one go, can't you?' Lucy said, as she started to do a seductive striptease, starting with her T shirt.

'I'll be the best fifteen minutes you've ever had.'

She laughed as she watched her man hurry out of his jogging bottoms and shirt.

'OK, ten minutes, and that's my final offer,' he said, as he pulled Lucy close to him and started to kiss her passionately.

***

Martin, Cath and Colin turned and stood as one as Phil Devers marched up to them.

'What the hell is going on here?' Devers said.

'I would have thought that was evident,' Martin replied, immediately regretting his levity.

'Don't take the piss,' Devers spat.

Colin glared at Martin, and then answered Devers, 'Look, Phil, it's not deliberate.'

'Of course it's deliberate; first you turn up at the scene of a murdered nurse; I mean who in their right mind would want to kill a nurse, anyway? And then you turn up at the hospital before even I'm made aware that *my* shooting victim is fit to be discharged, and then you snaffle him away.'

'It's sensitive,' Colin said.

'Some good your protection did; Broadbent is well and truly dead this time. And I'll be the one who is left with this whole crock of shit on my shoulders, while you lot rock on to your secret squirrel treehouse, like you also do.'

'You need to calm down, you'll have a stroke at this rate,' Martin said.

Devers turned to face Martin, and said, 'Stroke, stroke? I'll fucking stroke you with this in a minute,' as he shook a clenched fist in Martin's face.

'Well, forgive me for being a little prickly, but someone just tried to kill me, and I've spent thirty minutes sat on my neck with my balls around ears,' Martin snapped.

'Let's keep it civil, gentlemen,' Colin said, to both men.

'Well, tell me what's going on?' Devers said.

Then Colin's phone broke the heated conversation and all waited as Colin answered it. He turned away as he took the call, and Martin could hear him address the caller as "sir", and then confirm that Martin and Cath were alright. All three of them turned to face him as he ended the call.

'That was Paul Harding,' he started.

'What's he ringing you for?' Devers asked.

'To tell me that you, as of now, are on the "Need to Know" document.'

'What? Why?' Devers said.

'Because presumably, now you need to know,' Martin said.

Devers raised his fist towards Martin again and said, 'So help me God.'

'Martin: behave,' Cath shouted.

'Sorry,' Martin said, with genuine remorse and threw his hands in the air. 'It's been at trying day.'

Devers nodded and then turned back to face Colin.

'The sensitivity surrounded Tommy's status which had to be protected at all costs.'

'Status, what status?' Devers said.

Ignoring the question, Colin continued, 'And even though he is now dead, our duty of care remains in place regarding his status, and in particular towards our organisation.'

'OK, but again, what status?'

'Tommy Broadbent was - apparently - one of the top criminal informants Merseyside Police had,' Colin said. 'Though that was more due to his perceived criminal level, than any intel he actually came up with.'

Devers didn't reply straight away, he looked genuinely shocked. Then after a few seconds, he said, 'That toe rag, a top level snout?'

'It's true,' Cath said.

'I don't believe it, you idiots have been played.'

'We are not idiots, and if anyone has been played, it's Merseyside Police,' Cath added.

'Tommy Broadbent, a common snout. Are you sure?'

'Yes, because I recruited him, originally,' Martin added. 'And he now wanted out, and wanted to unburden himself.'

'Something big, something very big,' Cath added.

'Big enough to get him killed over. And it nearly killed us too,' Martin said.

'Any idea what?' Devers asked.

'That's the pisser, he was about to tell us when this happened,' Martin said, and then pointed at a low-loader as it started to lift their crushed car from the road onto its back. He hadn't seen the body being moved out, but it must have been.

'And Paul Harding wants us all to work together now; you'll still be running the investigations, but we'll carry on digging around in the shadows looking at the organised crime side of things. The worry is that something is about to happen,' Colin said.

'Understood,' Devers said. 'Full disclosure between us?'

'Yes, Cath is our Field Intel Analyst and will be your point of contact. But keep our involvement to yourself; we don't know whether Tommy had friends on our side of the law.'

'Jesus, you're kidding?'

'To be fair, we've seen no evidence of corruption, but your Chief Constable thought it prudent to assume so until we can prove otherwise.'

'The Chief's involved?'

'Yes.'

'So you, Martin, stop your dick waving and shake hands with Phil,' Cath said, which took Martin by surprise, and all of them laughed, which lifted the tension. 'Sorry, pal,' Martin said and offered Phil Devers his hand.

'None taken,' he said, as he took it and shook it.

'And Paul Harding wants you to pop in to see him when you get chance and he'll brief you in person,' Colin said.

Devers nodded, and then said, 'I've just been told that Tommy's long lost brother has been informed and will be making his way to Liverpool tomorrow morning, to ID the body. I was going to cover that as I've run out of detectives.'

'Do you want us to do that, free you up a bit?' Martin asked.

'Thanks that would be a great help. I've put back the actual post mortem until tomorrow evening, at the earliest; it's not like we don't know how he died. But if you could deal with his brother and document the ID, that would be top. Means I can crack on here, and fit in seeing Paul Harding instead.'

'Consider it done,' Martin said.

'There's just one other thing; well, two actually, that you should be aware of before you see Mr. Harding; just in case the paparazzi grip you first,' Colin said.

'Go on,' Devers said.

'Well, until you have actually had the post mortem done to legally confirm how Tommy died, this is technically not murder, correct?'

'I'm no Sherlock, but—' Martin started to say, until Colin waved his hand.

'Yes, button it,' Cath said, to Martin.

Devers nodded.

'Well, until then, even though it's blatantly obvious how Tommy died, it gives you the chance to say that the police are dealing with the incident as a fatal hit and run, until you know more.'

'Buy us some time?' Devers asked.

'Exactly, it may give us an initial advantage, especially if you say that the body in the back seat suffered disfiguring crush injuries, so the exact cause of death can only be properly determined once the Home Office post mortem has been done.'

'Not too sure how much help that will really give us, but if the head of CID wants me to do it, who am I to argue,' Devers said.

'I'm inclined to agree, but his second idea is a better one.'

'Go on.'

'Instead of saying that one, as of yet unidentified male, has died, say that all three of the car's occupants didn't make it.'

Martin looked up, fully attentive now.

'Paul reckons, that Martin and Cath here may be at risk; the killers won't know what Tommy has told them, or given them, so until we can evaluate any risk, they can operate under the radar and the villains will think there are no lose ends.'

Chapter Twenty-one

Micky Mann had a fun filled evening until he eventually made it home in the small hours. He initially crashed, but once most of the alcohol had worn off he didn't sleep well. His mind replayed to him the evil acts he'd committed. He hadn't expected his subconscious to torture him, he was a hard nut and had never been troubled before when he'd hurt people. Though he'd never killed before. He eventually dragged himself from his pit around eight. He felt knackered and hung over, dearly needing more sleep than his mind would allow. He hoped to break the circle of thoughts spinning around in his head.

He made a large mug of coffee and sat in the lounge of his one-bedroomed flat and tuned his 48" flat screen TV to a news channel. A reporter was doing a piece to camera with the crash scene in the background, though there was nothing left to see apart from police tape. According to the report, facts from the police were few at this stage, but they were treating it initially as a hit and run, but with an open mind; as the bodies were badly mangled and post mortems had yet to be done. Then the reporter said that she believed that all three of the crushed vehicle's passengers had lost their lives. So it was official; he was a quadruple murderer.

Then his phone trilled on top of the kitchen table and made him jump. He retrieved it and jumped back onto his settee as he answered the unknown caller. It was Kinsella, he thought it might be.

'Seen the news?'

'Just watching it now.'

'A top job my friend, and the boss is more than happy.'

'Did you see the boss last night?' Micky asked, not wishing to push his nose in too far, but Kinsella had said that he was to see or speak to the boss, when they parted, though he couldn't remember if he'd said, 'see' or 'speak'.

Kinsella answered without hesitation, 'Yes, and that's why I'm ringing you early. The boss has not only agreed to pay you a bonus but wants to meet you.'

'Meet me, why?'

'The boss likes to meet everyone who joins the firm.'

Micky hadn't expected this, he'd hoped for it, but hadn't really expected it. Not so soon. Things were really looking up. 'Wow, that's great, brilliant.'

'I put a good word in, so afterwards you can buy me that drink I didn't get last night.'

'Be a pleasure, mate.'

'I'll text you the details of the meet in a while,' Kinsella said, and then ended the call.

Suddenly, Micky felt his conscience lift along with his hangover, he emptied his mug and headed to shower, singing, 'I'm in the money; money, money, money.'

***

Martin and Cath grabbed a takeaway on their way home as neither had any appetite to cook. They were both whacked and didn't chat much, and Martin was relieved when Cath suggested they both have an early night; and not for the reasons that such a suggestion would normally have had on him. He slept well for a few hours but tossed and turned for the most part of the night. The crash replayed over and over in his dreams and seemed even more vivid than the real thing. In his reverie he was an omniscient observer, and as such he saw everything through a wide angle lens rather than the narrow focused perception of the real thing itself. He was aware of Cath constantly turning in her sleep and suspected she was on the same subconscious rollercoaster.

He eventually gave in around five and headed to the kitchen. He started to feel aches and pains that hadn't registered before. His neck and back ached on the left hand side; he recalled having to stretch to try and see Cath as they waited for Trumpton to free them from the wreckage. He made himself as comfortable as he could in an armchair, turned the gas fire on and sipped his tea as he flipped through the TV channels, keeping the volume low so as not to disturb Cath. He paused on a news channel, but turned over as soon as they started to report on the incident; he didn't need any reminders. He eventually settled on a channel showing an old Sci-Fi film, it would be enough to keep his mind occupied.

An hour later he felt a hand on his shoulder and realised he'd dozed off. He glanced at the hearth clock and was shocked to see that only an hour had passed; it felt like he'd been asleep for days, and it had been a blessed blank-minded rest. He smiled up at Cath as she walked around the chair and sat opposite him.

'What are you doing in here?'

Martin told her.

'Not my best night's kip either.'

'Have you any aches and pains?' he asked.

'Just my left shoulder where the seat belt bit, but it's OK. You had far less space behind that steering wheel.'

'We'll both live, unlike poor Tommy,' he said.

'You in a better mood, this morning? You were very rude to Phil Devers yesterday.'

'I know; I'll apologise again when I speak to him.'

'It was very unlike you.'

'It was; bad day at the office. Though, I'm not a huge fan of his to start with.'

'Why's that?'

'I've only met him a couple of times but have always found him a bit brash with an edge.'

'Well, if Paul Harding calls him one of his best DIs, then who are we to say different?'

Martin knew she was right.

'So what will today bring?' she asked.

'Me and Colin will cover the ID-ing at the mortuary and get a quick ID statement from the brother. That should put me back in Devers' good books.'

'On the brother, I only learnt of his existence yesterday, it was what I was checking out first thing from the Liverpool Office.'

'Ahead of the game as always.'

'And even though they are estranged, I could do with you hooking me up with him after you've done the official ID stuff, he should be able to give us something interesting on Tommy's background, or at least point us in the right direction.'

'More important than ever now, if we are to find out what the hell is going on, I'll set it up.'

'My research says he lives in Preston, so if you can confirm that, I could always see him at his home if he agrees?'

'Sounds like a plan.'

'I may as well head straight to our Preston office and await a call from you. I can soon be back in Liverpool if he'd rather see me there.'

'No worries, it might be a while though, we could do with having a nosy around Tommy's house while we have the brother, as estranged as they were, he'll no doubt want to visit it and will have next of kin stuff to sort out, whether he likes it or not.'

'OK, so who's first for the shower?' she asked.

'Ladies first.'

'Sexist pig,' Cath said, grinning, and then ran to the bathroom, before Martin could move.

'You win,' he shouted after her. 'I'll put the tea and toast on then.'

Chapter Twenty-two

Martin met Colin at the Liverpool Branch Office and they settled down in a quiet room and started to go through the events of the last two days. It was Colin's idea to sit down quietly and give themselves space and time to reflect. Hopefully, they'd find some clarity.

'Well, I've done my DCI's strategy bit by setting us up in here, so it's over to you the master tactician to come up with some answers,' Colin said, grinning.

'If I didn't know you better.'

'How did you sleep?'

'Shite.'

'How about Cath?'

'That'll be two shites,' Martin said, and then explained she wasn't coming there this morning, but had already headed to Preston to catch up with her enquiries into Tommy's background, and hoped to have a proper sit down with his brother later.

'I suppose we shouldn't brainstorm with only two of us, but as we are here, we may as well toss it around,' Colin said.

'I'll explain to Cath later, and bounce off her anything we come up with.'

'Should have rang you last night, but I was knackered, so God knows what you two felt like.'

'The first night after a serious drama is always the worst, I'm sure we'll all be fine by tomorrow.'

'It was a close thing.'

Then Martin realised in all that had happened after the incident, he hadn't thanked Cath, not properly, just an initial instinctive thanks. What an idiot. He told Colin.

'For what exactly?'

'For saving my life. I was so fixated on the other car, the gun barrel, and keeping maximum pressure on the brake pedal, I lost perception from the front, if only for a second or two. But that was enough. If she hadn't shouted "brace and duck" when she did, I'd have been decapitated, I'm sure. I was only distracted for a moment, but we seemed to have travelled far nearer to the trailer, and the unavoidable collision, in that instant.'

'Like you'd suddenly advanced in a disproportionate way?'

'Yeah, exactly. One instance we had several seconds before impact, time to glance away at the new threat, and then, boom.'

'In such extremely stressful situations one's perception of time can alter dramatically. You probably felt as if time had actually slowed.'

'On reflection, that's exactly how it felt.'

'I think it's something to do with the brain speeding up in order to find a solution, rather than time actually appearing to slow, though it can seem that way.'

'Well, I don't particularly want to experience it again. And I'll take Cath out for a slap up meal as soon as I can.'

'Don't forget the flowers and a bit of bling.'

Martin narrowed his eyes and said, 'Sure you two aren't working a scam on me here?'

'Well, someone has to.'

Both men laughed and then they went through the events of the last 48 hours.

It was clear that Tommy wasn't what everyone thought he was, but exactly what that meant was anyone's guess. He'd been about to impart something when the end came. He tried to recall his words verbatim and shared them with Colin, ' "It's just...OK; I'm not what you think, she runs the—" whatever that means?'

' "She", didn't, Cath say the guy at the club mentioned a woman who was in charge with Tommy? I knew we shouldn't have started without Cath.'

'She did, and as to what they are planning, it must involve the club?' Martin said.

'OCG, drugs, guns, women?'

'Any or all of the above. Hang on a mo.'

'What?'

'The club.' Martin said. 'We took him to his house and Cath went in with him, and then to the club where he nipped in alone.'

'Meaning?'

'Meaning we don't know what he did in the club. Do we know what was on his body?'

'Hang on I'll ring Phil Devers,' Colin said, and picked up his phone.

Martin went to refresh their mugs and returned as Colin was ending his call.

'About five hundred in cash, nothing else. No wallet, or cards, just the dosh.'

'He could have collected the cash from the club, or he could have dropped something off.'

'We'll need to have a look at that sharpish. I'll ring Phil and get one of his detectives to do a routine follow-up visit. Look less sus than us.'

Martin nodded and handed Colin a mug.

'Thanks, we'll continue this later with Cath, but it's been productive already.'

'Hopefully,' Martin said. 'What time are we expected at the mortuary?'

'Phil said he was just about to ring us, the ID has been brought forward, we've got to meet Tommy's brother there in forty-five minutes.'

Martin nodded and took a couple of slurps of his beverage before deciding it was too hot to neck quickly. Colin appeared to come to the same conclusion.

'Do you want me to drive?' Colin asked.

'I wouldn't mind, if you don't; just for today.'

'Not a problem.'

They both made their way into the garage, and were soon on their way into the city catching the back end of the morning's rush hour. It was nearing ten as they entered the hospital grounds.

'What's the brother called?' Martin asked.

'Bobby,' Colin answered. 'The elder of the two.'

'Tommy and Bobby?'

'Yep.'

'Sounds like their parents were fans of Cannon and Ball,' Martin quipped.

'Who wasn't?' Colin said, as he pulled into a parking spot at the back of the mortuary.

Mortuaries were never fun places, but Martin remembered the early years of his career when most were in old hospitals, often Victorian; eerie places with little regard to next of kin who had the sombre task which faced Bobby. Nowadays, they were much more professionally built. The actual examination rooms were bright and airy with huge air extraction systems. They even had a special room set aside for what was termed 'Dirty PMs' which related to the examination of bodies which were decomposed.

But Martin knew that even the fresh ones started to decay quickly, and gave off the most horrendous smell as soon as the pathologist's knife opened them up. As a young cop he'd always been advised to watch from the feet end, the stench was slightly less from there, to suck a mint, and to breathe through the nose. Thankfully, today they were not acting as exhibits officers covering the post mortem, that unpleasant task would fall to one of Phil Devers' DCs later. Now was just about the formal identification of the body. And Martin was relieved to see that this mortuary was one of the most modern ones with a separate room for the relatives to wait in, with fresh flowers, comfortable seating and soft furnishings. The room set aside for the ID was akin to a funeral parlour's Chapel of Rest.

The mortuary attendant showed Martin and Colin into the next-of-kin room while they awaited Bobby's arrival. Colin said he'd ring Phil Devers to just to keep an open dialogue with him while they waited. Martin quickly checked the ID room while he did. It was just down the corridor and Martin could see the body already in place. It was laid on a table with sheeting tied down over it, up to the neck. Done respectfully to cover the gruesome chest injuries. There was a separate veil over the head which Martin lifted and had a peek. Tommy looked at peace, and Martin was pleased to see that his face had not suffered any injuries; it would make it a bit easier for the brother.

He walked back into the next-of-kin room as Colin ended his call. 'Everything OK?'

'They have just found the gun. Discarded 100 metres down from the crash scene over a grassy mound at the side of the road.'

'That means there will be no forensics on it.'

Colin nodded.

'Took the search team a while to find it.'

'That's the problem, it wasn't the search team who found it,' Colin added.

'Who did?'

'Some poor sod taking Fido for his morning constitutional.'

'I bet Devers isn't happy. Especially, as it rained overnight.'

'Harding is less happy. The search team Inspector will be looking for a new role, apparently. Anyway, Harding wants to see us with Phil in his office once we are done here.'

Martin was about to acknowledge Colin when the door opened and the mortuary attendant popped his head around it. 'The next of kin, Mr. Bobby Broadbent is in reception, I just wanted to warn you that he is not a happy man; apparently he and the deceased fell out years ago.'

Martin thanked him and he shot off returning a minute later with a tall, stocky man in his mid-40s.

Colin introduced himself and Martin to Bobby, and said they were both so very sorry for his loss.

Bobby replied, 'Yes, yes, whatever. Can we get this over with; I'm a busy man and could do without all this bollocks.'

Chapter Twenty-three

Martin exchanged a look with Colin, and Bobby must have seen it as he then added, 'Look, it might sound harsh, but you don't know the history.'

Martin said, 'On that, would you be open to a chat afterwards, regardless of your relationship with Tommy? We do have to dig into his background as much as we can.'

'Like I say, I'm a busy man.'

'It can be later, at your home if you prefer. Our analyst is very nice and is in Preston. You do still live in Preston, don't you?'

'I do, but is this really necessary?'

Martin glanced at Colin, and he took the hint.

'As next of kin, I can tell you that we are now treating this as murder, though we wouldn't want that made public until after the post mortem examination has been done,' Colin said.

'It's why we have to be more thorough,' Martin added.

'Murder, ah? Doesn't surprise me; if you live his life I guess it is only a matter of time.'

'Can I ask why you were estranged?' Martin said.

'Because he's always been a thieving toe rag. He used to steal from me, and from Mum and Dad, and my patience eventually ran out. I've not seen him, or even spoken to him for years.'

'What about Mum and Dad?' Martin asked.

'Both gone, I'm afraid. And the bastard couldn't be bothered to attend either funeral. I made sure he knew by asking your lot to pass a message, both times, but he didn't reply. Didn't even send a card, let alone flowers. That did it for me, well and truly.'

Martin had to admit, he was starting to understand Bobby's hard attitude towards his brother. 'That must have hurt you. Any idea why Tommy didn't at least get in touch when your parents passed?'

'No idea.' Bobby said. 'Tell me; was he known to you lot before he died?'

Martin glanced at Colin again, and then said, 'I've known Tommy a long time, and to be honest, he was known to a lot of the local police.'

'You knowing him is no shock, and I know people can change, but if he had why didn't he get in touch? He knew where I was. I've lived in the same house in Preston for twenty years.'

Martin had no explanation for Bobby.

Colin jumped in, 'Come on, let's get the identification done. The sooner we get it over, the sooner we can leave you alone. My DS here has already written a short draft statement of identification for you to sign, so we can soon have you on your way, and perhaps talk to you again re his background when it's more convenient.'

Bobby nodded and his demeanour seemed to ease a little. Martin realised Colin was trying to keep him on side. The house search and Cath's chat with Bobby would have to wait.

Martin gestured towards the door, 'If you would follow me, it'll only take a minute. All three walked into the corridor where the mortuary attendant was waiting by the door to the room where Tommy lay; he held it open as they all trooped in.

The mood was now very sombre and Martin watched Bobby's face closely to see how he reacted. The body on its gurney was as it was before, in the centre of the small oblong room, but Martin noticed that the arms were now visible and crossed across its sheet-covered chest. It added to the gravitas of the occasion and looked more respectful. The attendant moved to one side, at the head, and Martin joined him so he could look across at Bobby who came to a halt next to Colin at the opposite side.

Irrespective of everything Bobby had said Martin could see anxiety and pain on his face as he stared at the cadaver in front of him. Then in an almost choreographed move, the attendant started to peel the veil backwards to reveal the head and face as Colin, said, 'Bobby is this body of your brother Tommy Broadbent?'

Martin glanced at the wall clock to record the time and looked at Bobby, whose eyes widened as he gaped at the corpse. He looked stunned, the poor man, so Martin said, 'You might have

106

been estranged, but it will still be a shock. Blood is blood after all.'

Bobby didn't answer, but continued to gaze at the body.

In the impasse, the attendant looked at Martin with a question on his face as he still held the veil aloft. Martin nodded to him, and he slowly replaced it over Tommy's face.

'Bobby, just for the record?' Colin asked.

Bobby turned to face Colin and asked, 'Who the hell is this?'

'Sorry?' Colin asked.

'Sure as hell looks like my brother, but that's not Tom Broadbent.'

'It's been a few years since you last saw him, and people change. But I can assure you that that is the body of Tommy Broadbent,' Martin said.

'Assure all you like, detective, but that's not my brother.'

'I've known him myself, on and off, for a couple of years,' Martin added.

'You may have known this guy,' Bobby said, pointing at the body. 'But that's not my brother: not unless he's regrown the little finger on his left hand.'

Martin, Colin and the attendant all shared a stunned look at each other, before all their gazes went straight to the crossed arms on the chest of the cadaver.

Martin zoomed in and could clearly see that all the digits of both hands were evident and totally intact.

'He caught it on a barbed wire fence at the back of our house, when we were kids. Tore the top half clean off. I got him home and while we awaited the ambulance I hopped over the wall to try and retrieve it. But the neighbour's dog beat me to it and wolfed it down in one.'

Chapter Twenty-four

Micky had been pacing around inside his flat; he'd tried watching telly and messing about on social media, but couldn't relax. He'd expected to get the call much earlier, and it was already early evening. He was starting to wonder if something had happened. He hoped not as he was excited: the thought of meeting the top boss, being brought into the inner circle, and getting a handsome payday was a triple result. Eventually, his phone buzzed to announce an incoming text; it was from Kinsella. He read it, sent a quick confirmation reply, and then had to Google where the hell the meeting location was. He'd never heard of Pontcysyllte Aqueduct, but soon learnt that it was a UNESCO World Heritage Site in North Wales, about an hour and a quarter's drive from Liverpool. Clearly, the boss wasn't taking any risks, and the more Micky thought about it, the more sense it made. A very secure location with a panoramic view. It just reinforced that he was joining a top crew.

He was on the road in five minutes. The route would take him through the Queensway Mersey Tunnel again, and down the A41 past the shipyards and the location of where all the fun had taken place the previous day. Although he wouldn't actually go down the road where the crash was, but pass parallel it, he felt a touch uneasy, and would do so until he was heading out of Birkenhead towards Chester.

Traffic was light and it was a beautifully clear evening. He made good time and arrived at a car park linked to the site just before 8 p.m. The aqueduct was impressive. It sat high in the sky above grassland and the River Dee. It ran for miles and carried a canal across the valley. According to Kinsella's text, there was a footpath which ran across the aqueduct next to the canal in the sky, and he was to meet Kinsella on his own, first, somewhere around midway. As he left his car he couldn't see any other vehicles, which although not unexpected at this time of day, he wondered where Kinsella's motor was. He'd initially figured that he would have been told to bring Jason in his motor, but guessed he was probably with the boss.

Micky followed the footpath from the car park and set off on the long trek across the bridge. In the distance he could see a figure leant on the railing looking outwards across the countryside. It certainly was a remote place and there was no way anyone could approach without being seen. The canal itself was empty of traffic, but as it would be dark in less than an hour he reckoned they would be undisturbed.

As he neared, he recognised the figure as Kinsella, who stood up but didn't turn to face him until he was with him. 'You've certainly picked a remote spot. Must admit I didn't know it existed,' Micky said.

'The boss is a very cautious man, he has to be. You can see for miles up here.'

'Fair enough.'

'You sure you weren't followed here?'

'Absolutely.'

'Another reason we use this spot is if you had been tailed, you'd have clocked them on the final approach as easy as anything.'

'Where is the boss?' Micky asked. He felt both nervous and excited.

'We'll give it a couple of minutes to ensure that we are alone, and then I'll text him to call him on. He's just at the other side,' Kinsella said, pointing the opposite way. It explained why Micky had not seen any other motors. They were obviously at the other end.

'He's so impressed with you; he's already lined up another little job for you.'

'Excellent stuff, I'll not let him down.'

Then Kinsella pulled an A5 sized brown envelope out from his jacket pocket and handed it to Micky. 'I thought the boss wanted to pay me himself?' he asked.

Kinsella drew his phone and manipulated it for a second or two and then put it away. He must have just texted the boss.

'Oh, he will, he's on his way, now.'

'So what's this?' Micky said, holding up the envelope.

'It's details of the next job; it'll be quick and simple, and nowhere near as messy as yesterday.'

Micky's heart sank as he realised the *next job* sounded like another killing. But he had to get a grip of himself; there was no going back now.

'And put the fucker away before you drop it. You can read and destroy it later,' Kinsella added.

Micky nodded and quickly folded the envelope in half and stuffed it into the back pocket of his jeans. He noted Kinsella look around; so followed his gaze but couldn't see anyone approaching. He was about to ask if it wouldn't be easier to walk across the rest of the viaduct and save the boss some bother, but decided it was probably better to keep his mouth shut. They obviously did things in a specific way.

Then Kinsella said, 'You keep a look out over there while he approaches,' pointing out from the railing, 'and only look round when he speaks to you.'

Micky was starting to wonder whether all this James Bond routine was a bit over the top, but he did as he was told, and leant on the railings with his arms and looked out across the lush vista, not totally sure what he was supposed to be looking for. Or was it more about not watching the boss approach. Probably the latter.

He was aware that Kinsella had stepped from his side, out of view, so must have moved to directly behind him. Then in a flash, he felt arms grab him around his knees and hoist him upwards, as if Kinsella was using him to do some sort of squat thrust style manoeuvre. 'Hey, what the fuck are...' was as far as Micky managed to say before the situation hit him. He was now off the ground and his waist was above the height of the handrail on top of the railings.

A huge force pushed him forward as he fought to throw himself backwards. At the same time, he was frantically trying to kick backwards with his heels, but in the instant that the whole episode had taken, he knew it was in vain. He was over the tipping point and felt the grip around his legs release as he cascaded head first over the side. He watched his entire life's movie reel dash at epic speed before his eyes. It paused on the scene of yesterday's crash, and then on the lifeless body of the nurse a millisecond before he hit the ground head first.

Chapter Twenty-five

'What the hell does this mean?' Paul Harding said, to no one in particular as he paced up and down his office. Martin, Colin, Cath and Devers were sat around a small conference table. Martin didn't have any answers, and no one else was jumping in with any hypotheses.

'Not Tommy Broadbent. Is the brother sure?'

Martin let Colin, as the senior rank; explain the finger and the dog story.

'Christ, you couldn't make it up,' Harding said, before turning to Martin. 'This finger thing, it was there when you first recruited him?'

'It was,' Martin said.

'Well, before we can answer the obvious question – as in, why? We need an answer to the even more obvious one. Where the hell is the real Tommy Broadbent?' Harding said, to no one in particular, again.

Then Devers chipped in, 'I've asked the pathologist to check whether he's had any plastic surgery.'

'OK, that's a start, good.'

Then Cath said, 'It's no wonder I've struggled so much to find any background; he hasn't got one.'

'It also explains his reluctance as a source, which both I and the two Johns experienced, Martin added.

'So why did he keeping put himself forward as a potential snout,' Harding asked Martin directly.

It was a good question and then it hit him. 'Maybe to keep a watching brief to pick up if we were showing interest in him.'

Everyone in the room turned to face Martin, and he continued, 'Think about it; he's living the life of the real Tommy Broadbent, probably just because of the striking similarities, and he even shares the same first name, but I'm guessing that was probably a bonus.'

'I get that,' Harding said, but how would he ever know if we had started an operation or official enquiry of any sort into the real Tommy Broadbent's activities? His handlers would never have passed that nugget the other way.'

'Unless they were corrupt?' Devers said.

'I'm as sure they are not, as I am, that no one in this room is bent. So unless I'm shown evidence to the contrary, let's assume that the two Johns ran it right,' Harding added.

'I'm not suggesting that, but if the cops ever started an investigation into him, the ethical dilemma that would have thrown up could only have had one outcome,' Martin said.

Silence followed as everyone considered what Martin had said.

Cath was the first to respond, 'Forgive me for not understanding the rules of informant handling, but what do you mean?'

Martin apologised, momentarily forgetting that Cath could not know. 'If he was being investigated for serious crime, he would not be able to continue as a snout. So by the very fact that he remained on the handlers' books, meant that the real Tommy Broadbent was free and in the clear with no cops chasing his arse.'

'My God, that makes sense. Perfect sense,' Colin added.

'And explains why after wanting out, he was far too dangerous to leave alive. He signed his own death warrant,' Martin added.

'And it means that every time he was tasked by his handlers to find out anything he could about A or B, then by default he would know we had an interest in A or B?' Colin added.

Martin nodded. The realisation that the organisation had effectively been infiltrated, if only as a consequence of Tommy keeping a watching brief, just added to the problems.

'Christ, we'll have to go through every contact sheet the two Johns wrote up to get an idea on what he may have learnt by default, and therefore be in a position to assess the damage,' Harding said.

'We can do that, if you wish?' Colin said, and Harding nodded.

'But first up we need to find the real Tommy Broadbent, like, as of yesterday. He's gone to a lot of trouble to stay under the radar while he does God knows what,' Harding added.

'Hopefully, all he was interested in was getting a heads up should we ever have started to look at 'him', Colin threw in.

'All we can do is pray so, but we need to check the worst case scenario,' Harding said. 'And if you guys can carry the brunt of this, Phil is up to his armpits with both murders.'

Martin, Colin and Cath all nodded, and Devers thanked them and then got to his feet, said his farewells and left them to crack on.

'Any idea where we should start?' Colin asked.

'I'll arrange a full search team to pull his house apart,' Martin said.

'And I'll dig deeper into the club; that's got to be the centre of whatever the real Tommy Broadbent is up to,' Cath added.

Harding then stood up, 'Right, I've now got the pleasure of bringing the chief constable up to date.'

***

Lucy Pinder was stretching out in an executive suite in one of central Manchester's 5-star hotels. Thirty odd miles away from Liverpool, but it could be thirty thousand. Each city had its own very distinct identity; and each rivalled the other. Dogs and cats. But both Mancunians and Scousers, alike, would argue infinitum as to who were the dogs and who were the cats. But as far as Lucy was concerned, it was the perfect place to house her and her partner while they were in the UK taking charge of business. Close enough to Liverpool to visit the club and do what had to be done, but they could also operate freely in Manchester totally unknown, and therefore untroubled.

She was ready to go out for dinner, and was wearing a brand new party dress covered in sequins. Sat in the lounge part of their suite she awaited Kinsella's call while her other half, who had just flown in, finished getting ready. She'd not long put the phone down, when it rang. It was Kinsella.

'Good news, Jason?'

'As arranged, the halfwit turned up like an expectant dog with his tail wagging.'

Perhaps Scousers were the cats, she mused. Maybe not as big as dogs, but with the guile and street smarts that their contemporaries could only dream of. 'Go on,' she urged.

'He's taken the dive, so it ends with him. One loose end tied up.'

113

'Excellent.'

'And I have a surprise for you.'

'Go on.'

'To make sure I've put some stuff in an envelope on him, so even Merseyside's thickest can't help but put the jigsaw together.'

'That's a bold shout if it has more than two pieces.'

They both laughed and Kinsella continued, 'It means they get to detect something for a change, and then by default, stop. This bit ends with him. The poor man must have been overwrought with guilt.'

They both laughed once more, and then she said, 'Seriously, you've done great. And he'll love the envelope bit. That was inspired.' She then ended the call just as her other half walked into the lounge.

'Jason?' he asked, as he took an armchair opposite her.

'Yes, and it's sorted. Micky the Mann is no more. The nurse killer the police are chasing is dead. It stops with him.'

'Let's hope so.'

Lucy then explained what Kinsella had told her.

'I love the envelope, bit; even the thickest plod will get that.'

'And if they connect Mickey and the dead nurse to Tommy, it all stops. All the car occupants are thought to have died, they'll surely pin Tommy's death on him, too. Case closed.'

'I like your new suit.'

'I love your dress.'

'We both scrub up well, but it has to be said, you look particularly good for a dead man.'

They both laughed and he poured them both a drink. He handed Lucy one of the glasses, with the stub of what remained of his left little finger wrapped against the stem of the glass. They clinked glasses together, and Lucy toasted, 'To the real Tommy Broadbent.'

'To me,' Broadbent replied. And then asked, 'How did you get on with Ted?'

'Just spoke to him, and told him to start to get the upstairs rooms ready.'

'He'll be solid, I'm sure.'

'In a way the other Tommy would not have been. He'd have been a pain and have got in the way of the new plans for the club.'

'Undoubtedly, and in any event, his real job was just to be me and to keep a watching brief.'

'And now he's dead, the watchers will stop looking.' She lifted her empty glass up and Broadbent took the hint and grabbed the bottle of Champagne and topped up her up.

'He's no relatives, so no one will miss him.'

'We found him down and out in the gutter with no family around him, and he can now head back down the gutter of life, or death, where he belongs,' she said.

'He'd have been dead years ago, if you hadn't found him. You've actually given him a good life, one that he wouldn't have had.'

'It was only ever supposed to be temporary,' Lucy said.

'Mind you, I've no family, apart from you; we had that much in common.'

'Your brother, Bobby?'

'He's dead to me, as I am to him. You have always been all the family I need.'

'You say the sweetest things to a gal. I know what you're after.'

Broadbent laughed and then said, 'I'll just have to be careful, and keep my face hidden while we set up the club for its new business model. You can face up for me. Though, I would like to do a flying visit once everything's in place.'

Lucy smiled her agreement, but she knew that the club aside, if what she had brewing came to fruition then she would need Tommy to front up a meeting over there, it would serve a dual purpose.

Chapter Twenty-six

It was good to get back to their Preston office the following day, as both Martin and Colin had a ton of paperwork to catch up on. Cath was energised in all things relating to the club Banging Sounds, and who was really behind it.

'I suspect they have people on wages who are working for intermediaries, for cash etc. etc. The chain could go on and on, and might never lead us to Broadbent,' she said, as the three of them finished off their brainstorming session, which Colin and Martin had started the previous day.

'Quite possibly, but there is something I don't get about the club?' Martin said.

'What's that?' Colin asked.

'Well, according to you, it makes money, but not a vast amount,' Martin said, aiming his comment at Cath.

'True; it's ticking over, but not in a particularly big way,' she answered.

'So what is its true worth?'

'As in its true meaning?' Colin said.

'Exactly.'

'Could just have been all part of the subterfuge; the place where "Tommy Broadbent" worked and could be seen,' Cath suggested.

'Also true, and it did achieve that; but it's a big expense if it was just part of false Tommy's cover.' Colin said.

'Be interesting to see what happens next,' Martin said.

'Perhaps they are planning something big and it involves the club. If so, I'll be watching,' Cath said.

'You said "they"?' Colin asked.

'Yeah, we still don't know who the woman is.'

'OK, Phil is doing the reactive investigations into who killed the nurse and Tommy. Incidentally, the CPS have told him that it is no longer in the public interest to allow the public to think we also died in the crash,' Colin said.

'It's not up to the CPS,' Martin said, feeling riled. The CPS seemed to be pushing their noses into the investigative side of things more and more; it was not part of their remit. 'We'll end up like the French if we are not careful, with an examining magistrate running everything.'

'It'll never get that bad, but they do have a point, so is Phil Devers is going to say that the two "passengers" survived the crash, but without saying who, or what, they are?'

'I guess that keeps our involvement - as police - out of it,' Martin said.

'And what about the brother, Bobby?'

'Leave him and the club side of it with me, if you wish?' Cath threw in.

'That would be great, and me and Martin can—' Colin started to say until his mobile rang and interrupted him.

As he took the call and Cath returned her attention to her computer screen, Martin headed to the canteen to grab a tray of brews and some toast. They really needed to invest in a kettle and a toaster for their office.

When he returned, Cath thanked him and dived in as he placed the tray down next to the printer. 'Colin?'

'Thanks, but it'll have to wait. That was Phil Devers on the phone; he's had North Wales CID on.'

Martin took a bite out of a slice and a slurp from his tea as Colin continued. 'Apparently, they have a beauty spot, a viaduct in the sky or something, and it's a favourite spot for those who love to fly without wings.'

'Or parachutes?' Martin asked.

'Exactly. Anyway, an odd one has come in. Some idiot has jumped to his death but has documentation on the body linking him to the death of Sarah, our nurse.'

'Really, now that is interesting,' Cath said.

'What kind of documentation?' Martin asked, trying not to spit crumbs everywhere.

'A suicide note and death bed confession, so to speak.'

'Even more interesting,' Cath said.

'They are treating it as suicide, but Phil wants you and I to join him at a briefing in Wrexham, North Wales in a couple of hours, so we'd better get going.'

'Who is the victim/murderer?' Cath asked.

'Don't really know, other than some known toe rag from Liverpool. Here,' Colin said, as he passed Cath a piece of paper. 'These are the deceased's details.'

'I'll do some preliminary checks while you are both en route,' Cath added.

'Cheers,' Colin said. 'You OK to drive today?' he asked Martin.

'Yeah, I'm fine, thanks,' Martin said, and grabbed the keys for their pool vehicle which were hung up on the wall. But the truth was he knew he'd be a bit nervous behind the wheel for a while longer yet, as anyone who has been in a bad crash will know.

They drove down the M6 and then west along the M56, which was remarkably event free. These motorways were always busy but often suffered horrendous tailbacks caused by accidents or breakdowns which were a daily event. Consequently, they arrived in good time and headed to Wrexham's police station canteen before the main briefing, which was due to start in twenty minutes. Cath had belled them en route to inform them that Mickey Mann was a doorman and thug who sold drugs and hurt people for money. He had a few convictions and was known to the city centre cops, and interestingly, he had worked the doors at Banging Sounds, but that could mean anything. Most doormen in the city centre would work a circuit of different doors, for different firms covering different clubs.

They had just sat down when they were joined by Phil Devers.

'Thanks for coming guys, I'm going to front the briefing with the Welsh SIO, a DI called Dai Jones, can you be eyes and ears at the back of the room? If anyone asks, I'll just say you are on my team. What they don't need to know, they don't need to know.'

Martin and Colin nodded.

'Thoughts?' Colin asked.

'Until we hear the details, I'll keep an open mind, but one, it all seems a bit convenient, and two, if Mickey Mann is, or was, our man, he's not the sort to take his own life in some guilt-tripped frenzy.'

More nods, and then Colin repeated what Cath had told them.

'Yeah, Mann was a nasty piece of work, and enjoyed the buzz of hurting people, but I wouldn't have had him down as a killer, though who knows.'

'You think he's been set up?' Martin said.

'Could be, but we did find clothing fibres on Sarah's body with gunshot residue on, so we have fast-tracked some clothing fibres from Mann to the lab this morning.'

'That would be nice,' Martin said.

'I don't expect a match. I mean what are the chances he's wearing the same clothes if he is our killer. That is, if he didn't burn them afterwards. But we have had a breakthrough on my way here, which is why I'm glad I caught you before we go in,' Phil said, as he glanced at his watch.

Martin instinctively did the same; they had five minutes.

'Go on,' Colin urged.

'Well, when they started to examine the clothing fibres from Sarah's body this morning, they also found a human hair which does not belong to the deceased.'

'Fabulous,' Martin said.

'But it will take time to extract the DNA from the hair root, and then search on the database for a match.'

'And Mann will be on the system,' Martin added.

'He will, but it'll be even quicker to compare the hair with one from Mann's body; the DNA analysis can follow, but at least we'll know.'

'Excellent,' Colin said.

Then Devers turned to face Martin, 'But we've got no forensics from the crash scene you were involved in, I'm afraid.'

'I never expected any, they didn't stop and then burnt their car,' Martin said.

'What about the gun the dog walker found?' Colin asked.

'Wiped clean with bleach wipes, and as it was thrown away, we can't even link it to the car: which was apparently stolen from a breaker's yard. Though the yard guy has been nicked and is getting the hard word as we speak, but don't hold your breath.'

'We won't; come on we'd better go,' Colin said, and all three stood and hurried out of the canteen.

Chapter Twenty-seven

The briefing room was on the ground floor of the police station, and a mixture of uniform officers and detectives were seated facing front. Martin and Colin stood at the back, and Martin reckoned there was about twenty staff in total. Phil made his way to the front and stood next to a detective in his fifties with striking white hair, it made him look older than he no doubt was. He identified himself to the room for the benefit of those who didn't know him, and thanked everyone for coming. It was Dai Jones. He quickly went through the basic facts and said they would treat it as suicide, as it appeared to be on face value, but would keep an open mind until they knew more. However, they would treat the crime scene as murder, so that no evidence was lost. All pretty standard stuff. You can always drop a murder investigation down to a suicide without loss of evidence, but not so the other way.

There was a big white screen behind Dai who nodded to someone at the front who activated a remote control, and the screen lit up. On it, Martin could see a photo of a piece of white paper with a several lines of typescript on it.

'This was found on the body in an envelope in the deceased's back pocket,' Dai started, and then turned to face the screen, 'and it reads: *"My name is Michael Mann from Toxtheth, Liverpool 8. I got involved with a nurse called Sarah; I used to supply her with Charlie. She had a problem. Anyways, she owed a lot of money, and as I fancied her I said she could pay off what she owed in other ways. I met her down by Canada Dock, expecting at least a blowie, but she got cold feet and said she was going to report me to the filth. I was carrying, and I know I shouldn't have been, but some geezer said he had the hump with me so it was just for self-defence in case I ran into him. Anyways, things got out of hand and I pulled the piece, just intending to scare Sarah but it went off. It was an accident, honest. I'm guilted up to fuck, and a mate told me that the filth were coming for me...."'*

Martin and Colin exchanged a look, and Dai continued, ' *"I know yous lot will never believe me with my form, and I can't go back inside and do a life stretch, so this is my only way out"*, the note is signed, also in typescript, ' *"Mickey Mann"*.'

Dai then turned to face Phil Devers, and continued, 'Irrespective of what we think of this note, and whether there is any truth to it, the deceased is obviously now of interest to DI Devers here from Liverpool, who has confirmed that a nurse named Sarah was shot to death at Canada Dock, Phil?'

Phil cleared his throat and was about speak when his attention was drawn to his phone vibrating in his hand. He gave the room his apologies as he turned away and quietly took a call. It didn't last long. He ended it and turned back to the front and looked at Dai Jones before continuing. 'That was the forensic science lab, and I can confirm that hair found on our murder victim is covered in gunshot residue, and it is the same gunshot residue as is present on her body; and that the hair is from the head of Micky Mann. It looks like he is our murderer after all.'

Back in the canteen, Martin and Colin were joined by Phil Devers. 'What do you two reckon?' he asked, as he took a seat.

'Too convenient,' Martin said.

'That note could have been written by a twelve year old,' Colin said.

'If it was, they'd have a higher IQ than Mann had, but I agree, it's all bollocks. The trouble is, the Welsh aren't going to make work for themselves without any supporting evidence,' Phil said.

'At least they are starting off as if it's homicide,' Colin said.

'For now. I've asked that the post mortem be carried out by a Home Office Pathologist instead of a local one, and Dai was resistant until I said Merseyside would pick up the bill. I hope you'll back me when I give Harding the good news.'

'Consider it done, it needs to be a thorough one,' Colin said.

'What about the railings?' Martin asked.

'What about them?' Phil asked.

'Not that we are going to miss Mickey the toe rag, but if it is murder here, he may have struggled, pre-launch. There may be forensics on the railings themselves.'

'Good point, I'll ask Dai to get their CSIs to check the mid-section above where he was found.'

'And if it is murder, with a convenient death bed confession, then someone has gone to a lot of trouble to bring things to a close; at least from our attention.'

'It all leads back to the real Tommy Broadbent; not that we can actually prove that he's done anything wrong; yet,' Colin said.

'We'll keep on the Tommy trail, and leave you to manage the murder times two, attempt murder times two, and the murder/suicide liaison,' Martin said, with a grin on his face.

'When you put it like that; can we swap?' Phil said.

'At least your offences are actually detected,' Martin added.

'Oh well, I'd better get off home then and put my trotters up,' Phil said, rolling his eyes.

'Joking apart, have we got any intel coming in which mentions the club?' Martin asked.

'Nothing, and if we do, I'll pipe it straight through to Cath. But what I can tell you is that the fake Tommy handed over no intel at all to the two Johns in the last couple of months, or more, and they had not tasked him with anything, either.'

'So nothing could have gone in the wrong way, even by accident?' Martin said.

'Nil, zilch. I know that doesn't help,' Phil said. 'Better go and grab Dai before he shoots off, sort out the viaduct railing examination.'

'Can you ask him to keep it as suicide as far as the press are concerned? If the criminals think their ruse has worked, then at least we keep an advantage,' Colin said, as Phil rose to his feet.

'Will do. What's your next move?' Phil asked.

'I've absolutely no idea, but you'll be the first to know,' Colin added, and Phil grinned before he turned and hurried out of the canteen.

'Well?' Colin asked Martin.

'All I know is that to go to all this trouble, someone is very keen to keep a clean sheet.'

Colin nodded.

Martin knew that reactive CID always had their hands full, but at least they had clues to follow, whereas with proactive investigations it was always about following intelligence more than hard facts, to try and catch someone before they commit the substantive offence, or nab them in the act. He'd done both kinds of investigations, and had always thought what they did at NWROCU was more fun, but now he wasn't quite so sure. Hopefully, Cath would come up with some leads after she'd spoken to Bobby Broadbent, if anyone could charm someone who wasn't predisposed to talk with you, it was Cath. Which left the club as an obvious other starting point.

'We could pay the club Banging Sounds a visit; speak to the barman Cath met, or the woman, or whoever else is running it? Pretend we are City Centre CID under Phil's command following up on the accident, now that it's official that fake Tommy was killed?'

'Good idea, gives us a chance to have a nosey around Tommy's office, see if he did leave something behind,' Colin said.

'Not that I expect to find much, but shall we do his house first, there may be more chance of someone being at the club preparing to open, later?' Martin asked.

'Sounds like a plan, come on then,' Colin finished with.

DOUBLE CROSS

Chapter Twenty-eight

'Are you sure about this?' Lucy asked, as she and Broadbent climbed into the hire car.

'I've got a baseball hat and sunglasses on, and no one gives a shit. I mean that was part of his brief, be a front for me and appear legit so the heat lifts,' Broadbent said.

'I get that, but now he's dead, it's even better for you, as you are totally off the radar and can never go back on it.'

'I know, I know, but if we are going to run the new business from there, as much as I trust you - and I so totally do - I'd like a look around. It's been years since I've been in there.'

Lucy knew that the new business apart, if what she had planned next came off, she'd need Tommy's kudos to front some meetings with some very serious players to get it green lit. 'OK,' she said.

'Ted's trustworthy enough, isn't he?'

'I wouldn't have promoted him if he was not. And anyway, he knows I have Kinsella lurking in the background as my enforcer.'

'Fair enough.'

Lucy said that she'd drive, that way Tommy could slouch in the passenger seat.

Sixty minutes later, they were heading along Liverpool's iconic waterfront with the Liver Building in the foreground with its two sculptured Liver birds clearly on view on top.

'Would you look at that? Warms the heart to see those two girls again,' Broadbent said, as he stared up at the building.

'Never mind that, keep your head down,' she said.

He grinned at her and then complied.

Five minutes later, they were on Dale Street, and approaching the front of the club. It sat on the street, pavement fronted, with a small street down one side and a pedestrian walkway down the other. The club was detached from the other buildings in the road, and had a small yard at the rear which doubled as a car park. She drove down the side street and parked at the back. The rear fire door was shut. 'If you hang on I'll go in the front and open the back door, saves putting your pretty face about unnecessarily.'

Broadbent smiled his agreement and she quickly got out and headed for the alleyway. As they'd passed the front of the club she'd noticed that the shutters over the front doors were three-quarters up, so knew Ted was already there.

She found him behind the bar restocking the bottled beer fridges, he turned as she approached.

'Hi Lucy, it's good to see you. How are you?'

'All good thanks. Any dramas?'

'None; just had some press around after the shooting in the cathedral, and a couple of plod, but all basic stuff.'

'Excellent. How are the rooms upstairs coming on?'

'Just needed a good clean really, it's a long time since this place was a hotel. New beds and furniture, and all five are now en suite as well.'

'Top behaviour. Not that we'll be advertising on Hotels and Inns dot com. But they need to be comfortable as well as functional.'

'All sweet.'

'And what of the staff?'

'I never liked or trusted the staff Tommy hired, and know I shouldn't speak ill of the dead, but I didn't really agree much with Tommy - club-wise - if I'm being brutal. That's why I was always glad to see you, as he deferred to you when you dropped in.'

Lucy smiled, and said, 'Well, you are running the show now so we have to keep things secure.'

'I get that, I'm afraid Tommy wouldn't have easily agreed to everything. In fact, I couldn't understand why you tolerated him, if you don't mind me saying.'

'He had uses you could never have known about, but are about to find out. Anyway, what about the staff?'

'I fired them all and have rehired people from the right side of the tracks.'

Lucy grinned and said, 'You mean the wrong side of the tracks?'

They both laughed and Ted said, 'They are the original three wise monkeys and I would trust my life with any of them. We all grew up on the same street in Croxteth.'

'That'll do for me. And now that you are management, and in our inner circle, I've got a little surprise for you.'

'I like surprises.'

Lucy walked over to the rear fire door and opened it with the bar and waved for Broadbent to join her. He was soon at the door and came in with his hat and glasses still on. He followed her over to where Ted was stood. 'This is my other half with whom I run the business; the mysterious Mr. Lucy, as you call him.'

'Good to meet you at long last, boss,' Ted said.

Lucy watched and smiled as Broadbent held his hand out and said, 'Always good to put a face to a name. I know we have spoken many times on the phone, but it's good to meet you in the flesh. Lucy says great things about how you can be trusted.'

'Absolutely, boss,' Ted said, as the two men shook hands.

Then Broadbent took his hat and glasses off, and grinned at Ted, and said, 'Ta da!'

Ted's eyes widened in shock, and he said, 'Fuck, what?'

Lucy and Broadbent burst out laughing, and Lucy said, 'Don't worry it's not a ghost. I'll explain while you pour us both a drink.'

'Well, at least the hat and glasses worked,' Broadbent said.

'Yep,' Lucy said, and then turned to Ted; 'two double scotches, and whatever you are having.'

'Cheers, I think a need a drink.'

Lucy quickly told Ted how they had found Broadbent's perfect doppelgänger in the gutter, just about the time that the real Broadbent was feeling the heat, and needed to disappear over to Holland for a while.

'What was his real name?' Ted asked.

'Can't remember his last name, but get this, his name was Tommy; how's that for a bonus?' Broadbent said.

'That was pretty inspired, if you don't mind me saying so,' Ted said.

'Not at all. It just rolled on a bit longer than we first intended, for reasons I'll not go into now,' Broadbent said.

'Must admit, it explains a lot,' Ted said.

'How do you mean?' Broadbent asked.

'There was always this sort of reluctance about him; everything was hard work,' Ted said.

'I'll drink to that,' Lucy said, and then emptied her glass. 'Come on you, we need to check the office and then do one.'

Broadbent nodded and emptied his glass.

'And I need to get a shift on, we open in two hours,' Ted said.

Lucy then headed upstairs, there were two stairways in the place, the main one at the front near the main doors and toilets, and a fire escape one which led down to the back of the club and ended near the fire door. The landing ran from front to back with a view over the dancefloor on the right-hand side - as you walked, front to back - with seven rooms on the left which were on the outside wall side; above the alleyway. The first five were bedrooms, then an office, and then a bigger office, which was more of a mini meeting room in size. Lucy led Broadbent into the small office and went straight to the safe situated behind a mahogany desk. It was a combination locked one and as she put in the code, Broadbent sat down in a worn Chesterfield on the door side of the desk.

Inside, was the takings tin which housed the previous days' cash. The amount looked low. Though, she had noticed over time how the cash monies became less and less as more people used plastic over the bar. So, if the fake Tommy had helped himself, it would be hard to tell, and it couldn't have amounted to much. Not that they could do anything about it now. But what was interesting was what was under the tin, stuck to its base over time; she nearly missed it, and would have done if she'd left the heavy tin in situ. It was Broadbent's real passport. It was eight years' old now. They had given it to fake Tommy when they had taken him on. Broadbent had used a bent one ever since, and fake Tommy was told not to travel with it, and only ever use it for ID purposes; and as he didn't need it now, the real Broadbent may as well have it back. She grinned at the photo and tossed it over to him. 'Here, a present for you.'

Broadbent caught it and opened the first page and looked inside. 'God, have I aged that much?'

'Looks that way. And your nose is bent,' she answered, and laughed.

When they first hired fake Tommy they had to talk him into having his nose broken so he would look even more like Broadbent. But while Broadbent had been in Holland, he had had his straightened, Lucy had forced him to, said she couldn't stand his snoring. 'Well, at least you can use a genuine passport now if you want? Stop you shiting yourself with the snide one.'

'True, but it might be a bit risky, all things considered,' Broadbent said, sliding the document into his pocket.

'Come on, time to do one,' Lucy said.

'I'll just have a peek in the rooms while you say goodbye to Ted, see you out back in a jiff,' he said, and headed back onto the corridor.

'Don't be long,' Lucy said, as she headed for the rear stairs.

Chapter Twenty-nine

Martin and Colin hadn't expected to find anything of much interest at Tommy's and hadn't been disappointed. Though they did find some correspondence which was years old in the name Thomas Dorchester, Martin would pass that on to both Phil and Cath. If this was his real name then the visit had been worth it. Somewhere, there could be a family relative who'd not heard from Tommy for many years, and was about to get some bad news.

'Come on, let's do the club next, see if we can't get any info out of whoever is running the place, get a look into his office and try and work out what he popped in for after you'd picked him,' Colin said.

Fifteen minutes later, they pulled into the private car park - come yard - at the rear of Banging Sounds. There was a rental car parked up near a rear steel door, which was closed, so they'd have to trot around to the front. They got out and walked down an alleyway and Martin was relieved to find that the shutters were up and the front door unlocked. Colin walked in first. The place was dimly lit with just some lights on behind the bar. A middle-aged man appeared from one end of the bar and made a bee-line for them.

'We're not open for a couple of hours, you'll have to leave.'

Martin produced his warrant card and introduced them both, and said, 'Just need to ask a couple of questions and we'll be out of your way. Firstly, who are you?'

'I'm Ted the manager,' Ted said, and then looked over their heads, before settling back on them. 'Look, can I sit you over there,' he said, and pointed to a table to the side of the place which was underneath an upstairs landing.

'Why can't we sit here?' Martin said, pointing to a couple of bar stools. 'We won't keep you long.'

'Er, they've been sterilised, COVID-wise, those tables on the other side of the dance floor have yet to be done,' Ted said.

Martin looked at Colin, who nodded, they didn't want to cause the guy any extra work and therefore piss him off, so they both turned and walked away from the bar, across the dance floor and chose the middle table of three under the upstairs, and sat down. As they did, Martin could hear footsteps above on the landing.

Ted joined them, and said, 'That'll be the cleaners, they'd have my bollocks if I'd cocked up their routines.'

'What is upstairs?' Colin asked.

'It's private up there, out of bounds to the public. Anyway, how can I help you?'

Martin was listening to the footsteps, first one set, and then a second, heading towards the rear of the club. Colin gave Ted the old, "we are detectives investigating the fatal car crash in Birkenhead and we believe the deceased man was the manager here bla, bla, bla" routine.

'Yes, Tommy Broadbent,' Ted said, with great accent to his words.

'Well, go on,' Colin said.

'He was my boss, but I'm now the manager.'

'That didn't take long,' Colin said, as Martin was half-listening and half-following the footsteps which sounded like they were now on a metallic staircase.

'Well, things have to carry on,' Ted said.

The footsteps came to a stop and Martin peered over Ted's shoulder expecting to see two cleaners emerge. It might be worth having a word with them while they were here.

'So who actually owns this place?' Colin asked.

'It's a business consortium from Holland; I can't really tell you any more than that. I deal with a representative from there, mainly via email.'

Then Colin told Ted about Tommy popping into the club on the day he was killed. Ted said he knew that Tommy had popped to his office upstairs, but didn't elaborate.

'Any chance of a peek in there?' Colin asked.

Martin was fully expecting a "no, go get a warrant" answer, but was amazed when Ted sprang to his feet and readily agreed. 'This way,' he added, pointing to the main stairs near the front door, which Martin thought odd as the rear steps were closer. But Ted set off, so they followed and as they were climbing the stairs, Martin could hear the footsteps at the other end start up again, going down.

They walked along a sort of gantry of a landing past several closed doors and then Ted led them into an office, which was the penultimate door on the corridor. He took them in and showed them the safe, and even opened it, and explained its sole occupant; the petty cash tin. This was obviously where Tommy had got his money that was found on his body. If he had dropped something off, it wasn't here now. 'And nothing else has been moved from here since?' Martin asked.

'Such as?' Ted said.

'Don't know, anything?'

'Only I have access, so no.'

'OK. Any chance of two minutes with your cleaners?' Martin asked.

'Sure, I'll go and get them,' Ted said, who then turned and left.

Again, his answer had surprised Martin, 'He seems very helpful for some reason.'

'Maybe, it's just the press he doesn't like.' Colin answered.

Martin then glanced at Colin who read his mind and said, 'Be quick, I'll listen out for his footsteps on the wooden landing.'

Martin quickly opened all the drawers in the desk, but they were empty. He then pointed to the desk, which just had a blotter, laptop and a desk phone on it. The laptop was closed shut, and Martin knew he really couldn't go near that without a warrant; a warrant he wouldn't be able to justify, especially if the device wasn't Tommy's.

Then the door opened and in walked, Ted. There had been no sound of footsteps; he'd probably tiptoed to try and catch them out.

'I'm sorry, we've missed them, they've both gone,' Ted said.

'But I thought they hadn't done the tables where we sat?' Martin asked.

Ted paused and then said, 'I must have been wrong.'

Colin then pushed for some background on Tommy; had he any family or friends and that sort of thing? All Ted's answers were negative. Too negative, he must have known something about Tommy's personal life, it's impossible to work with someone and not know some stuff.

Martin asked about the laptop, and as expected, it apparently belonged to the club and then Ted threw in that Tommy never used it, he left Ted to do all the admin, even though he had only been a barman. He said it was one reason why they never got on, professionally; which if true, he could understand.

Martin also noticed something else about Ted; since he had returned to the office, his demeanour had hardened, he was far less accommodating or friendly, and appeared more like Cath had described him. He asked if they were done, and when Colin said they were but may have to return to speak to the cleaners, he ushered them out as quickly as he could. He promised to speak to the cleaners and get in touch if they knew anything of interest. Martin knew this was bullshit as Ted hadn't asked for any contact details from them, and doubted he would remember their names five minutes later.

They left via the front and made their way to the back of the club, the same way they had come in, and Martin noticed that the rental car had gone. He also noticed that the rear steel fire door was ajar. Why hadn't Ted showed them out that way? It would have been a lot quicker. Probably just being an arse with them.

Chapter Thirty

'Hurry up and get in you idiot,' Lucy snapped at Broadbent, as she ran around the front of the rental and jumped into the driver's seat. She started the engine as Broadbent climbed in the passenger side and set off before he'd closed the door probably.

'Hey,' he shouted, as he then managed to slam the door shut.

'Do you want to get caught, and blow everything?'

'You worry too much; we got out alright, didn't we?'

'You sometimes don't worry enough, that was close,' she said, as she drove back onto Dale Street and turned away from the club, and headed towards the city centre. She only calmed down once they had left Dale Street and were safely away.

'You heard them, they said they were investigating the crash where "Tommy Broadbent" died, so imagine their surprise if they'd seen you? "Oh, hi Tommy" they'd no doubt say, "Glad you are not really dead, it means we can all go home now".'

'I know, I know, but with Ted's help we managed it. You must admit it gives you a buzz, though? Reminds you that you are truly still alive?'

Lucy looked at Broadbent and grinned, the bastard had that way of making her smile even though she was still mad. 'Well, it certainly gave us a buzz, that's for sure. But if you think that's a buzz; wait until you see the surprise I'm planning for you,' she said, before concentrating on her driving. The quicker they were out of the city and headed back towards Manchester, the safer she'd feel.

'Yeah, you keep teasing me with all this stuff. Come on give me a hint; we are partners after all.'

'I will soon, I just need to prove it works, first.'

'Is it to do with the girls?' he asked.

'No, they are just going to be a short term source of income. I think it would be too dangerous to run them for too long, don't you?'

'Yeah, but if we keep it tight, and only allow clients whom we invite, it might help to keep it quiet longer than we'd first thought.'

'True, but you know how you boys like to talk and brag about what you and your tiny appendages get up to.'

'Hey, less of the tiny.'

'Present company accepted, of course,' Lucy said, and flashed him a smile.

'So how do you mean, "Prove it works"?'

'All in good time, but if it does, we are going to need you to sell it to your Neanderthal misogynist mates.'

'I can't wait,' Broadbent said, before settling down into a slouch.

Lucy drove them onto West Derby Road heading due east out of Liverpool towards Queens Drive, from where they would pick up the A580 - the East Lancashire Road - which would take them straight to Manchester.

***

Martin and Colin had only just left the club when Martin's phone rang through the car's Bluetooth. It was Cath, and she sounded excited. 'What is it?' he asked.

'Just had Merseyside Police Intel Unit on, do you remember the armed robber Clayton Rigby?'

'Not *the* Clayton Rigby?' Martin asked.

'The very same.'

Martin and Colin shared a look of astonishment. Two years ago they had spent months investigating a robbery firm from Salford who used to specialise in committing robbery on banks, cash-in-transit, booking shops and any retail premises which they deemed to be cash rich. Martin had run the surveillance and strike teams on Rigby and his firm, and had taken them down on a pavement outside a Barclays bank in St. Helens. All were armed, and all were arrested in an armed strike. Everything went textbook; all four gang members ended up on their arses on the pavement, plasti-cuffed up, with their individual weapons made safe and laid next to them as the guy with the video camera

135

recorded everything, so the jury would be able to see exactly how the arrests had gone down, and who had which gun.

Then four separate police vans turned up to ferry the prisoners to the nearest Custody Suite when it all went wrong. All four men started to resist their escorting officers before they could get them cleanly into the back of the police vans. Rigby head-butted the officer leading him and ran off with his hands still cuffed in front of him, into a nearby housing estate and escaped.

The other three were all flattened and contained, and later convicted and given long terms of imprisonment. But all three had refused to even acknowledge who Rigby was, let alone where he might be. That had been two years ago and no end of digging had turned him up. 'Please tell me he's been arrested somewhere?' Martin said to Cath.

'Not yet, but plans are being put in place. They reckon they will know where he'll be as of 7 a.m. tomorrow morning. There's a briefing to be held at out Liverpool Branch Office and I thought you might like to be on it?'

'Cath, you're a star. How good's the intel?'

'According to them, it's A1.'

'It sounds very specific?'

'Doesn't it. I take it you are in?'

'Try and stop me,' he said, and then told Cath he'd drop Colin off and head home early, and get his head down, he'd catch up with her tomorrow.

'Works for me, I'll be working late anyhow, I've arranged to see Bobby Broadbent this evening,' she said.

Martin acknowledged that, and Colin asked her if she wanted him to accompany her. She thanked him and said she'd be OK; he may as well have an early finish, too. Colin thanked her and they ended the party call.

'Stephanie will think there is something wrong, two earlier nights in a row,' Colin said.

'Join me in the morning, if you want?' Martin suggested, but Colin declined. Said it was time he spent some while in the office, he'd become behind on the organisational stuff.

136

Martin nodded, but his mind was racing. They had done everything they could think of in an effort to trace Rigby. Watched and followed his close family and known associates. Tasked numerous informants with the carrot of a five grand reward. Sent out undercover officers, and even bugged his parent's house for a short time, to try and pick up where he was hiding. But nothing, zilch. They had eventually effectively given up, until any fresh information gave them a lead, which had never happened. Until now. He'd love to know where the Merseyside Intel Unit had got their gen from, but knew they wouldn't be able to share that. But it did sound specific, down to a point in time and not just a place. This led Martin to surmise it was a one-off opportunity, not one to be cocked-up.

Chapter Thirty-one

Lucy parked their motor in the underground car park, and she and Broadbent headed up to their room on the fifteenth floor of the hotel. Once back in the apartment, her phone started to ping and bleep. She began to navigate her way through the variety of messages from a variety of social media and telephone text platforms, and grinned as she absorbed what they all said.

'You seem popular?' Broadbent said, as he appeared from the bathroom.

'Yeah, it's from my secret lover.'

'Now, I know that's not true; I'm more than enough for you,' he said, before grabbing at his own crotch.

'If it all goes well, you'll be pulling your little friend for real, trust me.'

'The suspense is killing me.'

'All in good time, it won't be long now. I just want to show you, rather than tell you. You'll see.'

'Well, I may as well leave you to it for half an hour; I fancy a pint at that Irish boozer down the street.'

'OK, but keep your head down.'

'Will do, they have loads of TVs in there; I'll just watch some sport over a pint. Text me when you're done and we can go out for a bite.'

Lucy nodded and then a thought hit her, 'Leave that passport behind, just in case. Just be your luck to get turned over and lose it.'

'I'd like to see some mug try, but you're right,' he said, before pulling the passport out of his pocket and throwing it towards to glass coffee table. But as it landed, something emerged from within its pages. 'What's that?' he said.

'Have a look.'

Broadbent picked up the passport and pulled a small plastic card from within it. He then quickly checked through the remainder of the document before returning his attention to the card. Lucy could see that it was white and credit card sized, but with no writing or anything on it. Broadbent turned it over, the rear was also blank.

'Looks like a hotel room key card,' she said.

'It's certainly a key card for something,' he said, and handed it to her.

Lucy took it, but could see no hotel logo or other such identifying feature on it. 'Interesting, I think we'll keep hold of that until we work out what it's for.'

'Well, whatever it's for, old Tommy won't need it now,' Broadbent said, and laughed, before she put it back on the table next to the passport.

Then Lucy's phone buzzed again drawing her attention back to it, and Broadbent waved and headed towards the door.

***

Martin was at their Liverpool Branch Office early and was pleased to learn that the other officers involved had no idea what the morning's operation was about, or more importantly, who it was about. Even the armed strike team didn't know who the subject was. All they had been given were photos and plans of an end terraced house with which to plan their assault. It would be a rapid entry. The DI running the show was Shelia Jorden, who Martin knew vaguely, but more by way of her excellent reputation. She was a redhead in her forties and was a career DI with apparently no aspiration to continue up the ladder. As she had once put it the last time the two had conversed, 'DCIs get very little extra money, but are fitted out for a tailor-made desk.' She clocked Martin at the rear of the briefing room and walked over.

'Hi, long time no see, you good?' she asked.

'Us redheads have to stick together,' he said.

'You're not a redhead.'

'I just hide it well.'

'Up yours, Draker.'

They both laughed. 'I could have you for making a hair-ist remark,' she added, and they laughed again. 'Seriously though, I bet you are excited?'

'Am I, love to know where he's been for the last two years?'

'I bet.'

'And where the current intel has come from?'

'Me too.'

'What's the plan?'

Shelia then explained that the intel said that Rigby had moved into a rental property the day before under a false name. They had put an obs van on the address straight away, but no one had been seen entering or leaving the property.

'How do we know he's actually there?' Martin asked.

'The lights were turned on and off and the curtains drawn to by a figure roughly matching Rigby's description.'

'Is that it?' Martin said, trying not to sound too sceptical.

Shelia threw her hands in the air and then pointed to herself and then to the sidearm of a firearms officer stood nearby and said, 'Messenger - gun.'

Martin smiled an apology.

'I have naturally questioned it, but have been told in no uncertain terms that the intel is good. Rigby is in there, but he won't stop too long. He moves around continuously, and if he smells something he's not happy with - real or imagined - he does one.'

'That's why we have never caught up with him, I guess,' Martin said, ensuring he sounded more conciliatory.

'Which is why, no one but you and I know who the subject is, I'll brief them just before the strike so they know what they are facing. At the main briefing I'll just describe him as a very dangerous and violent fugitive who would not hesitate to shoot a policeman.'

'That should get their attention.'

'That's the idea.'

'But why 7 a.m.? Sounds very specific.'

'Because we are sending our "meter reader" to confirm that he is there. And as Rigby is a new tenant, it fits with doing it as early as possible on his first full day in the property.'

'Ah! A great plan. I take it that the property hasn't got a Smart meter, though?'

'I'm a redhead, not a blonde.'

'Now, that is hair-ist.'

Shelia grinned and then rushed off. Ten minutes later, she briefed everyone. There were two teams of six armed response officers whose job it was to do the rapid entry, a DS and three DCs who were there to arrest the subject and search the place for any additional evidence, and Martin and Shelia who would be in the command car. The fact that she refused to name the subject just added to the buzz in the room, but she was determined that if it was a negative search, no one could accuse her team of having loose lips. It was an easy finger to point if the intel turned out to be incorrect, especially from those who provided the information in the first place. Cops were often very defensive when things went tits up.

Briefing over, and everyone sure of their role, they synchronised watches - 0610 hours - and then rolled out. She told everyone to be on plot for 0640.

Martin joined Shelia in the command car, and they were soon near to the target address in a quite side street in the Anfield district of Liverpool. The road was straight out of the TV sitcom Bread, from the late 80s. All the houses were pavement-fronted with their doorsteps and stone door surrounds painted white. The forward RV was behind an ambulance station which was one minute away. Each of the two ARV crews of six left the RV and made their ways to prearranged plots, metres away from the front and back of the property; which was a 1930s back-to-back house. The rear team had to climb into someone else's back yard ready to jump over the wall into the rear of the target address when ordered to go. They shouldn't be in the other person's yard long, and as the house at the rear was all in darkness with its curtains drawn to, Shelia decided not to disturb the owners.

As soon as the armed officers had entered the target address and secured the prisoner and the property, they would join the party. Shelia then called for radio silence as the undercover officer dressed as a meter reader did his knock. There was deathly silence in the command car, and Martin found himself holding his breath. They could hear the knocking on the front door, via the 'meter reader's' open mike, and then silence; and then more knocking followed by more silence. Then the undercover officer whispered over the radio, *'I'm getting no reply, I'm going to have to leave it, to keep going would look unnatural.'*

Shelia agreed and the OP reported not seeing him leave, and also added that there had been no movement inside the property, the curtains were still drawn with the lights off.

'The lazy bastard probably can't be arsed answering the door,' Shelia mused out loud.

'Sounds like it,' Martin agreed.

'It's going to be fully light soon.'

'Agreed.'

Then Shelia picked up her radio mike and said, *'All units, this is Alpha One; confirming that the target is an armed robber from Manchester, who you will all know by name; which is Clayton Rigby. He is believed to still carry, or have immediate access to firearms for his own protection. All teams acknowledge.'*

All the teams then acknowledged the intel update and then Shelia spoke into the mike once more, *'All teams, this Alpha one: strike, strike, strike.'*

Chapter Thirty-two

Martin and Shelia sat in silence awaiting the initial situation report. It would only take minutes, but would feel like hours. It was always the most nervous part of any operation. They moved their position to the target address's street, but held back by 50 metres. The thought of seeing Rigby brought out in handcuffs was tantalisingly close now. Then the firearms unit sergeant came over the radio to announce that the downstairs was now clear and secure. They decided to approach on foot.

As they made their way towards the property, Martin saw the upstairs front bedroom curtains being opened by one of the firearms officers, though he'd no way of knowing whether Rigby would be in the front, or rear bedroom. But it did mean it was now safe to approach the house from the front aspect. 'Come on, let's get in there,' he said to Shelia, who he guessed had seen what he had too, as she smiled and said, 'Yep, can't wait.'

'He's robbed his last bank,' Martin added.

They reached the house and were about to walk through the door when another of the firearms officers declared, over the net, that all the upstairs rooms were secure, including the loft space. Then the sergeant leading the firearms teams came back on the radio, *'Bravo One to Alpha One, I'm afraid it's a negative search. No one present at the property.'*

The words dug in through Martin's earpiece straight into his brain, ' "No one present" how the hell.' he said, to no one in particular.

Then Bravo One continued, *'Bravo One to Alpha One, there's more, but you need to see this. Please make your way to the bathroom of the property.'*

Martin just looked quizzically at Shelia as they both rushed inside.

The bathroom was at the top of the stairs to the rear of the property, it was small with a just a shower, sink, WC and a mirrored wall cabinet. It felt even smaller with Shelia, Martin and an embarrassed looking firearms' sergeant squeezed inside.

Martin immediately noted that the bathroom window was wide open, but the sergeant wasn't looking at that.

'Here,' he said, and pointed at the glass-fronted cabinet.

Both Martin and Shelia followed his instructions and then Martin saw what all the fuss was about. Written on the mirror, in what looked like toothpaste, were the words, "TOO SLOW".

Sixty minutes later, Martin and Shelia were back at the Liverpool Branch Office, joined in the conference room by Colin and Cath who had legged it up from Preston. The door burst open and in walked Paul Harding who looked flushed to say the least. He initially started on Shelia. 'How the hell did he find out?' But before she could answer, he added, 'One of your lot must be bent; incompetent, or both.'

Martin saw Shelia take a moment and a deep breath before she briefly outlined the operation. She did so calmly and without emotive language, which Martin wouldn't have been able to do in her position. But he jumped in as soon as she had finished, and said, 'It's not Shelia's fault.'

'Well, whose damn fault is it?'

'She didn't even tell the strike team who the target was until a second before they went in. Just on the off-chance it turned out like it did.'

This seemed to calm Harding a little as he hesitated and then apologised to Shelia.

'None taken, I'm sure: much,' she said.

Martin admired her for saying that. He liked her all the more for it. Harding spun around and she quickly put her hands up.

'I guess I deserved that; you are dismissed Shelia, but thanks for trying,' Harding said.

Shelia spun around and winked at Martin before she left the room. As soon as the door closed, Harding carried on, ' "Too Slow" too fucking slow: who the fucking hell does that toss pot think he is?'

'One who is not as smart as he is arrogant. If he hadn't left that cheeky note, then we'd be none the wiser. Now we are,' Martin said.

'He's got a point, boss,' Colin jumped in with.

'I realise this, and irrespective of what it hints at, I withdraw my earlier outburst. I know it's not at the door of NWROCU. Which means it's on us, here at Merseyside Police. I've already asked the head of Intelligence to provenience the source of the intel, and then work it backwards.'

'Can I ask if it came from a live source, sir?' Cath asked.

'No you can't, but yes it did. The trouble is this is not the first failed op we have had recently.'

Martin, Colin and Cath exchanged a joint look of incredulity.

'This is the third failed job this month. Sue Claire - ACC Crime - is going to have my bollocks for this.'

Then his phone rang and Harding sighed as he looked at the screen, he took the call and walked to the rear of the room as he spoke. Martin heard him use the work 'Ma'am'.

Two minutes later, he ended the call and was back. 'That was ACC Claire demanding my attendance forthwith; we'll have to chat later. But suffice to say, unless I can talk her around, she is minded to halt all intelligence led operations until we can find out what's going wrong and plug it.'

'What about your ongoing undercover operations?' Colin asked.

'Including them.'

'May I ask how many you have live at the moment?'

'Three. This is a nightmare. You guys find Rigby, fast. Then maybe the arrogant twat can tell us where he got *his* intel from?' Harding finished with, and then hurried out of the room.

'Sorry for Mr. Harding's use of the word twat, Cath; other terms for scumbags are available,' Martin said.

Cath smiled, but Colin did not. Then his phone rang and he took the call. Martin could tell that it was from Phil Devers, but not much else.

Two minutes later, Colin ended the call and turned to face Martin and Cath. 'It just gets better and better. That was Phil Devers if you hadn't guessed, and his hunch has paid off; or not, depending on your point of view.'

Martin didn't like the sound of this.

'The PM on Mann's body has identified ante mortem injuries to the top of both of his knees consistent with coming forcefully into contact with a hard blunt object. And the CSI sweep of the hand railing across the viaduct has found crushed fibres on the top edge, which are a match to fibres taken from the knee area of the trousers Mann was wearing.'

'So it is murder, as we suspected,' Martin said.

'I'm afraid so, and even though the offence is on North Wales, Merseyside police will have to stay heavily involved. This'll put Harding over the edge.'

'I don't fancy Phil's next phone call,' Martin said, trying not to grin at the unintended pun.

'I told him I'd do it.'

'That's bleeding good of you, Col.'

'Isn't it. And I'd better do it before he gets to the ACC's office; just in case she gets piped off first,' Colin said, as he slowly pulled his mobile phone back out of his pocket.

'What can we do?' Cath asked.

'Go and find Clayton Rigby, and fast.'

And with that, Martin and Cath hurried out of the room.

'Where do we try first?' she asked Martin, as they headed towards to garage.

'I've absolutely no idea.'

'Let's go back into the main office; I'll give the taxi firms a try first. He's had to leg it at short notice, unprepared, leaving what he had behind,' Cath said.

'Needing transport out of the area, immediately. Good thinking, it's worth a try,' Martin said, and they both headed back inside.

Martin knew that a lot of city centre taxi firms had a "ring-around" system with each other. It was a way of getting information or warnings out to other drivers very quickly. The police could use it in emergencies so long as they didn't abuse it with non-urgent stuff. And the payback for the drivers was the knowledge that whenever any one of them was in trouble, the police would respond in numbers. Martin also knew that only certain individuals had access to the system to prevent its overuse. Cath being one of them. He left her to it and went to make a brew.

Three minutes later, as he walked into the general office where Cath was, with two mugs of tea, she looked up grinning. 'No time for that, we've hit the jackpot.'

'What?'

'City Cabs from Anfield picked up a guy in the next street at the right time who matches the description of Rigby. The driver said he looked rushed and was perspiring.'

'Where did he take him?'

'OK, not quite the jackpot, he didn't take him to an address, but dropped him in Manchester city centre.'

'Manchester? That's a fair cab ride.'

'Yeah, he told the cabbie to put his foot down and gave him a hundred quid.'

'This just gets better. Where did he drop him?'

'In the centre near Piccadilly Gardens, and watched him walk away and go into the nearest boozer. That was about thirty minutes ago, the driver is still on his way back.'

'Let's get a shift on,' Martin said, as he fished his car keys from his pocket and then started running back towards the garage with Cath right behind him. Then he stopped. He needed to check something with Colin. Cath ran into the back of him.

They were soon mobile and Martin drove using all his advanced driver skills to get to the M62 as quickly as he could. The motorway would be quicker than the East Lancashire Road, but they would hit a wall when they turned onto the M602 into Salford. But hopefully, they would be at the boozer in forty or so minutes. He did consider whether he should ring Greater Manchester but it would take too long to organise, which was in-part, why he'd stopped and rung Colin before they'd set off. Rigby was a potentially armed and now on full alert. Colin agreed that to arrange a full armed operation was out of the question, and the troops they had used earlier had all gone back to their normal armed response vehicle duties.

But as they were responding to hot intel in a fluid movement, Colin had granted Martin authority to arm himself for protection purposes before he left Liverpool. Colin would arrange for a Manchester ARV to be close by and able to respond if the situation escalated to a spontaneous firearms situation. His job was to quietly enter the boozer and then call it in if he saw Rigby inside. He explained all this to Cath as they gunned it down the motorway. Then he gave her the bad news; Colin had ordered that she was not to enter the pub with him.

'So what? Sit outside and miss all the fun?' she said.

In an attempt to change the subject he asked her how she had got on with Bobby Broadbent the previous evening.

'Not good, will have to go back,' she answered.

'Why's that?'

'Although I'd arranged a time, he was out when I got there, and didn't answer his phone, so I left a message.'

'That's weird.'

'I know, anyway, nice try Draker, but I'm coming into the pub with you, we'll look more natural as a couple.'

'But it's a potentially dangerous armed situation.'

'And I'm supposed to be a *field* intelligence officer.'

'But it's an armed op.'

'It's only an armed op, if he is in there. And if he is, we quietly leave and call in the cavalry: isn't that the plan?'

He had to admit that technically, she had a point. 'But Colin had ordered—'

She interrupted him with, 'What Colin doesn't know can't hurt him.'

'You're impossible.'

'I know, now step on it,' she said, grinning.

Chapter Thirty-three

Lucy smiled as she finished her last call. She was awaiting just one more before she'd be able to show Broadbent what she'd been secretly trialling behind the scenes. She'd already had a text claiming it had all gone to plan, but she needed to hear it from the man himself. This, and his gratitude, would be crucial going forward. Then her phone rang again and startled her from her thoughts. She looked at the screen and smiled even wider. She pressed the green icon and said, 'I've been waiting to hear from you.'

'Lucy, I'm sorry I ever doubted you. But how the hell could you have known?' the caller said.

Broadbent and Lucy had known Clayton Rigby for many years; he was one of those serious criminals they trusted. He was part of a small band who was a member of that exclusive club, but nevertheless, they hadn't spoken for some time. They hadn't needed to, until recently. She could hear a lot of background noise. 'Where are you?' she asked.

'In a boozer, catching my breath,' Clayton answered.

'Well, don't use my name, then.'

'Sorry, forgive me; I'm only just calming down. I'll switch back on in a sec. But as grateful as I am, how the hell did you know?'

'The how is not important for the moment, and I'll let you into the secret later. I'm just glad you got out in time; we didn't have the intel very long before I belled you.'

'By the skin of my dick. To be honest, I nearly didn't, I've been very careful when arranging my new gaffs, and I'd only been in this one a matter of hours, which had tempted me to wing it.'

'I'm glad you didn't, though it would have proved the system, even if you had been nicked.'

'Sorry, I didn't quite get that, there's a lot of clatter in here, and apparently twenty-two men are running around a park chasing a ball, or so the six TVs say so.'

'Doesn't matter.'

'I owe you and Tommy, large, just say how much? I won't quibble.'

'Interestingly, how much would think is fair, given the circumstances?'

'Ten grand, easy, if I'm being honest with a friend.'

Lucy smiled and then said, 'If you do me a mega favour, you can have the first one on the house; how does that sound?'

'Sounds amazing. Anything, just name it.'

'Can you get your arse to a hotel in Manchester this afternoon, when I'll be able to explain more?'

'Sure thing; I'm in Manchester already.'

'Perfect, I'll text you the details. Enjoy your football.'

'Wrong shaped ball for me: this lot spend 90 minutes pretending to be hurt with a twisted sock, or whatever, whereas my lot spend 80 minutes pretending not to be hurt whilst running off a few broken ribs.'

Lucy laughed and was about to end the call, when Clayton spoke again.

'And to be fair, what you did for me today was actually worth twenty large of any serious player's money.'

She smiled even wider on hearing this, and then ended the call, before she started to write Broadbent a text.

***

Martin pulled up outside the address and immediately wondered if they had the right place or not. It was a plush wine and specialist gin bar and not the sort of place Martin would have expected a Salford armed robber to frequent. He glanced at Cath and could see the uncertainty on her face, too.

'Perhaps it was just the first lush house he saw?' she said.

Martin looked around the street, which was a fairly major road just down from Piccadilly Gardens on the edge of Manchester's creative Northern Quarter. Opposite was an Irish bar called Old Nell's Drinking Tavern. 'That looks more like it. You think the taxi driver got it wrong?' But before Cath could answer Martin's phone rang, he answered it allowing the incoming call to travel through the car's speakers.

'Hi Boss, it's Alpha Romeo Seven here. We are parked up around the corner from your location; just call us in if you need us.'

'Thanks, Romeo Seven, we are just about to recce it now, and then probably the Irish bar opposite, shouldn't keep you too long.'

Romeo Seven acknowledged Martin and the call ended, before he turned to face Cath, 'Come on, let's stick to the intel first, and then try the other one.'

As soon as they walked into the wine and gin bar, Martin knew it was a bum steer. The place was tiny, one of these modern micro pubs which were all the rage. There was only a handful of people in, it was not long after eleven and didn't look as if it had been open long. Martin double checked with the lone barman by showing him a mugshot of Rigby.

'If he walked in here, mate, I'd have been straight on the phone to your lot,' the barman said, and shuddered. Martin glanced at the photo and got what he meant. Rigby would have looked more at home in an Adams Family portrait - he looked like Uncle Fester's uglier brother. He thanked him and quickly left. Once outside Cath said, 'Looks nice in there, we should give it a try next time we are out in the city centre?'

Martin, nodded, and then said, 'Come on.'

They both crossed the road and walked into the Irish pub which was already half full. It had hard wooden floors with several TV's along the walls showing a re-run of one of last night's FA Cup third round matches. But nothing much else of interest. It was quickly apparent that Rigby wasn't inside. Martin checked with first barman who told him that he'd only just started, so he called his mate over. Cath asked what time they opened.

'Nine o'clock,' the second barman answered.

Then Martin showed him the Adams Family inset and asked his redundant question. But then saw the man's eyes widen.

'You've only just missed him,' he said.

'You sure?' Martin asked.

'Defo, he was here for about an hour, sat on his own looking like trouble, so I kept a close eye on him, especially as I was on my own until eleven.'

'Any idea which direction he went in?' Cath asked.'

'Sorry, love, I was just glad to see him leave.'

'How long since?' Martin asked.

'Five, maybe ten minutes ago.'

Martin thanked the guy and left him his calling card on the off chance that Rigby came back. The barman took it and nodded.

As soon as they were back outside, he turned to face Cath, 'Twice in the same day, I can't believe it.'

'Nor me,' Cath said, and then looked all around.

Martin followed her gaze but knew it was hopeless, from here he could have gone anywhere.

'Harding will be pleased,' Cath said.

But before Martin could answer, his phone started to ring, it was Colin, he groaned as he took the call.

Chapter Thirty-four

Ten minutes after texting Broadbent he was back in the hotel room and Lucy turned and looked as he entered. 'Enjoy your pint of Ireland's favourite beer?'

'It was too busy in there, unlike yesterday afternoon, so I thought it more prudent to try the wine bar opposite, which was almost empty. Then I went for a wander around Piccadilly Gardens.'

'Nice.'

'I take it that you have finally got something to share with me?'

'I have, and the proof of it is on his way over here.'

'Who's that?'

'Clayton Rigby.'

'That old blagger; he's hotter than me. Be good to see him again.'

'You're ice cold now you're dead.'

'True.'

'But for us, he'd be locked up now, facing a twenty stretch.'

'How come?'

'I'll go into it all properly once Clayton's here, but I'll brief you with the preliminaries, first; come and sit with me.'

Broadbent then joined Lucy at the occasional table near the window. 'You remember when we first came across Tommy Dorchester sat begging for his supper in Preston?'

'Of course, nearly fell over when I saw him.'

'Well, they do say we all have one person who looks just like us somewhere in the world.'

'I know, but not outside Preston railway station.'

'Anyway, his job was just to appear as you to the outside the world. To seem to have gone straight, and run the club. And it worked, the heat went away, and only the most trusted knew different.'

'I never thought it would work so well, I always thought someone would blow out the con to the filth.'

'That was why we had him offer himself up to them as a snout, so we could try and monitor things, and at least give us a head start if it turned to rat shit. Even though we'd moved to Amsterdam.'

'I know all this, Luce.'

'I know you do, but with him keeping tabs on the filth, it got me thinking.'

'Go on.'

Lucy took a deep breath and then explained how she had had the idea of infiltrating the cops with several fake informants for the specific reason of keeping an ear open on their interest in any particular named criminal they chose.

'How the hell are we going to find a number of blokes down on their luck, like Dorchester was, who also just happen to look like a particular criminal?' Broadbent asked.

'We don't. We hired Dorchester as he looked like you. That was his job start to finish. Putting him into the cops was a secondary idea; and it worked. We gave him titbits to feed in to keep their interest in him going, and he found out what and who they were really interested in at any one time.'

'Granted.'

Lucy carried on, and explained her vision of getting someone to infiltrate the cops using their own, real details and background, but with a specific criminal as their primary responsibility. 'Take Clayton Rigby, for example.'

'I'm starting to get the picture. But we'll have to make sure we get the right geezers in, and it'll cost a lot.'

Lucy accepted this, but then elaborated that they sell it as a sort of insurance policy. Take someone like Clayton who had been on the run for two years, he would be an ideal candidate to sell it to as he knows he is red hot, and facing twenty years if caught.

'Is that what happened?'

'Yes and no. I chose Clayton without him knowing.'

'And?'

'Thanks to us, I was able to tip him off that the cops were going through his door this morning. He was reluctant to believe me at first as he'd only just moved in, but I was able to convince him, but without explaining how I knew. I'll script him up when he gets here.'

'He owes us large, then.'

'Does he,' Lucy said, and then went on to explain the intel her fake informant had been able to give her.

'So how did it work in practice?'

Lucy then explained that the fake snout had told his handlers that he knew Clayton well and was aware that he was moving around the North West never staying long in one place. 'The police of course tasked him, together with other real informants to find out more. Then they came back and asked our man to confirm an address they had been given. I rang Clayton and it shocked him that I knew. The details were correct.'

'Where did the cops get their other info from?'

'We'll never know that, but without our man in place we would never have picked it up, and Clayton would have been nicked.'

Broadbent whistled and then went to the minibar and poured them both a gin and tonic. 'This calls for a drink,' he said, and handed Lucy one as he re-joined her. 'We will need pretend snouts we can absolutely trust. And they won't be cheap to run.'

'I know, but think of the possibilities?'

'You've done great, but there is a lot to think about before it's a goer.'

'I realise that, but we have proved that the concept can work, with Clayton.'

'How much is he going to pay us?'

'Could be twenty grand, but I've suggested a freebie.'

Broadbent was just taking a sip of his drink and then spat it out. 'What?'

'There's a reason for that as there is much more to tell you,' Lucy said, as she glanced at her watch. 'But it'll have to keep until Clayton's gone, he's due here any minute.'

'OK, but who did you use as the fake snout. I mean, that's the potential weak link bit, if you don't mind me saying?'

'I know it is, and I know it will all take some thinking through. That is why we needed someone we could absolutely trust to run the pilot.'

'So who did you use?'

'Paul.'

'What, your brother, Paul?'

'Yeah, an ideal choice.'

Broadbent burst out laughing and added, 'You sly old cow.'

'He's only been on the cops books for a couple of weeks, we had no idea how long it would run for, which is why I wanted to keep it a surprise. I didn't want to bring you shite, but proof, before I explained it all to you. I hope you don't mind?'

'With something potentially this good, it's been worth the wait. Luce, you are a star.'

'You can thank me properly, later.'

'Now you're talking,' Broadbent said, with a leer on his face.

'By buying me a five-star dinner, I meant, you arsehole.'

They both laughed. And then she added, 'We've had a couple of surprise spin offs, too.'

'How do you mean?'

'Advance knowledge about a couple of low level drug raids; both compromised thanks to us, and both dealers involved have since paid Paul, not knowing how or from whom the info came, and without knowing in whose debt they really are.'

'This just gets better. How much?' Broadbent asked.

'Five grand from each, but I told Paul to keep it all in lieu of his wages.'

'I like it more and more. If we run this right, titbits like that could cover our expenses, at least in part, if not in total.'

'Told you the possibilities were endless.' Then there was a loud knock at the door. 'That'll be Clayton.'

'You stay there, Luce, I'll get it,' Broadbent said, as he rose to his feet, and then headed towards the door.

Chapter Thirty-five

Martin was relieved when Colin told him to stay with Cath and follow any leads they could come up with in tracing Clayton Rigby. Meanwhile, he would have the pleasure of an audience with Paul Harding; he was hoping he may have calmed down since Colin had rung to give him the bad news. He said he'd meet with them later. The first thing they did was access the Irish bar's CCTV, which confirmed Clayton Rigby wearing a baseball cap pulled down low, had been there. It was definitively him, but not so clear as to meet the standard required for a formal ID, not that they needed one, but it confirmed what the barman had said. It seemed that Clayton had either chosen his boozer well, or had just dropped lucky, as there was no CCTV in the street, apart from the wine and gin bar's CCTV, opposite, but that only covered its front door, so was looking the wrong way.

Next, they visited the local police and put them on alert for Rigby, all the cops in Manchester were sent an update and photo, if he was seen wandering about, he'd be nicked. But Martin had to concede Cath's point that they didn't even know if he was still in Manchester. The locals said that their circulation also went to all the city's transport hubs and to the British Transport Police, but more out of protocol than hope. They eventually gave up for the day and headed back towards their Preston base to take stock and rethink.

'We definitely need to do some sort of covert infiltration into Banging Sounds, it's our only point of reference into finding the real Tommy Broadbent and the mysterious woman who it seems was really running the club,' Martin said.

'Yeah, she was obviously the link between the two Tommys,' Cath said.

'What about his estranged brother?' Martin asked.

'I left a note asking him to call, as well as a voicemail, to which he hasn't replied to either, so we may as well give it a cold knock.'

157

Martin looked at his watch; it would be six-ish by the time they arrived back in Preston, dinner-time, always a good time of day to knock on a door. He hoped they'd have more luck, but didn't expect it to lead anywhere, the brothers hadn't communicated in years.

As they drove up the M6, the mood in the car was flat. It was the first time that they had stopped to catch their breath and Martin was still reeling from the day's events, as he knew Cath would be, too. If missing Rigby at his house by minutes wasn't bad enough, to miss him by seconds at the Irish bar was like United losing to Liverpool and City in back-to-back games; unthinkable. But at least Rigby had dropped a bollock with his cheeky message; though it opened up a whole host of further questions and dilemmas.

It was twenty past six when they pulled up outside Bobby's semi-detached home in a quiet side street, on the west side of Preston in the Lea district. A large ex-council house built soon after the last world war, it was on a huge estate, that was mostly built in the 60s when the social planners thought it a good idea to construct massive council estates on the outsides of towns and cities. And apart from all the problems which grew from having a lot of villains living in one community, it was a nightmare for the honest and hardworking folk who just needed somewhere to live. The other problem, of course came when the towns and cities grew outward and ending up enveloping these estates. The only bigger cock up these planners came up with was the high rise flats; another weapons-grade fuck up. Those idiots had much to answer for.

Martin noticed a Ford Mondeo in the driveway as they pulled up.

'That wasn't there last night,' Cath said, as they alighted from their vehicle.

Martin nodded and followed her down the path, but they didn't need to knock on the door, as it was opened as soon as they approached. Bobby was stood there and quickly moved to one side, and said, 'Get in, quick.'

They both did and he shut the front door and led them into the lounge, before turning around to face them. 'No offence, but you two couldn't look more like plod if you had a tit on your heads.'

'And what if we do look like cops…' Martin said, which he never thought they did.

'You are not Preston police, are you?'

'No, but we have an office here,' Martin said, still none the wiser.

'This is not the sort of area where people have the police making house calls. Well, not without a sledgehammer and a search warrant.'

Now Martin understood.

Cath said, 'But you agreed to meet me?'

'Yes, at the cop shop, not bleeding here. That's where I was last night, when you came here. No one tell you?'

Cath shook her head, and then said, 'I did leave messages, but don't worry, no one saw me knock.'

'You're kidding; this street is fully of nosey fuckers and drug dealers' lookouts, especially in the evening time, so please make this quick, and then leave me alone.'

Martin took a back seat and let Cath talk. She outlined that they were obviously trying to trace his brother Tommy Broadbent, and were just after any background information, however old, that might give them a clue. Bobby asked what he had done, *this time*. And Cath glanced at Martin for help.

'If I'm being honest, I'm not sure; but what I do know is that people loosely connected to him keep turning up dead. Also, someone tried to run us to off the road after having shot and killed the guy you saw on the slab, who'd gone to a lot of trouble to appear legit,' Martin said.

Bobby nodded and then asked about the guy the on the slab. Martin told him that they think they knew who he was, but hadn't traced any relatives yet. 'He was just someone who looked like your brother.'

Then Cath asked him if he had heard of the club Banging Sounds, which he said he had not. She told him how the lookalike Tommy had been running it for ages under the veil of respectability. Martin saw the shock on Bobby's face.

'Christ, if I'd know that, I might have been tempted to pay him a visit, if only to pass on a piece of my mind. All I knew was that his last known address was in Liverpool, which is where the messages were left, courtesy of your lot, to inform him of Mum's and then Dad's passing. When he never responded to them, I was totally finished with him.'

Cath pushed on, asking Bobby if he knew of any old friends or associates they could approach.

'He was a loner, well, he always appeared that way. He did have a tight circle around him, but always kept things very close to his chest. Helped him play the big "I am", added mystic to him, or at least he thought so. Always been the same, even as a kid. But just before we stopped talking, he became even more reclusive. Apart from that tart of course. She was the only one; you'd have thought she was family.'

Martin and Cath exchanged a look and Cath pressed on, 'Which tart?'

'Never met her, some bird called Lucy, that's all I know, apart from the fact that what little contact we had ended after she came on the scene.'

'Is that why you became estranged?' Cath asked.

Martin noticed that Bobby didn't answer straight away; he looked like he was considering something, but then said, 'Yeah, I guess. Look are you done? The street dealers will be out soon and they will clock you in a second.'

Martin knew that they had to keep Bobby onside and thanked him for his time, Cath promised that if they needed to talk again, she'd ring and set up somewhere to meet well away from his home or even police stations. He nodded but added that he doubted he could add any more, but at least he didn't slam the door shut to that. They left his house and had a quick scope around as they hurriedly got back into their car. Martin couldn't see anyone obvious. 'He was more receptive than at the mortuary,' he said, as they drove away.

'What do you reckon?' Cath asked.

'He only faltered at the end. I reckon there is more to their breakup than he's told us,' he answered.

'Agreed,' Cath said. 'And this Lucy woman is new information.'

'I bet she's your mystery woman from the club?'

'Just what I was thinking.'

'Come on, let's go and see how Colin has got on with Harding, he should be back in the office now.'

Martin and Cath arrived back at their satellite office in Preston to find Colin already there. They quickly brought him up to speed between them.

'So you reckon he's holding back on some of it?'

'Defo: as Cath was questioning him I was observing. The only time he hesitated was when she asked about the reasons for their estrangement. Tried to make it all about the lack of contact after their parents' deaths.'

'But as we know, they were estranged before then,' Cath added.

'That's certainly how it came across at the mortuary,' Colin said.

'And this Lucy sounds interesting.'

'He's certainly not a fan of hers,' Martin added.

'Which tends to lead back to the club,' Colin said.

'Exactly,' Cath and Martin manged to say in unison.

'Becoming quite the double act, you two,' Colin said, and laughed.

Martin then asked how it had gone with Paul Harding.

'As you can know, he's not happy. The "Too Slow" line has nearly put him over the top, and Sue Claire ACC - Crime has suspended all intel-led ops - as expected - including the undercover ones. The UCs and the snouts are being given exit strategies, such as coming down with COVID, but Harding wants a resolution quickly, as they can't spin out the bullshit for too long.'

Both Martin and Cath nodded and let Colin carry on. Apparently, they are as happy as they can be with the dead fake

Tommy, as in, he hadn't given his handlers anything for ages, and nor had they tasked him.

'What about the source behind naming Clayton Rigby's address?' Cath asked.

'I got the impression it had come in bits from various sources, and they just pieced it together.'

'The old jigsaw intel picture?' Cath said.

'Exactly, so working backwards it's almost impossible to know where the problem is,' Colin said.

'It could easily be a snout who gave them the final piece of the puzzle, as in the street number, and then bottled it and piped Rigby off,' Martin said.

'These things happen,' Cath said.

'I said that, trying to reassure him; as in, it may just have been a one-off bit of back luck,' Colin said.

'Which is true,' Martin said, before asking if either of them fancied a brew.

They both said that they'd love one before Colin, added, 'That's when Harding confirmed what he let slip at our last meeting; about the two other jobs going wrong.'

'What sort of jobs were they?'

'Low level drug raids, which appeared nailed on, but both came up empty.'

'Happens,' Cath said, again.

'Yeah, but apparently, in both instances, the police said the dealers were cocky, as if they knew in advance, one actually said, "I've just sold my last bag half an hour ago, so you'll find nothing here, nob heads" which didn't go down well.'

'Ah, this just gets better,' Martin said.

'I know: we need a break; if only to stop Harding having a heart attack,' Colin said.

'In that case shall we sack the brew; who fancies a pint instead?' Cath asked.

Both Martin and Colin agreed to go for one, but only one. Tomorrow would be another busy day.

Chapter Thirty-six

Lucy, Broadbent and Clayton got past their introductions and were all sat around the table with a drink.

'I have to say, Lucy, I'm still getting over the shock,' said Clayton.

'And to think that you nearly ignored me.'

'Yeah, sorry about that, but I only moved in the gaff yesterday and I've been so careful with each move I've done. And if I'm being honest, I thought I'd slipped off the cops' radar a bit, not that I've ever been complacent.'

'Looks like you owe Lucy, large?' Broadbent said.

'Look, I won't quibble, it's worth the twenty.'

'What would it be worth if we could keep a watching brief over things for you?' Lucy said.

'For that level of security, I'm sure we could come to a healthy arrangement, even if you do throw me a freebie for this first time. Incidentally, just name whatever you want me to do and it will be done. But first, tell me how you've managed it?'

'Go and grab three more drinks from the mini-bar and I will,' Lucy said.

Clayton quickly obliged and as soon as he was sat back down he said, 'I'm assuming you've got a bent cop at a high level? Don't know how you've managed it, I've been trying for years to buy a decent one, but have failed. There aren't as many around as there used to be.'

'Even better than that,' Lucy said, and then explained the whole fake Tommy bit and then the pilot scheme with her brother. When she had finished, Clayton sat back in his chair and whistled.

'One hell of a scam. But why me?' Clayton asked.

'You were a natural choice; we knew you, you are on your toes, red hot, and you are in the North West,' she answered.

Clayton nodded and cocked his head to one side signifying his understanding and then asked, 'What's the favour you want?'

'We have plans, big plans and we need you to help us with it. You are our proof it works.'

'Absolutely, just holler exactly what and when?'

'Will do. It'll be Tommy who will be driving it, so he will call you in.'

Clayton nodded and Broadbent grinned at Lucy as he raised an eyebrow. She accepted that she had not had enough time to fully brief Broadbent with her plans for the next phase of the scheme. It would be at a level where his kudos and reputation would be needed to sell it, and Clayton's standing and evidence that it works would hold it up. She was sure Broadbent would be fully onside when she explained it in detail after Clayton left.

'Any chance of meeting your brother so I can shake his hand?' Clayton asked.

'Probably better that we limit when you two actually meet.'

'Operational security, I get it, but please buy him a drink on me,' Clayton said, before pulling his wallet out. He counted out two piles of fifty pound notes, and said, 'A five hundred pound drink for Paul, and another five hundred quid should buy you two a couple of bottles of Louis Roederer's finest Cristal. On me, the very least I can do, for now.'

Both Lucy and Broadbent thanked Clayton as he rose to his feet.

'One last thing,' Lucy said.

'On operational security: Paul reckons the cops were given a street but with no house number, and then they suddenly had a house number but with no street. That's why they guessed at putting the two together before asking Paul to confirm it. That's when I rang you and we both discovered that they had surmised correctly,' she said.

Clayton nodded and said, 'Meaning a real snout was grassing on me.'

'At least one, you need to play it very close to your chest going forward.'

'Thanks, I will,' he said, as he walked towards the door, and then he stopped and turned around as he started to open it, and said, 'And if I find out who is grassing on me for real, I'll shoot the bastard. So if your Paul picks up anything on that front, I'll be much appreciative and will pay you for that separate.'

Lucy and Broadbent both raised their glasses together in agreement and Clayton nodded and left.

'Well, that went well,' Broadbent said, as the room door closed to.

Lucy was about to answer when her phone buzzed. Spookily, it was her brother Paul. She told Broadbent who was calling as she took the call.

'Sis, we have a problem,' Paul started with, 'I need to tell you something urgently.'

Lucy sat in silence as she listened to Paul. Just when everything was starting to come together, especially, as their businesses in Holland had all gone south, this pilot with Clayton and Paul was the start of something new. Bigger and better. And now this. Once Paul had finished, she thanked him, and mused that perversely, but for the pilot scheme with Paul, she'd still be none the wiser. Broadbent obviously knew something was wrong as he had sat mutely, watching her intently as she had mainly ummed and ahhed her side of the conversation.

She ended the call and tuned to face Broadbent. 'We have a problem, Houston.'

'I gathered that much.'

'You are no longer dead.'

'What? Course I am; Kinsella made sure of it. He even saw the other Tommy being carried into the morgue.'

'I know that,' she said.

'And hopefully, now in a pauper's grave.'

'Yes, a pauper as he has no possessions to speak of, his house was rented, and he's no relatives?' she said.

'Exactly.'

'And as he has no next of kin, it was the cops who formally identified him.'

'Exactly,' he said.

'Except, apparently that's when the problems kicked in.'

'How, he's no family; it must have been the cops who formally ID-ed him?'

'Yes, but they first tried to ID him with his brother.'

'He hasn't got a brother.'

'No, but you bloody have.'

Lucy saw the look of utter shock on Broadbent's face as the realisation kicked in.

'Bobby. Shit.'

'Bobby Shit, indeed. We never reckoned on that.'

'How the hell did they find out about my tit of a brother?'

'I've no idea, but he said it wasn't you.'

'Are we sure, I mean, I've not seen him in years and Tommy Dorchester and me were dead ringers?'

Lucy then pointed at the missing finger, or half a finger on Broadbent's hand, and said,' told you we should have cut his off.'

'Like breaking his nose wasn't enough?'

'Apparently not,' Lucy spat back.

'OK, let's move on.'

'According to Paul, certain snouts were told by their handlers that the body in the car was not you, and that his real identity would be revealed to the coroner soon. They've been tasked with finding the real you.'

'Look, I was always going to have to stay in the shadows, once *dead*, so I still have to.'

'Yes, but now they are looking for you; when the plan was that they would never need to look for you again.'

'I know, I know,' Broadbent said, getting to his feet. He then started to pace the room in thought.

Lucy guessed exactly what he might be thinking.

Confirming it, Broadbent said, 'Look, why would he say anything now, after all these years. If he was going to, he would have done so a long time ago.'

'Granted, but now the cops will be all over him trying to find the real you. It stirs things up,' she said. 'Plus, we can't just go back to Holland. Especially, with this new venture around the corner.'

'We'll monitor it, I'm sure it'll be fine.'

'I told you to go to your parents funerals, rebuild things a bit; keep him sweet.'

'I wanted to; but trust me; it would have done more harm than good. He didn't want me there.'

'I need to think.'

Broadbent took the hint and refilled their glasses, when he returned Lucy said, 'And Paul's been told by his handlers that apart from any info on *you,* there will be no contact for a couple of weeks.'

'Is he worried?'

'He shat at first, naturally, but now reckons whatever is going on is nothing to do with him.'

'I wonder what *is* going on.'

'He hopes to find out afterwards.'

'Going forward, again, do you want to fill me in on where you see this scheme going?'

Lucy quickly outlined what she had in mind, and after she'd finished, Broadbent looked amazed. 'I like it, much better than the one-off I guessed you were going to suggest.'

Lucy smiled and nodded.

'We will need some serious geezers,' he said.

'That's where you come in. You have the clout.'

'I need to give it some thought.'

'And we need to make sure we have no problems hanging over us before we make the approaches, or we'll look toxic and unprofessional,' Lucy added.

'I know, I know. I'll give it all some thought while I take a shower. I think we can still afford to celebrate tonight.'

Lucy smiled her agreement and watched Broadbent as he stood and walked into the bathroom. She waited until she could hear him in the shower and then picked up her phone. She dialled a number and Kinsella answered on the first ring. 'You busy?'

'Just looking to sort a couple of things, no biggie,' Kinsella answered.

'Anything I should know about?'

'Nothing to trouble you. I'd tell you if it was.'

'OK, look, I can't talk for long and will have to fill you in properly later on, maybe tomorrow. But I need you to do something sensitive.'

'Go on,' Kinsella answered.

'I need you to keep a close, but very discrete watch on Bobby in Preston.'

'What, Bobby as in Tommy's brother?'

'Yes, but let's keep this between you and me, for now.

Kinsella didn't answer, so after a few seconds, Lucy said, 'Look, this won't blow back on you. I just need to know his comings and goings, what he's up to, visitors, that sort of thing.'

'Major problem?'

'Not as such with Bobby, but the police know that the guy you shot is not our Tommy, so Bobby may be under their spotlight, that's all. I just don't want to over worry Tommy just yet.'

'Shit, how did that happen?'

Lucy gave Kinsella an abridged version of what Paul had told her, and promised to elaborate when she had more time.

'Damn, damn, damn,' Kinsella said, with more emphasis than Lucy expected.

'Go to go, laters,' she said, and ended the call as Broadbent entered the main room with a towel wrapped around his waist.

'Who was that?'

'Just Kinsella reporting in.'

'You tell him about the other Tommy?'

'Yep.'

'Bet he was pissed off?'

'He was, he really was,' she said, as she rose to her feet. 'Anyway, my turn in the bathroom.'

Chapter Thirty-seven

The following day, Martin and Cath were back at their desks in the Preston office having spent the previous evening separate at their own respective homes. Nothing was wrong between them, but they both said they felt flat after the day's events and needed to sort stuff out at home, such as laundry; and Martin was really glad of an early night. He was sure Cath was too, a chance to recharge one's batteries and switch off from the job by way of distraction. Martin knew that was not always possibly as the subconscious mind had a way of interrupting things, but it would have been nigh on impossible had Cath and he spent the evening together; the conversation would have naturally turned back to work. That was the one down side of both working for the same firm; exacerbated when they were working the same case.

Cath said she would keep digging in an effort to try and find any relatives for Tommy Dorchester – as they now knew for sure was his real name – and keep an eye on Bobby, too.

'It's Bobby that particularly niggles me,' she said, 'there's more to the brothers falling out than he's telling us.'

'Defo.'

'What about you?'

'I had a quick word with Colin before he shot off to the Branch Managers' monthly tea party, and ran an idea past him which he has told me to get on with.'

'Sounds interesting, give, Draker,' she said, and smiled.

'Well, as we keep saying, the club is our only starting point. And as ACC Claire has suspended all intel led ops in Liverpool, for the moment, we can't even task any real snouts.'

'Didn't know you had any in Merseyside,' Cath said, still grinning.

'If I had, I'd have to kill you rather than tell you, but sadly, I haven't; well not in Liverpool. But the likes of the two Johns have, but currently everyone has their hands tied behind their backs; other than receiving anything to do with Broadbent.'

'We are flying blind,' Cath said.

169

'That's exactly what Harding said, apparently, to the ACC, of whom he is desperately trying to get to reverse her kneejerk decision.'

Cath said, 'I sense a "but" coming?'

'No flies on you. But it also provides an opportunity. Normally, it can take ages to get a fully licenced level one undercover officer. Nearly impossible at short notice, unless there is a threat to life situation.'

'I thought you could get one from anywhere in the UK?' Cath said.

'You can, technically, but they are always so busy everywhere, plus, we really want one who is imbedded locally and knows what's going on.'

'Got you.'

'And as all the active ones in Liverpool are currently working on their exit strategies, I suggested to Colin that we grab one and put him or her into Banging Sounds to try and pick up some intel.'

'Can't do any harm.'

'But before we approach one, we need a proper recce of the place. I know Colin and I went in when it was closed, but we need to get the vibe of the place when it's open, and as we've already been in as cops, we are out of it.'

'I get that.'

'And due to the sensitivities involved, it's probably risky putting a local intel detective in there.'

'I get that, too.'

'And seeing that you've already been in as a member of the press…'

'You want me to do a revisit?' Cath's face lit up, 'now you're talking. I'd love to.'

'And you'd be taking your new role as a *field* intelligence officer to a new level.'

'Just tell me what you want me to do.'

'I'll drop you off and be around the corner somewhere should you need me, but you shouldn't, as it's not about taking any risks, or even gathering serious intel; though any spin offs in that direction would obviously be a bonus. But it is about setting the scene for the level one undercover officer, so they can plan their strategy.'

'When were you thinking?'

'Tonight, so we've a lot to go through before then, sorting out your cover story, authorities etc.'

'Sound like fun,' Cath said.

'Just a quick in and out really, perhaps a glass of something and then don't push your luck. See what kind of clientele are in, and if this mysterious Lucy is there. I know we have no idea what she looks like, but if she is supposed to be in charge that might be self-evident,' Martin said. 'But you are just eyes ears, not there to engage in a way a trained undercover operative would.'

'Understood. Plus, it's a legitimate question to ask about her as it was Ted who let it slip when I paid my first visit,' Cath pointed out.

'That had slipped my mind, nice one. I just wished I hadn't gone in with Colin; I could have joined you,' Martin added.

Cath then gave him one of her disapproving looks, and he threw his hands up in the air in surrender.

***

Cath was really excited about going covertly into the club to recce it ahead of the undercover operative. In reality, it wasn't much different than when she'd winged it on her first visit, and from a point of view of doing what was expected, it wasn't too arduous a task. But she was so excited because it was a first; a first in so far as she was doing it officially. To the onlooker, that would make no sense, but she knew her new job as a *field* intelligence officer was on trial. It was a new role allowing analysts to gather intel in the field in a variety of roles. This was once the preserve of warrant holding detectives, but as the jobs by definition didn't need a badge, it was being opened up to civilian police staffers for the first time. If anything went wrong, she was only too aware how fickle the authority to continue could become. She could end up back tied to a desk being fed intel to analyse from officers, and the hopes and aspirations of other intelligence analysts could be dashed.

She knew with every step Colin allowed her to take, she was breaking new ground for others to follow; so no pressure then.

By early evening, she and Martin had gone over things a hundred times, including her two ways out or the club if she felt threatened; one way, was a covert intervention, where Martin would enter as a detective doing his own non-Cath related enquiry, to allow her an opportunity to leave during the impasse that would create. The second exit was a more serious one; Martin would have a bunch of local uniforms at the ready to crash in; not that they would be told why, or indeed where, until needed. The first response would be triggered by a pre-arranged text to Martin with the letter A on it; the second, more urgent one would be simply a blank text.

Martin had stressed it should be a doddle and no escape strategy should be needed; but it was good tradecraft to prepare for one, and tick the 'just in case' box.

'Come on, we'd better get going,' he said, as he returned from the little boys' room.

Cath glanced at her watch, ten to eight, she nodded and picked up her grip handbag.

DOUBLE CROSS

Chapter Thirty-eight

It was approaching nine as they turned onto Dale Street, in Liverpool, and Cath was getting herself together as Martin slowed and pulled over short of the club. It was still light, just, but would be dark in half an hour. The neon sign above the club's double-door entrance was visible over a mixture of light and dark patches on the street. Stood in the shadows offset to one side of the entrance were two doormen. Both huge brutish looking individuals, both wearing Crombie style coats, which she guessed was required dress for bouncers. The doorman nearest the door was bald; the other had long dark hair.

'I'll be one minute away and will constantly watch my phone screen,' Martin said.

Cath nodded.

'Don't forget: A equals me, and blank equals the cavalry.'

'Where are they?'

'Back of a van on the waterfront; literally two minutes away, though they don't know that.'

'Reassuring to know. I'll ring you when I'm leaving.'

'I'll pick you up here, same spot.'

Cath nodded again and swiftly alighted from the vehicle and glanced as Martin drove away. She looked up as she approached the door. The long haired lover from Liverpool only glanced at her, but the bald guy seemed to be looking at her with a fixed stare which she found a little unsettling. Though, looking intimidating was their game, she knew, and ignored him.

As she was about to walk through the door the bald one said, 'Can I help you, love?'

She felt like saying, "I'm not your love, and no you can't help me as I don't do drugs" but instead said, 'All good thanks, evening fellas.'

The long haired lover just glanced again, but baldy held his fixed stare and grunted. It was then that she noticed a wicked scar across the man's head which only added to his menacing look. She wondered if these sorts gave themselves scars on purpose to enhance their vileness.

The door closed behind her and she quickly took in the club again. It looked very different from last time. The bar to her right had three staff working it, with several punters either stood at it, or on bar stools. Piped music filled the air, and a handful of young women were dancing on the small dancefloor in front of the bar. A sign advertised some wicked DJ she had never heard of who would be starting his gig in an hour's time. She realised they had chosen their time well. It would no doubt be bedlam after that. Beyond the dancefloor was a small stage with all the music equipment on it, under the upstairs corridor which was the private bit. It had several doors off it which were all closed.

She walked to the bar and was quickly served by a middle-aged woman. She chose to sit on a bar stool nearest the door at the edge of the bar. It gave her a good vantage point and was close to the exit. There was no sign of the guy she'd met last time that Martin said had introduced himself to him as Ted. Neither was there any sign of a boss-like woman; whatever a boss-like woman was supposed to look like.

No one paid her any attention, and she ordered a second G & T as the first one hadn't touched the sides. Then she saw baldy step inside the front door, and stand looking into the club, which she thought was a bit strange. But he hadn't been there a minute, when raised voices outside were evident, and then two rough looking youths hustled their way into the place. Well, one did, as the second one suddenly went into reverse, courtesy of the long haired lover who yanked him backwards by his collar. She heard him say, 'I told yous. Yous two are still barred.'

Baldy spun around in time to block youth number one. 'You heard my mate; out. Last chance.'

Youth number one who only looked about sixteen, but was built like Baldy's twin, said, 'Fuck you, tosser, I'm having a drink on my manor, and—'

Youth number one didn't get the chance to finish his sentence as Baldy's fist smashed into his face. This was quickly followed by a savage head-butt, and Cath wondered if that was how he had got his scar. The youth went down hard. He was still conscious but all the bravado and bluster had been knocked out of him. Then Baldy followed up with a totally unnecessary kick to the torso. He was joined by the long haired lover with no sign of youth two behind him. Both bouncers then dragged the youth out, who was still regaining what few faculties he had as he went into swear mode.

Cath shuddered, and turned to look away. Straight into the face of the barman she had first met, who was now stood directly in front of her.

'What the fuck do you want?' he said.

She noticed him nod some sort of Neanderthal communication to Baldy as he continued out the door. She turned back to face the barman and stepped off her stool, mainly to gain some height, but also to get him out of her private space. Once upright, she answered him, 'Lovely place you run here.'

Nodding over her shoulder, 'Every club gets dickheads, so if you are thinking of printing that—' he started to say.

Cath cut him off to reassure him. 'I'm just after some more background on Tommy Broadbent now he has been involved in a fatal accident.'

'Like I told you before, I don't talk to the press, and even if I did, I didn't know anything about his personal life. We weren't besties, so I took little interest. Now he's gone, and I'm in charge; that's it.'

'Congratulations Ted. Well, now you are the boss, you surely have added responsibilities, like the image of this place to keep.'

'How do you know my name, I never gave you my name?' Ted said.

'I am journalist, Ted, it's not rocket science and what's the big deal?'

'There isn't one.'

Cath noticed that he had calmed a little, not exactly warm, but somehow the fact that she knew his name had had an effect. She had no idea why. But carried on, 'Look, I promise I'm not here to rubbish your club; in fact the way your door staff dealt with those two thugs was swift and efficient.' She nearly chocked on her own words as she said them. But it seemed to have the desired effect as Ted seemed to ease even more.

'We run a tight ship and don't let thugs in.'

'Very glad to hear it. We are just considering running a human interest story on Tommy, that's all. One which will get the readers to empathise with the poor man, nothing more. The place where he worked is incidental really, other than any quotes saying what a nice man he was and suchlike. But I'm guessing I'm not getting that sort of quote from you?'

'You'll be getting no quotes from me, so if you're done?'

Cath realised she would get little more from Ted, but at least she had the layout of the place in her head, knew what sort of entertainment they offered, and what sort of doormen they used; the latter probably being quite important to an undercover officer planning her or his strategy. She had just one last roll of the dice. 'Perhaps the owner/manager could add something?'

'I'm the manager and the owner is an overseas consortium,' Ted said.

'But I thought you said that Tommy ran the place with a lady? A lady who actually did the running as Tommy was secondary to her, or that he deferred to her? I can't recall your exact words.'

'Er well, I shouldn't have, er I mean, she just oversees sometimes, that's all. Pops in occasionally. I probably made more of her position just to diss Tommy. It was me who used to prop him up,' Ted said, looking and sounding on the back foot for the first time.

'An overseer from overseas?'

'If you like. Look, I have a club to run.'

'Lucy, that's her name isn't it?'

Ted's demeanour had gone from aggressive to rattled and now full circle to scared.

'I never gave you her name,' Ted stuttered.

'So her name is Lucy? Can you give me a mobile number for her; I just want to get a quote on her dead ex-manager, that's all? Can't see why she'd mind that?'

'She's abroad and I don't have her overseas number, and I'm not at liberty to give her UK number out. If you leave me yours I'll pass it on, along with your request. Best I can do, now please leave.'

Cath had pushed it as far as she dared, but had learnt a lot in the process. She quickly pulled out a made up calling card with a made up name on it together with a burner phone's number on it, courtesy of Martin's preparations for her. She handed it to Ted who looked at it and said, 'Which paper did you say you worked for?'

'I didn't, I'm freelance, so I write and sell to many regional and national ones. Thanks for your time,' she said, noting a look of relief on Ted's face. Cath was buzzing as adrenaline surged through her. She'd turned Ted on his head, and was enjoying the confidence it had given her. She spun around just as Baldy was heading straight for them.

'Problem, Ted?' Baldy asked.

'No, all good thanks,' Ted said, in what Cath noted was in a deferential sort of way.

She smiled as she sidestepped Baldy, and walked briskly towards the door. She could feel both their eyes burning into her back as she left. She then remembered she hadn't rung Martin and didn't fancy hanging around outside waiting for him, so decided to head off in any direction and ring him once she was clear.

Long haired lover just gave her the slightest glance as she left. Then to her joy she saw Martin parked where he had dropped her off. She hurried across the road and quickly got in as he started the engine.

'As it's dark now, thought I'd park in the shadows and wait.'

'You couldn't have timed it better.'

'How did it go?'

'Very, very well, considering. You are so right about doing things physically, you learn so much more.'

'Can't wait to hear.'

'Let's head home, I'll tell you all about it on the way.'

Martin nodded and the car accelerated forward. Cath risked a glance as they passed the front of the club. She saw that Baldy was back outside, and staring intently at them as they drove past. She shuddered, she was glad to be out of his company.

Chapter Thirty-nine

Jason Kinsella wasn't a deep man, but he was a ruthless one, and what he lacked in education or social skills, he made up for in street smarts. His senses were honed in any manner of ways, and he never forgot a face. First, it's about familiarity, he knows he's seen it before. Then it's time; a feeling as to when; is it a face from the past, or a recent one? This bit jumps out first. He knew it was recent. Then, it's all about context: a sighting, or more; a conversation. Then, it's about threat assessment. That's what is really important; and he can't evaluate the latter until the former are recognised. And they don't teach that in school.

Straight away, he knew he'd seen the women entering the club, before. And recently, too.

He spoke to her and listened to her answer. This told him that he had not spoken to her before. He decided to see what she was up to and have another look at her, so he told Frankie to remain outside and stay alert. They'd had a whisper that the Slyne brothers were hustling their way around the pubs and clubs trying to give it the big "I am". They were just a couple of spotty tossers, but it put the paying punters off. Frankie had already had a run in with them the week before. It had all been handbags and gob, but if they came back he'd told Frankie it was time for pain-assisted learning.

He entered the club and saw the bird on a bar stool on her own, she'd obviously not met anyone inside. There was just one drink in front of her, but she could be waiting for someone. Then the Slyne brothers tried barging their way in which took his attention.

They were soon sorted, and once outside he followed up his head butting of one, by catching up the other, and giving him a similar headache. This was their final warning, so they'd better listen.

He ducked back inside to see Ted talking to the bird, but she did one as he approached. He watched her walk out and then turned back to Ted, 'Who the fuck was that?'

'Just some tart from the press.'

'Press. Fuck the press want?'

Then Ted banged on about dead Tommy and some sop story she wanted to write. Said he gave her rock all, and all was sweet.

'It fucking better be. There are big plans coming, and the last thing Lucy and Tommy want is the press nosing around.'

'Yeah, I get that. Do you want me to tell Lucy?' Ted asked.

'Nah. If she needs to know anything, then that's my job. You just run this bar and get ready for those rooms upstairs to start earning their keep.'

Ted looked relieved and then scuttled off behind the bar. Jason wandered back outside and turned to Frankie, 'Where did that posh tart go?'

'Over there,' Frankie said, and pointed to a motor parked about fifty metres away. Jason saw its headlights turn on and heard its engine start. Someone was picking her up.

'What about those two nob heads; the Slime brothers? I not sure they are too quick on the uptake,' Frankie asked.

'If they are thick enough to come back, we'll drag them around the back and you can pick one to shoot. Do his foot or summat; see if they get the message then,' Jason said, as he watched the car approach.

But as he had said the word "shoot" it frigging hit him. When he'd shot Tommy the stooge, she'd been one of the passengers in the car. He was sure of it. Memory search complete. 'Fuck me,' he said, as the car passed the club doors. He saw the woman looking straight at him, and as she did, he got a profile glimpse of the driver. And this time his memory skills were instant. All about context. He was as sure as he could be that he was the other one in the motor that day; the driver then, too.

What had Ted said? She was press. That was all they needed. And if she was from the press then the other one, driving, must be press too. His two loose ends had just become seriously looser.

After five minutes pacing up and down and telling Frankie to shut up, he decided he'd better ring Lucy. He was conscious that she was out to dinner with Tommy, so texted first.

Five minutes later she rang back, said she was powdering her nose, and Kinsella could hear a spacious echoing sound behind her speech.

'What's so urgent?' she asked.

'You remember the two who picked dead Tommy up from the hospital?'

'Yeah, the two you reckoned were mates, but in any case hadn't had time to chat before you intervened? And are presumed dead.'

'Yeah, those two.'

'Go on.'

'Well, it turns out that they were not just some accomplices who he'd scrounged a lift from. And they are not dead.'

'Don't tell me they are plod, Jason, it's bad enough the cops now know he was not our Tommy.'

'Not that bad, thank God, but nearly as bad; the press,' he said, and then gave Lucy a quick rundown on the evening's events.

'And you just let her walk away?'

'I only made her as she was driving off, and I was working from a fleeting glance I'd had on the day, when at the time I'd been concentrating on shooting the stooge Tommy.'

Lucy didn't answer straight away, and Jason could hear a tap running followed by a hand dryer. When that finally stopped she came back on the line, calmer. A timely intervention.

'OK, fair enough. You've done well to remember her at all, I guess. And we now know they must have survived, contrary to what the media have said.'

'Thanks.'

'If it's just some sob story, no problem. And Tommy could only have told them about his fake status, and as that's now out of the bag, what can they do?' Lucy said, sounding as if she was thinking out loud as much as asking Kinsella.

'He'd no knowledge of what the club bedrooms are to be used for, so that's safe,' Kinsella said, trying to reassure Lucy.

'True, but if the press are planning to run the fake Tommy thing as a story – and to be honest, why wouldn't they – it could have serious implications for us. How can we sell the infiltration concept to other villains when our business model gets splashed all over the red tops? It would kill it.'

'What do you want me to do?'

'We don't want to bring more attention to us, so I guess it all depends what they are planning to do. If it's just a sob story, then let them get on with it,' she said.

'And if dead Tommy has grassed and they are planning an exposé?'

'Then kill them, but it will have to look like an accident, if possible, but kill them.'

Chapter Forty

The following morning, Martin and Cath were in their Preston office before Colin, and Martin was just about to head to the canteen when Colin walked in with a tray supporting three steaming hot mugs of coffee and a large plate overflowing with buttered toast.

'Thought I'd treat you,' he said, as he placed the tray down on the printer table.

'We really must invest in our own kettle and toaster,' Martin said.

'And a mini-fridge wouldn't go a miss,' Cath added.

'We should; anyway, for now, dig in,' Colin said. And all three did.

Sat at his desk wiping crumbs from his chin, Colin said, 'You did a great job last night, by all accounts.'

'Thanks,' Cath said, and smiled at Martin.

'So what is the upshot?' Colin asked.

'The club appears legit, but for the several rooms upstairs; the majority look like they are to be used for something less legit,' Cath said.

'Prostitution?' Colin asked.

'A good guess, but it could be worse than just prostitution.'

'Such as?'

Martin let Cath give Colin all the news, it was her gig after all, and concentrated on having an unequal amount of toast as they talked.

'People trafficking; with or without enforced prostitution.'

'The scourge of our time.'

'Totally. And Ted who is now "running" the bar is just a paid lackey in my opinion.'

'Expand?'

'Well, he obviously defers to this Lucy character, of whom he looked scared of once he realised I had her name. And when the doorman Baldy approached, I got the distinct impression that he was really running the show.'

'Hey, leave some for us,' Colin said, turning to Martin.

There were just two slices of toast left, so Martin apologised and offered them to Colin and Cath, who both took a slice. 'I'll go and get some more, if you wish?'

'I'm OK,' Colin said.

'Me too, but the kettle and toaster are on you,' Cath said.

Martin just smiled. He was sure he had a spare kettle at home - if it worked - so his greed might only cost him a toaster.

'We could do with knowing who the doorman is,' Colin said.

'That's my mission for today,' Cath answered.

'Did you get a look?' Colin asked, turning to Martin.

'Only a glimpse, so not too good really, given the lighting, and the fact that I was driving.'

'Conclusions?'

Cath smiled her acquiesce to Martin; it was his turn to speak. 'We still can't prove any serious criminal offences,' he started with.

'I know, that bothers me, or more accurately, is starting to bother the Quadrant Super,' Colin said.

Martin knew that the North West region's operations were run by two detective superintendents, and it was they who gave Colin the budget to run ops. And notwithstanding, that three murders were now linked to what they were doing, and crimes don't come much more serious than murder, homicides were still the preserve of local police forces and the regional homicide unit, and not the NWROCU. They needed to show organised criminality to stay within their own terms of reference.

'But on the plus side, someone has gone to a lot time, trouble and money to present the fake Tommy; and therefore by default, he must in hiding for a very good reason. We could just do with proving what that is, or more importantly, be able to show that it revolves around organised criminality?'

'Which it obviously does,' Colin said.

'Unless Phil Devers or his Welsh counterpart makes a breakthrough on their investigations, and ones which show the organised crime element, we are stuck with the club,' Martin said.

'And following on from Cath's excellent recce last night, let's concentrate on that.'

183

'We've also got the real brother of the real Tommy; I'm convinced he can give us more, not just on Tommy and what he is up to, but also on his partner Lucy, who we know is really running the club,' Cath added.

'Thanks to you,' Martin said.

'OK: well, Martin and I can go and find ourselves a temporarily out-of-work undercover officer, thanks to Sue Claire's kneejerk suspension of intel-led ops, and you can concentrate on ID-ing Baldy?' Colin said to Cath.

Cath nodded and then added, 'And I'll try and set up a meet with Bobby somewhere neutral.'

The briefing over, they all attended to admin and other office tasks, such as review of authorities, and Martin sat with Colin and wrote up their operational policy log. The latter task was always mundane and time consuming. Each decision had to be recorded together with the rationale for it. Martin hated these logs. They were the same as were used on murder enquiries, and he could understand their need with homicides, but not on their live ops. It was just added bureaucratic quagmire. By 11.30 a.m. they were done, including the recoding of the last decision; to meet UCO 585 for lunch to discuss strategy. This entry was made in the sister log, which was marked sensitive - eyes only. He'd actually done a ring around the day before, and arranged a meeting for lunchtime today. So he gave Colin a prod when it was time to leave.

Cath had bailed nearly two hours previous; she said she was sick of being passed around by Liverpool City Council and the Security Industry Authority, in her attempts to obtain a list of licenced doormen who worked at banging Sounds. The SIA was run by the Home Office but Martin knew the City Council would have a list, and maybe more, with regard to background on the club, and had suggested a physical visit.

'As you always say, "you can't beat a physical visit",' Cath had answered.

'As last night proved,' Martin said.

Cath had smiled and collected her things, and was gone. He said he'd catch her later.

DOUBLE CROSS

It was now twelve thirty and Martin pulled into the car park behind a village boozer on the outskirts of Preston on its northern side. Halfway between Preston and Lancaster, near to a small market town called Garstang. A perfect venue to meet a UC, who, until a day or two ago, was operating in Liverpool.

Colin said he could buy the drinks as a fine for nicking most of the toast, so Martin headed to the bar and bought two lagers. The pub looked very old with low a ceiling and oak beams which actually looked genuine. There were a few couples dotted about enjoying lunch, but the place was only a quarter full, if that, perfect. Colin had located a table and four chairs in the arch of the pub's large front bay window, and Martin brought the ale over and sat down.

'How will we recognise the UC?' Colin asked.

'The UC will recognise us,' he answered. And five minutes later a black woman in her thirties with her hair tied back behind her head strode into the pub. She was tall with the build of an athlete and wearing smart casuals. She made directly over to their table and stuck out her hand. 'Hi, I'm Gilly,' she said, warmly.

Both Martin and Colin stood and reciprocated and Martin asked her what she wanted to drink.

'Any fruit juice will do me, thanks.'

Martin headed to the bar and returned with her drink.

'So how did you know who we were?' Colin asked.

'Spoke to Martin last night and he described you both,' she said, and then grinned.

'What?' Colin asked.

'That is why I only recognised Martin,' she added, and laughed.

'Kettle, toaster and mini-fridge, for that,' Colin said to Martin.

Fair enough.

'Anyway, gents, before you start to pitch a job to me, I have to warn you, that if it's in any way to do with Liverpool, it may be sometime before I could consider it. Martin was elusive as to where the job was, but unfortunately, all operations in Liverpool have been suspended,' Gilly said.

'Yes, we realise that,' Martin said.

185

'Until further notice,' she said.

'On the express orders of ACC Claire,' Colin added.

'That's right,' Gilly said.

'Which is why we hoped you might be able to fit in a quick little job for us while you're not too busy?' Martin asked.

'Sorry? You mean in Liverpool?'

'Erm yes, but it's only a little job,' Martin said,

'Sue Claire will never authorise it,' she said.

'Well, as we are NWROCU, our own ACC will do that,' Colin said. 'And before you ask, I've already checked.'

'Wouldn't that piss Sue Claire off?'

'She won't know about it,' Colin said.

'That's the beauty of undercover jobs; they are secret,' Martin added.

'Just while you're not busy,' Colin said.

'A quick in and out job,' Martin added.

Gilly didn't answer right away, but took a swig of her fruit juice and then said, 'A quick in and out, you say?'

'Yep. It's just a simple small job,' Martin said.

'How small?'

'Tiny,' Colin said.

'How simple?'

'As simple as—' Martin started to say.

'He is,' Colin interrupted with, pointing at Martin.

'You are like a double act, you two.'

All three laughed which lifted the tension Martin could feel was starting to build.

'And if I don't like it, I walk away?'

'Absolutely,' Martin said.

'OK; let's hear it, but first you can put a vodka in that juice,' she said, pointing at her glass.

'No problems and I'll fetch some menus, too,' he answered.

He smiled as he headed to the bar, but he knew that, as with all undercover operations, the final say is with the operative; their role is voluntary and they can't be ordered to do it.

Chapter Forty-one

Cath was still buzzing a little from the previous evening's visit to Banging Sounds, and although, in the wider scheme of things, it had been a simple deployment, it was still breaking new ground for her as a *field* intelligence analyst. If she continued not to cock things up, too much, the sky was the limit. She could envisage the day when civilian police staffers were fully fledged undercover officers, surveillance experts and informant handlers. After all, that's what happened in the security services. They are all technically, civilians, with no powers of arrest. It was time the cops caught up, and it would release a lot of detectives to do all the detecting. She knew there was a national shortage of detectives and had been for some time.

She thought about all this as she drove down the A59 past Lancashire Police Headquarters south of Preston, en route to Liverpool. Recalling her efforts on the phone with the SIA, they had a guy called Frank Holland on the books who was listed as working for Banging Sounds, among other venues, and the description matched the long haired lover, but she'd drawn a blank with baldy, and she'd have thought that his scarred head would have stood out. Same result at the City Council, though the woman she had spoken to in their licencing department had sounded vague. Cath guessed the woman either didn't know the answers to her questions, or was just fobbing her off; hence the personal approach.

She arrived at the council buildings at 10.30 a.m. and left none the wiser at 11.30 a.m. She'd managed to track down the woman she'd spoken to on the phone, who had not looked best pleased by the personal treatment. Perhaps, the physical approach was not always best. That said, she got the feeling that the woman was being vague as she was a numpty, and didn't know anymore. What Cath did manage to illicit, was Ted's full details now that he had taken over the licence, and the club's owner was listed as a limited company registered in the Netherlands. She decided to go for a coffee at the nearest Costa or Starbucks and reassess if there was anything else she could do whilst in Liverpool. She loved the coffee produced by these modern coffee houses but hated the exorbitant wait involved. She knew it took a little while to produce quality, freshly made coffee, but couldn't help thinking that the business model was flawed. If they could reduce the wait, say by having more machines for starters, then surely they would sell more. But what did she know. She just hated queuing, contrary to the French stereotypical view of the British.

Eventually, she had her flat white and was sat in a quiet corner. The wait had provided one positive, though; it had allowed her mind to wander towards Bobby Broadbent. He was definitely worth a follow-up visit. She sent him a quick text asking to meet someone neutral later. She decided to use the burner phone from last night, just to be on the safe side. She knew there was a Costa and a Starbucks situated on the re-vamped Preston Docks, so suggested one of those. She promised not to keep him long and would not need to bother him again. She wasn't sure her last comment was entirely truthful, but it might help to tease him out to meet her.

Cath quickly finished her lukewarm flat white and looked up at the queue, considering a refill, but the damn backlog was even worse. Then she revisited her conversations with the council woman, Jennifer, she'd said her name was, and a sudden realisation hit her. Maybe the reason why she couldn't trace Baldy via the security licencing authorities, was staring her in the face. What if he wasn't licenced? To be honest, he looked the sort who'd done time inside and was possibly barred from working the doors; officially. She knew that doormen had to wear their licences on their arms and tried to remember from last night. But she couldn't recall seeing anything on their arms, there may have been, but she was not looking for it. A lesson for next time: note everything.

She left the coffee shop and decided to grab a sandwich from a local Deli, and eat it next to a rural space and watch the world go by. She'd just finished and her burner phone announced an incoming text; must be from Bobby, which was a good sign. She pulled it out of her coat pocket, but before she could read it, the device rang an incoming call from a number which was withheld. She stared at it unsure, it must be Bobby, or it could be from Martin dialling through a switchboard. She took the call before it rang off, 'Hello.' she said, fully expecting to hear Martin's voice, not knowing why he hadn't rung her personal phone.

'I know I gave you a bit of a hard time, well, not so much a hard time, but I wasn't over friendly, but that's my job; no offence,' the male caller said.

'Sorry, who is this?'

'I was on the door last night when you called into the club and spoke to Ted,' he said.

Baldy. 'Oh yes,' she stuttered, as she sought to get some authority back into her voice. 'Are you the one who approached as I was leaving?'

'Yep, Ted gave me your card,' Baldy said.

Of course, the card. 'OK, how can I help you?'

'It's' more how I can help you. I hear you want to write a story about old Tommy who used to run the club?'

'Yes that's right,' Cath said, after clearing her throat. She could hear the confidence back in her own voice.

'Is that all it's about?'

'Yes, honestly, I've no interest in decrying his memory or debasing the club in any way.'

'Huh?'

Cath immediately regretted her choice of words, and said, 'I'm not after slagging anyone one off. Just a small piece about how sad it all is; being shot and then surviving only to be killed in a dreadful car accident.' Cath wasn't aware what Phil Devers had released to the pubic yet about the accident, but she knew at some stage they would have to come clean that Tommy was shot dead, though she hoped he could keep her and Martin's true details out of it for a while longer. And even if it was public knowledge that Tommy had been murdered, it didn't really alter her cover story about doing a human interest piece. And she could always drop the 'story' if she felt it could cause her trouble. All this flashed through her mind in an instant while she waited for Baldy to answer.

'OK. Look, I know he didn't get on overly with Ted, but I always found him a decent geezer and I'd be happy to meet up and chat about him if that's what you're after? But because of the way Ted is towards him, it would better somewhere away from the club.'

This, she hadn't expected. 'Great, just tell me when and where?'

'How about now, let's get it done?'

'Yeah, sure, I'm in Liverpool at the moment.'

'I'll text you the postcode, I know somewhere just outside the city centre where no one will see us, say in thirty minutes, if that suits you?'

'Yeah, sure,' she replied, and then the phone went dead before she could ask any more questions. She wondered whether she should run it past Martin first. But she was conscious that there was no way he could get over here in time, even if he wasn't meeting the UC officer, but a quick chat could help. She pulled out her private phone and tried Martin's number as she walked back to her car, but it rang straight to voicemail. He must still be in the middle of discussions with the UC, so she left a quick message, she'd speak with him later.

Then she remembered the text on her burner phone and quickly swapped devices; it was from Bobby and he said he was happy to meet her at the Costa which was inside the foyer of the Odeon cinema on the Docks. He suggested five o'clock; perfect. She sent him a quick reply to confirm, and then her phone buzzed again. It was the postcode of some back street boozer, apparently, close to Bootle Docks on the north side of the city. Brilliant, she thought, today was turning into a success after all. She just hoped that Martin and Colin were having as much luck with the UC.

Chapter Forty-two

Cath drove along Derby Road out of the city, with the waterfront and any number of Liverpool's docks to her left. The road was edged with vast tall buildings and warehouses supporting the port trade, intermingled with newer retail outlets where clearly once had also been port related buildings. The docks were still very much active and busy but not the global force they had once been. As she approached the northern district of Bootle, the Sat Nav told her to keep going as the road name changed to Primrose Road. Somewhere between Bootle and the next township, Seaforth, which were only a couple of miles apart, the device directed her to turn right and she would be at her destination.

On her left hand side she saw The Longshoreman's Arms, which was a pavement-fronted pub built in polished red brickwork, which seemed to bulge outward. The mortar was almost white as where the huge stone lintels and columns around the windows and the doorway. She could see the entrance to a small car park just passed the main building, as her text from Baldy had mentioned, and she pulled in there and parked. Hers was the only motor there. She wondered whether Baldy had parked in the street, or whether he lived within walking distance; this could be his local. The thought reassured her; he'd be well known, presumably.

She checked her phones, nothing back from Martin yet, and then got out and locked her car. She walked around to the front and was deciding whether to wait a minute or two, or just go in, when she heard a voice. She looked towards the sound and saw Baldy crossing the road on foot a little higher up. He must live local she guessed. This time she would make sure she sucked up every bit of detail.

He was still wearing his Crombie coat from the previous evening but his head was covered with a baseball cap and he was wearing sunglasses. If he hadn't have shouted, she wouldn't have recognised him. Though, seeing him in a baseball cap somehow added a familiar look.

'This way,' he said, as he briskly walked past her into the pub's doorway, and as she turned to follow, she suddenly realised that she didn't even know his real name.

Inside, there was a circular bar in the middle of a single room which had a very Victorian feel to it. Alcoves with ornate glass partitions above bench seats gave each snug area the look of a Waltzer carriage from the funfairs; except these ones didn't spin around, well, not without several drinks inside you. The place was only a quarter full, but Cath was glad to see people inside. The lone barman nodded at Baldy; another reassuring act.

Baldy asked her what she wanted to drink and pointed towards an empty alcove, so she sat down keeping a dark wood table in front of her. He was soon back with her fruit juice and a pint of ale and plonked himself opposite. Weirdly, he had kept his sunglasses on and she wasn't really sure why. It wasn't as if she hadn't seen him without them. Maybe he was just nervous talking to the press?

'So you want to do a sob story about Tommy?' he started with, which she thought was a disingenuous choice of words, seeing as Tommy was such a friend.

'Can I ask who I'm speaking with?' she answered his question with her own.

'Jay, or JK: most folk call me JK,' he said, without hesitation.

'OK, Jay, yep, I was just after some background from a human interest point of view, that's all.'

'Well, I can't tell you much, he was a loner, no bird, no mates to speak of, in fact, I don't know of any other friends but me, and I wouldn't exactly call him a mate if I'm being honest. But I got on OK with him.'

'Family?'

'None at all, that much I'm sure of. So I can save you time digging in that hole.'

'You're not giving me much padding to his life.'

'There's not much to give, as you can see.'

'It's just such a tragic set of circumstances,' she said.

'The way I heard it, the shooting in the church was a case of mistaken identity, and the accident was, well, you know,

192

accidents happen don't they?' Jay said. But Cath noticed him lean in closer towards her when he mentioned the accident, and if she could have seen his eyes she wouldn't be surprised to see if he wasn't scrutinising her. It flashed through her mind whether he already knew it hadn't been an accident. Damn, she should have spoken with Phil Devers before the meeting to double check what had, and had not, been released to the press. She decided to cover both bases and said, 'To be honest, it doesn't really matter how he died; it's still such a tragedy that he did.'

Baldy didn't respond, but she noticed he sat back a little. 'So what do you mean about mistaken identity?' she asked, moving things on.

'Just what I heard, I mean, who in the world would want to harm or even kill the likes of Tommy. He wasn't an active villain. That was all in his past, I believe, so he hadn't pissed anyone off.'

She wondered whether she should point out that Tommy Broadbent was considered by the police as potentially still a very active criminal, but decided against it. If he was playing her it would make no difference and she would be effectively giving away police intel.

'Have you ever met Tommy?' Jay asked, as he leaned inwards again, not much of a lean, probably didn't even know he was doing it. What Martin would call a non-verbal tell. But it was clear to her. She was being scrutinised again. 'How could I have?'

'Just wondered if you'd spoken to him while he was in the hospital?'

The question threw her a bit, what would it matter to Jay if she had, but in keeping with her story, she decided to keep it low key. 'No, I never got the chance to talk to him.' Changing track she asked about the club's supposed co-manager/owner's representative; or whatever title the mysterious Lucy held.

'I'm just a bouncer, Ted will no doubt deal with her, but she's probably just a go-between on behalf of the company which owns the club.'

'Did you ever meet her?'

'No.'

'Or see her?'

'No, look what is this?'

'I just thought that Lucy might have an opinion and comment on Tommy, that's all. Ted said he'd pass on my request with my number to her.'

She noticed that Jay was back in his forward position again, and that he'd moved after she said Lucy's name. Interesting.

'Well, I'd just let that request arrive then,' he said, before leaning back once more. 'But I wouldn't expect a call; they didn't get on, so she would have nothing good to say about Tommy in any event.'

Cath decided not to push it further, and then Jay leaned back farther and drained his glass. Cath asked him if he wanted a refill, but he declined, said he had to be somewhere else in ten. The meeting was clearly over. She thanked him for his time and they left the pub together, he just nodded at her as he crossed the street and disappeared into the estate. Cath was relieved to reach her car and get back inside it, and didn't hang about. Once she was back on the main road she relaxed and ran the meeting back through her mind. She hadn't learnt much, and had left with more questions than she had arrived with. It had been all staged and she had been the interviewee, but she felt like she had passed the test; whatever the test had been. This meant that Jay was hiding something, something he didn't want her to find. Plus, he reacted negatively that she knew Lucy's name.

Her phone rang via the car's Bluetooth, it was Martin.

'Christ, Cath, are you OK?'

She refrained from giving him her "I'm a big girl" speech, she knew he was just concerned. 'Yeah, it was a doddle, didn't learn much, but will fill you in when I get back.'

Martin said OK and briefly told her about their meeting with Gilly the UC officer, and that she was up for being deployed. He'd fill her on properly when he saw her.

***

Kinsella rang Lucy as soon as he was out of sight of the pub.

'How'd it go?'

'It's definitely her I saw in the motor that picked Tommy up from the hospital.'

'I see. So do we have a problem?'

'Not sure. She was convincing that she is just after doing a "human interest story" as she puts it, and if that's the case, it's like you said: safer to leave alone and not draw attention.'

'It's a tough call. Do we kill her and bring on a spotlight; even if it looks like an accident, or do we run with it?' Lucy said.

'On the plus, I'm as happy as I can be that she accepts that Tommy has no family or friends, and in particular, no family, so a dead end of which I've saved her time in not going down.'

'That helps. Why do you think she's not admitted to being in the motor?'

'Perhaps the cops have told her to keep quiet, for now. It's not uncommon for them to hold details back to give them a head start trying work it all out.'

'True, are you worried about the police?'

'They couldn't find a blade of grass on a football pitch.'

'But if she was in the car, then she must know Tommy was shot, so why not say so to you. It makes this "human interest story" thing sound a load of bollocks.'

Kinsella thought before he answered, replayed the final seconds of the shooting of Tommy in his head. 'It's highly possible the way it happened, that she does not know he was shot. She knew they were being followed, even chased, but in the end, that HGV backing out in front of them was just a fluke of luck. I just wanted to make sure by shooting him.'

It was obviously Lucy's turn to consider things as an impasse ensued. 'That trailer nearly got me and Micky too. Though if it had got Micky it would have saved me a job,' Kinsella said, and then laughed at his own black humour.

'We are about to set up a meet to sell our idea to some very influential people, if the fake Tommy story surfaces before then, we could be stuffed.'

'What happens when it comes out eventually, like at the Coroner's inquest?'

'I've thought about that, we can limit the damage; he's just a sad loser who lived off someone else's reputation as he happened to look like him. That's all the cops can really surmise. They don't know the half of it. OK, they know he was a low level grass, but not why; and that bit will never be made public in a Coroner's court, which actually helps us immensely. And by then, weeks will have passed anyway, and the deals will have been done. But a story now by the press could rock the confidence of the people we have in mind to approach.'

Kinsella guessed Lucy was thinking out loud more than speaking to him.

Then she said, 'Let's keep a close watch and you keep in touch with her, ask to see any story before it goes to print, and if she hesitates, then smell a rat. Then say you have found something salacious to add, meet her and kill her.'

'OK,' he said again, not too sure how he was supposed to keep such a close watch. He had her name, 'Jill Garvey', a mobile number, but little else. He pulled the calling card Ted had given him from his pocket and looked at it, but there was nothing else on it. Which he already knew.

'And if you see anything that concerns you, and you need to act fast, just take executive action. I trust your judgement. You're about the only fucker I do trust at the moment.'

'Accident?'

'If possible, but if not...' Lucy answered, leaving her sentence unfinished.

'What about her driver mate?'

'I'd forgotten about him; maybe he was just the driver.'

'If I have to move in, I'll try and get that out of her, first. Though to be honest, the way he drove that motor he was clearly a professional driver, so probably just hired help.'

'I'll leave that call with you. It sounds like we have a plan. And don't forget that other fucker; we should have dealt with him years ago.'

'Do you want me to just keep watching, or pay him a visit and warn him off?'

'Again, your call: do what you have to when you need to.'

'Fair enough; you'll owe me a few drinks once we can meet up.'

'Trust me, once this is all sorted, I'll give you a night out you'll not forget. Got to go, his nibs is coming in,' Lucy said, and then the line went dead.

Kinsella had wondered whether to tell her that the press woman knew her first name, but thought it might just further spook her unnecessarily. And her abrupt end to the call had made the decision for him. Then he smiled at her last remark as he picked up his pace, his motor was just around the next corner.

Chapter Forty-three

Martin was relieved when Cath answered her phone and said she was on her way back, it sounded like she had had an eventful morning, but he would have to have a quiet word with her about meeting unsavoury people with no backup. He was conscious of not denting her enthusiasm, or coming across as patronising; which is where it became tricky being her boyfriend and supervisor. Not that she needed much supervision. He'd just say it was standard policy, so next time, he or someone else, could be parked around the corner. He'd be careful not to make it a big deal. He hoped Colin's plan to get her sworn in as a Special, and thereafter have access to some defensive training, came to fruition.

But all in all, it looked like they were all having a better day. The UC, Gilly, or whatever her real name was, had agreed to spend a few nights in Banging Sounds. They knew it was speculative; and couldn't expect to catch Tommy in there, but if they could ID and house Lucy, then they could concentrate on her, and she would no doubt lead them to the main man. Once they had explained all this to Gilly, she'd agreed to it. She was well known around all the city's pubs and clubs in her undercover persona, though she'd not been in Banging Sounds for some time. She also had a mate who could go in with her so she would not stand out. It was all a gamble, but worth a shout. At least they were doing something.

Cath arrived back and brought Colin and him up-to-speed fully, as they did her. 'It sounds like this Jay knows more than he is letting on.' Martin said.

'I think he is very concerned about drawing undue attention to Tommy and the club. I think the place is, or about to be used as a high class brothel,' she said.

'That would fit,' Colin said.

'And may explain why Tommy wanted out.'

'Agreed,' Cath said.

'And to think he was just about to open up when he was killed.' Martin added.

'Still not the best of reasons to kill someone. After all, he was providing the real Tommy a unique service being his legit face. Once gone, that mask would not be replaceable,' Colin added.

'He must have really pissed them off,' Martin said.

'And become a liability, for some reason,' Cath threw in.

'And this Lucy, sounds more and more interesting judging by Jay's reaction to her name.'

'Totally. I'll have a deeper go at trying to trace her.'

They discussed their plans for the rest of the day, and Martin was relieved when Colin stepped in and had a quiet word with Cath about having backup in certain scenarios. He stressed that she was continuously breaking new ground and she seemed to take it well. Then he said he needed some quiet time so he could concentrate on getting all the required authorities done for Gilly. Martin was to arrange for some officers from Liverpool to be available as backup, as would Martin be, who Colin wanted armed as well, to cover all bases. Though getting the firearms authority through would be the hardest bit as they had no intelligence that firearms were to be involved at all.

'How are you going to swing that last bit?' Martin asked.

'I'm going to request that you alone are armed for purely defensive reasons as the subjects are suspected as being behind the shooting of Tommy and the death in North Wales,' Colin said.

'Pity we can't prove that.'

'That is why I need some peace to choose my words.'

'You should become a novelist when you retire from the cops.'

'Nobody would believe any "faction" I could come up with. They'd say it's too farfetched.'

Martin smiled and then Cath said she was due to meet Bobby Broadbent at the Costa on Preston Docks at five, and did she need any backup. Martin wondered if she was proving a point, but she appeared genuine.

'Bobby's not any kind of threat, so no, Cath, but we will be here if needed. Five to ten minutes away,' Colin said.

'So what are you up to?' Colin asked, as Martin put his coat on.

'Off to buy a kettle and toaster before the shops close,' he answered.

***

Lucy sat opposite Broadbent around the table in their hotel room, each with a fresh mug of coffee. It was approaching late afternoon and Broadbent had told her that he had come up with a list of five top drawer villains he thought worthy of approach, and more importantly, safe to approach. She didn't know who Broadbent had chosen, but he said she knew two of them, if only by association. For all Broadbent's limitations, of which there were many - which she usually had to manage around - this was where he came into his forte. He had a reputation she could only aspire to, a standing which was mainly built from ancient deeds and she knew was nearly as false as fake Tommy's persona. But the higher echelons of the organised criminal world was still very much a misogynistic place, and this was where Broadbent was needed to make her plans a success.

She'd explained in detail, over dinner the previous evening, that to market what they had as a one-off supply would be a nightmare to implement and manage. It was far better sold as an ongoing insurance policy; and because any insurance policy expends dead money - until it's needed - they had to pick those to approach very carefully. She reminded him how grateful Clayton Rigby had been, and although the timings couldn't have been better, the more in the shit their would-be clients were, the better their chances of success. And with Clayton there to tell his story, hopefully, they would clinch it.

'Are you sure you have the right prospective clients?' she asked Broadbent.

'As sure as I can be.'

This didn't overfill her with confidence. 'It only takes two, maybe three to turn us down, and then tell all their contacts that what we are offering is shit and dangerous, and it all comes tumbling down,' she said, starting to feel stressed.

'Sometimes you treat me like a numpty; don't you think I know this?'

Lucy didn't answer him, but instead asked, 'OK, so who is first on your list?'

Broadbent then rearranged some papers on the table in front of him into a set order. He picked up the top one and said, 'Mad Micky Moffatt.'

'He sounds a charmer.'

'He is.'

'If we get this right and roll it out with success, you do realise we could go nationwide with it. Keep it for the select few, but on a national scale; we'd make millions. It'd make our losses over in Holland look like small change,' she said.

'I know, I know; chill, will you.'

Saying "chill" was another of Broadbent's annoying habits; she sat back in her chair and took a deep breath. And then as if reading her, he said, 'And don't let the name put you off.'

'Go on.'

'He may be a grumpy, violent bastard - or a proper moody, naughty geezer, as our colleagues in the south might say - but he is as sharp as your stilettos. People often make that mistake about him, at their cost.'

'OK, I'm sorry, I'm just a bit tense having put so much into this; I'd hate to see it fail now.'

'I know, and me too; my reputation would be shit thereafter.'

And what about my growing status. She didn't say.

Lucy looked on as Broadbent read his notes and picked up his phone. He turned to face her. 'Moffatt is a well-known robber in Manchester. He used to be part of the infamous Quality Street Gang, and although they had their heydays in the 70s, 80 and 90s; most of them are now senior figures who oversee and run - or allow - robbery teams to operate in their areas. Moffatt is now Salford based, and no one does a blag on his manor without his approval. But here's the thing; he has to keep his nose off the street, or has had to for the last six months as he's wanted for killing his lover in a violent domestic. And there isn't a real snout anywhere in the North West who would dare grass on him.

They all know that he'd start with their families before moving on to them.'

'So how the hell is he going to buy in to what we are selling?' Lucy spat.

'Because, believing no one would dare grass on you, and knowing no one is, are two entirely different things.'

Lucy smiled; she had to admit he had a point.

'And the filth have often tried and failed miserably to get anyone to talk about him; so they would do cartwheels at the prospect of signing up a snout who was offering to do just that.'

Lucy was quite surprised with Broadbent's clever reckoning; maybe she'd done him down in her mind, he'd just made an even better point. 'Come on then,' she said, excitedly.

It was Broadbent's turn to smile as he dialled a number; he held the phone away from his face and put the loudspeaker on. She immediately heard the call ringing out. And then it was answered.

'Who is this?' the recipient asked.

'It's Tommy Broadbent, here Micky, I hope you are well, pal?' Broadbent said.

'Fuck me, Tommy the ghost, thought you were dead-ish?' Moffatt said, and then roared with laughter.

'As Mark Twain once said, "Rumours of my death have been greatly exaggerated".'

'Stop being a clever-arsed poncy twat, and tell me what you want?'

Broadbent glanced at Lucy and rolled his eyes, before he continued.

'I have a business proposal to put to you.'

'Not interested, pal.'

'Wait; what if I could offer you a way of knowing what the filth is being told about you.'

'Never happen, I'd cut off their granny's tits; for starters.'

'And be able to tell you what they were asking in relation to you, as and when you popped back on their radars.'

There was a pause this time before Moffatt spoke, 'You got a bent cop on the books?'

'Something potentially far better than that, but no more over the phone. I'm setting up a meeting of a chosen few top geezers, to put it to you all. You in?'

'I guess I should hear you out; where?'

'I'll text you the details of exactly where and when, but it'll be in Liverpool.'

'That shithole.'

Lucy realised that Moffatt was a Manc through and through.

'If I come all that way and it's shite, I'll have to give you a slap, no offence.'

Broadbent held three fingers up to Lucy to signify, that it's only thirty miles between Salford and Liverpool, or so she guessed he was saying.

'Fair enough,' Broadbent answered.

'And if I don't like whoever you've got in that room, I'll slap you for potentially exposing me to dog shit.'

'Fair enough,' Broadbent repeated.

'OK, text me the details, and for fuck sake use code,' Moffatt said, and then the line went dead.

Chapter Forty-four

Cath knew that Preston Docks had undergone a massive investment and re-imagined construction, transforming it from its heyday as an inland port to a popular retail place full of food outlets, pubs, a marina, motor parks, elite flats and more. But she had yet to visit it, and was pleasantly surprised. It reminded her of Manchester's redeveloped Salford Quays, but on a smaller scale. She soon found the Odeon cinema which had a Costa coffee shop within its vacuous entrance foyer. She clocked Bobby Broadbent straight away sat at one of two easy chairs at a table nearest the entrance. It was discretely apart from the main seating area, which was good. Salutations over, she noted that his coffee was nearly done, she glanced at the wall clock, just after five, she wasn't late so he must have been early. She asked him if he wanted a top up, to which he said yes, so she then began the agonising wait to be served.

She eventually returned with two coffees and sat opposite Bobby. 'Thanks for agreeing to see me.'

'You said it would be the last time.'

'Of course,' she lied, or suspected so.

'OK, what more can I tell you?'

'First up, why did you and Tommy really fall out?'

She noticed Bobby pause, take a deep breath followed by a sip of his coffee, and then he spoke, 'Things had been going downhill for a while, he was always sponging off Mum and Dad, which I never did, and it wound me up. Particularly, as he was often treated as the prodigal son.'

Cath smiled her best empathetic smile and Bobby carried on.

'Then one day when he had not been around for months, he waltzed back to Preston and hit them with another bullshit story, and lifted five grand from them, which was by far the most he'd ever borrowed. I say "borrowed" he never ever paid anything back. I had it out with him and things became heated.'

'What happened?'

'The spiteful little bastard told me that he was the favourite, which I'd already worked out long ago. And then he told me why.'

Cath took a sip of coffee and watched Bobby intensely as he paused to do the same. She could tell that what he was saying still evoked pain. He was telling her the truth.

Bobby continued, 'He said that he was full blood - to use some stupid street term - and that I was not. Initially, I disregarded it as just some nasty attempt to insult me, but he was off and running. He went on to claim that Mum had an affair of which I was the product. My Dad, whom I adored, was not my real dad. I floored him there and then.'

'As painful as that was, it might still have been rubbish.' Cath said, as sympathetically as she could.

'We were in their house, alone at the time, or so I thought. In our row, we'd not heard the front door. Mum rushed in to stop us, which on seeing her we both did. I fronted her, and in my blind rage, I accused her.'

'What did she say?'

'She denied it, but I could see it in her eyes. I said that I would go and ask Dad when he got home and she nearly had a fit and made me promise not to. That I had no idea what that would do to him.'

'Take a break,' Cath said, she could see how much torment Bobby was in. He drank some more coffee and then continued.

'So you'll understand how disappointed I was to find that the guy on the slab was not my brother.'

Cath just nodded. She totally understood now.

'The fact that Mum freaked so much told me all I needed to know: not only was it true, but Dad can't have known, and I couldn't break his heart, I loved him too much.'

'So I guess that was the end of you and Tommy?'

'It was.'

'How about your relationship with your mum?'

'It was never the same; I wanted to know the details but didn't want to hear them, if that makes sense.'

Cath nodded, it did.

'So, it was never mentioned again. My feelings cooled towards Mum, but I had to keep up the pretence for Dad's sake. He was a sharp guy and would have soon picked up on a bad vibe. It was hard, but it became the new normal. I was almost relieved when Mum passed first, and I know that sounds harsh, but it was just me and Dad then. Those last couple of years with Dad were some of my happiest.'

Cath wasn't sure what to say next, so finished her coffee.

'So you can see why I hate my brother and if I knew where he was, I'd tell you in a heartbeat.'

'I believe you. What can you tell me about Lucy?'

'She made Tommy worse, if that was possible. I only met her once, a big tall slender Nigerian, stunningly attractive, but with hard soulless eyes. She thought they were the new Bonnie and Clyde.'

A huge impasse seemed to seep in and Cath could tell that Bobby was wrestling with something else. She decided to take a hint from Martin, who always reckoned that as uncomfortable as impasses could be, they were always best left to deepen. Eventually, the person you were talking to would feel the pressure to fill the void, and when they did; it was usually the truth they used to do it with. So Cath sat in silence and was surprised just how heavy the pressure of the emptiness became. She could see it weighing heavily on Bobby, too.

Eventually, he said, 'OK: there's more you should know, but not here. I got the bus here, do you have a car?'

'Yes, it's parked on the huge car park at the back of this place.'

'OK, let's chat there, then you can drop me off,' Bobby said, and was quickly on his feet.

Cath followed and then overtook him outside to lead him to her car. She could tell that gold dust was coming; she just hoped that the break didn't close him down. She hurriedly led Bobby down the side of the large multi-screen cinema to a vast flat car park at its rear. There were very few cars on it. It was so big she could see a leaner driver being put through her paces in one corner of it.

Once they were both inside her car, she turned to face Bobby who thankfully carried on.

'Tommy has killed someone.'

This was indeed gold dust Cath thought, shocked. Especially, as they had been struggling to prove any offences against him; certainly anything hands on. Again she just let Bobby carry on.

'I'm sure he and Lucy put something in her tea; brought on a heart attack. She had a dicky ticker, and was getting old, nobody suspected anything suspicious.'

Cath was desperate to know who, but kept quiet.

'She'd outlived her use, I guess. I never really understood why.'

'Why didn't you go to the cops, it was obviously someone you knew?' she did ask.

'Couldn't prove it, and I didn't like her that much.'

Cath knew that she had to remain non accusatory, so chose her most sympathetic voice, 'You know, if the police knew something was wrong, then a full post mortem might have shown up any unusual additives in the blood.'

'I was in two minds; I couldn't be sure, and I couldn't prove which one had done it even if they had found something.'

Cath knew that where there were no suspicions and a history of ill health - and even when a doctor couldn't issue a death certificate - a post mortem was superficial. In the case of someone with a bad heart, the pathologist would go straight to the heart, find that it had failed and that would be that. And she understood what Bobby was saying, even if he had spoken out and an adulterant had been found by a further, more intense examination, it would be impossible to prove who actually put it there. Could even prove suicide. But she didn't understand why Booby, who so despised Tommy, didn't go to the cops irrespective of how hard it would be to prove a case. So she asked him.

'I had a better idea: I thought, OK, I could go to the police and cause him a lot of distress, but with probably no outcome, or I could use it against him. Or more accurately, use what he didn't know, against him.'

'Go on.'

'I told him that I had proof, told him I had found the discarded bottle.'

'And had you?'

'No, but it worked. He never questioned whether the bottle I claimed to have hidden was the one or not.'

'That amounts to an admission that he, and, or her, had done it,' Cath said.

Bobby nodded and added, 'And that they had thrown the bottle away, somewhere where I might have found it, which I never did. Reckon it went in the wheelie bin which was emptied on the same day. But by the time I looked, it had already been emptied, but Tommy wasn't to know that.'

'So what was the better idea?'

'That he stays away forever. And that included family funerals. I'd go through the motions of getting the police to leave messages, but I didn't expect to see him. After Mum and Dad, our Uncle went, he was the last.'

'So him not attending your family funerals was not the cause of your further disquiet, but a trade off?'

'Exactly. I hated him, and Dad left me everything in his will, which did surprise me, but didn't amount to much, they'd lived in a council house all their lives, but what he did leave me meant a lot. And it meant more knowing that Tommy got nothing.'

'I can't thank you enough for being so open with me, it certainly explains a lot of things, and I truly believe you don't know where Tommy or Lucy is. But, as and when we get hold of them, we will have to put the suspicious death to them, even if it leads nowhere.'

'I get that, but you'll have them then, so they will be gone anyhow,' Bobby said, and then looked through the windscreen in obvious thought, before he turned back to face Cath and said, 'Tell, me you will have enough to put them away regardless, for all their other criminal acts, of which I'm sure are plentiful. I couldn't stand it, if they walked free from everything; especially as I would have lost my lever over them.'

Cath had no choice but to "tactically lie" to quote another Martin-ism; for the greater good, and said, 'You've no need to worry, and the historical murder will be the cherry on the cake; a cake with no file inside.'

Bobby smiled at her comment and said, 'OK.'

'But I will need a name to have any chance of putting that cherry on top.'

'You know, I've never felt this good in years. I don't know what it is about you, but you are a good listener. I feel unburdened. I feel good to be alive now and able to carry on with my life afresh. Or I will when I let this last bit out.'

Cath had to nearly bite her bottom lip to stop herself from replying. It had to come in Bobby's own time. It had to flow unsolicited.

And then it did. He looked through the windscreen, again and she saw his eyes focus, so she glanced too. It was just a figure heading past them towards the cinema. But she knew whoever it was couldn't hear them. Bobby clearly disregarded the distraction and turned back to face her.

'The murder victim was our mu__'

That was as far as Bobby managed, but Cath was in no doubt that he was saying 'Mum'. But that realisation would come later. What happened next would be etched in her memory until the day she died. As Bobby started to say the word 'mum' the windscreen exploded into a spider's web. A network of striations broken only by a hole on Bobby's side. The opening a match to the blackened and burnt one in the left side of his head. Blood, bone and brain matter ricocheted off his seat's headrest before his skull hit it, which then lolled forward. The gore splashed around the car in an instant as time slowed to a crawl; accentuating each grisly aspect of what had just happened. Shocked to inertia, Cath started to take in what had just occurred. First, glancing at the lifeless body of Bobby with the right half of his head missing, and then forward at the shape of a man in dark clothing running away from them; the cinemagoer from a moment before.

Then she looked at herself in the driver's mirror and saw blood splatters across her face; she started screaming, uncontrollably. She was sure she would never stop.

Chapter Forty-five

Lucy listened as Broadbent's phone rang. She thought it was about to go to answerphone before it was eventually answered, with, 'Who the fuck is this?' Broadbent really knew some charming folk.

'It's me, Tommy,' Broadbent said.

'Don't know no Tommys. So tell me where you got this number from?' the recipient said.

Broadbent had told her that number two on the list was a guy from Cheshire called Sid. A career fraudster who had a penchant for ripping off old ladies out of their life savings with a charm she couldn't image he had, based from his comments so far. According to Broadbent, Cheshire police were sick and tired of Scousers considering the middleclass well-to-do folk of Cheshire as fair game, and were actively targeting the likes of Sid.

'Yes you do; it's Tommy Broadbent.'

'Fuck me, I thought you were dead,' Sid replied.

Broadbent then went through his Mark Twain routine which Lucy was sure would start to grate before long. And then he pitched their proposal.

'Sounds interesting; I've always thought of plod down here as a bunch of sheep shaggers, but somehow they have been getting some results,' Sid said, and then went on to list a number of names who had had their collars felt recently, before he finished off with, 'Count me in, could do with some insurance.'

'Two out of two,' Broadbent said, before briefing her on number three; someone called Johnny the Jemmy, on account that he started life as a standout burglar, and still was, though he had progressed to footballers gaffs and similar. But then Broadbent warned her that he made Mad Mickey Moffatt look like a choirboy.

The call was answered straight away and after Broadbent had gone through his preamble, which Lucy noted was getting shorter and more polished; Johnny's response was also brief, but less polished.

'I'd heard you'd gone straight, and if you're back from the Dam, it means you are in the shit, or hot. Therefore, I'm not interested, so don't call again and bin my number,' Johnny said, before ending the call.

Broadbent just shrugged his shoulders before picking up the next piece of paper. If Lucy thought Johnny was brief, the next guy made him look verbose.

'Fuck off and don't call me again,' the guy spat, before ending the call. Broadbent had only got as far as the introduction.

Broadbent then picked up the last piece of paper.

'Keeping the best until last?' she asked.

'I went to school in Preston with this guy, so in or out, I know he's solid,' Broadbent said and then went on to describe Jack Jackson. Broadbent said he'd forgotten his real first name as at school he'd always been called Jack, from his surname, and it had stuck. It might be Derek, but he couldn't be sure. But whatever it was, Jack had been relieved when the nickname took off.

'What's wrong with being called Derek?'

'Might not be Derek, but whatever it was, he hated it, apparently only his mother got away with using it; anyone else got a slap,' Broadbent explained. And then gave Lucy a potted history. Apparently, he enjoyed hurting people, but was primarily a Class A drug dealer. He operated in Central Lancashire, and Liverpool where he was equally well known. Cocaine and Crack were his main commodities. And although he would sound grumpy, he wasn't really, but that hadn't stopped him getting a further nickname of 'Happy Jack' but never to his face.

According to Broadbent's sources, the North West Regional Organised Crime Unit was breathing down his neck, so he reckoned he would jump at what they had to offer. This turned out to be the case. When Broadbent ended the call, he was smiling.

'You look a lot more pleased than he sounded.'

'Trust me, that Jack's happy voice; you should hear him when he's pissed off,' he said, and they both burst out laughing.

Lucy sat back in her chair and could feel all the tension of the last few days start to lift. They now had three confirmed, which would be enough. Truth be known it would be hard work trying to run five scams at once. All they had to do now was to identify three would-be snouts to use to infiltrate the police, and if Paul her brother still wanted to play, then they would only need to find two. The hard bit would be the 'sales meeting', as she called it. And it would be Broadbent who would be the head seller, though she was banking on Clayton Rigby to swing it with his tale. It was all coming together nicely. 'Any thoughts on who to hire as our infiltrators?' she asked.

'That bit will be easy. As soon as we send one into plod talking about one of our clients, the cops will fall over themselves, and if they prove to be shite, then we can always replace them. Pay off the original ones saying that the client is no longer interested in our service or something like that.'

'They'll need to keep their mouths shut,' Lucy said.

'There you go again; leave it to me,' Broadbent said, as he pulled his coat on. He wasn't smiling.

Lucy gave him her Marilyn Monroe look and his face cracked.

'OK, I know, but the stress is off now. I'll go and grab some shampoo from the shop on the corner, and then we can celebrate.'

'Excellent idea,' she said, and watched him as he left the room and the door swung to. It had only just clicked shut when her phone went off. It was Kinsella. 'How's it going?' she asked.

'Bad, bad shit.'

Just when she was on a high. She asked what was up.

'You know you said I could take executive action if it was time-urgent.'

Lucy groaned inwardly as she said, 'Yes.'

'Well, I've had to.'

'Go on.'

'Tommy's brother.'

'Bobby, what about him?'

'I had to, Lucy.'

'Had to what?'

'Shoot him. He's dead.'

'Fuck sake; why?'

'I caught him having a private chat in a car and it looked well sus.'

'Who was he talking to, Five-O?' she asked, and wondered how Kinsella had come to the conclusion that the conversation was that bad. Though she knew if they were digging into the real Tommy's background, sooner or later, Bobby would, or could become a liability. But he was still Broadbent's brother; estranged or not.

Then Kinsella answered, 'Not the cops; worse.'

What could be worse than the filth? 'Who then?'

'That bitch from the press I met this morning.'

'Her! How?'

'I don't know, but they were having a private one-to-one in a motor at the back of a cinema in Preston.'

Lucy had to admit, it sounded bad, very bad. And they had no way of knowing what Bobby had, or had not told the woman. 'You shot him, you say?'

'Had to act fast.'

'What about her?'

'Fucking gun jammed, had to leg it.'

'You need to finish her off.'

'I know; I'll set up a meet with her.'

'Let me know when it's done.'

'Of course. At least then, there are no more loose ends.'

That was true.

'What about Tommy?' Kinsella asked, with clear fear in his voice.

'Leave him to me. He doesn't need to know, yet. Would serve no purpose. I'll judge as to when, or indeed, if.'

'Thanks,' Kinsella said, sounding relived.

Then Lucy heard the door start to open; Broadbent must have forgotten his wallet or something. 'Got to go,' she said, and ended the call.

Chapter Forty-six

Martin didn't sleep much; he was too concerned about Cath. He spent most of the night holding her and calming her when the nightmares came. At one stage she was shouting, "Get it off me" and clawing at her face. He knew she was in for a rough few nights, but the first would be the worst. The memory of what she had endured would fade in time, but would never go away. She would have to learn to live with it; put it in a mental Pandora's Box - it's what he does - but she would need help and support. Colin had already arranged for her to see the force psychologist in the coming weeks, which she had accepted. But she had refused to go on sick leave. She said the solitude would only feed the demons, she would be best kept busy; plus, she was desperate to help catch the killer in any way she could. Martin got all that. He was never any good alone with his thoughts after a major drama. Though he had suggested she have at least one day off, but she was having none of it. He could only hope that by holding her all night, she got some rest, albeit disturbed.

The investigation into the murder of Bobby Broadbent was immediately handed to the North West Regional Homicide Unit, and a DI named Vinnie Palmer was the effective lead on it. He had asked Martin if Bobby had any next of kin they could contact. To get their hands on Tommy Broadbent to deliver a death warning message; now wouldn't that be nice. "Your brother's dead, and oh, by the way, you're nicked". But they were no nearer to finding Tommy, or Lucy in real terms.

Gilly the UC had gone into Banging Sounds the previous night and a DS from the Liverpool office provided cover in Martin's absence, though he hoped to be there tonight. The DS had been good enough to leave him an update on his phone, which he'd just read; apparently the place was quiet and there was nothing to report. Often the way with such speculative jobs, it could take time, time they didn't have.

He brought Cath a brew as she stirred and asked the stupid question everyone asks in these situations; "How are you feeling?" This was said more in hope. But Cath came back with the stock answer of "not too bad", anyway.

An hour later, they were on the road, and an hour after that they arrived at their office at 8 a.m. Colin asked his own stupid questions and Cath gave the expected replies. Then Colin turned to Martin and said, 'While Cath is working I want you with her, and armed, at all times.'

Martin nodded. Cath didn't, but neither did she object, she'd have known it was a prerequisite for her not being on sick leave.

'Any developments with the murder?' Cath asked.

'They are still doing all the scene stuff, and there is a lot of forensics in your car.'

'Just glad it was the firm's car and not my own.'

'But in other news, I've had Phil Devers on, and he says that his Welsh counterpart - Dai Jones - has found a witness to their job.'

Both Martin and Cath turned to face Colin.

'Apparently, house-to-house enquires in a village near to the access to the viaduct has turned up a potential witness. Someone saw a rough looking bloke driving away from the scene at speed at the right time. Might be nothing, but the witness is being properly interviewed by detectives this morning. Phil will keep me updated.'

'Some potential good news, for a change,' Martin said. 'If we can ID him, he could lead us to Tommy and Lucy.'

'We live in hope.'

Then a phone in Cath's bag rang and she went to fish it out to take the call, Colin quietly asked Martin, how Cath really was. He told him about the nightmares and promised to keep a close watch on her. They then turned around as Cath finished her call. She was smiling.

'That was my burner phone,' she started with.

Martin and Colin were all ears.

'The bouncer guy, Jay, says he might know where dead Tommy's business partner is, if I'm interested in approaching her for comment about Tommy.'

'Lucy.' Martin said.

215

'He never used a name, but did say "her". But he wants cash; I bought some time by saying I'd have to speak to my editor.'

'How much?' Colin asked.

'Just a grand, but he reckons he knows where she is living. Too good to miss.'

'Too good indeed,' Colin said. 'Incidentally, I checked with Phil when we spoke earlier, and they have not realised the full details of the "car crash" yet, but he reckons they will have to by tomorrow.'

'Timing's excellent, then,' Martin said.

'I'll arrange a grand from petty cash, if you can ring him back and set up a meet,' Colin said to Cath.

'Will do.'

'And you get yourself to the armoury,' he said, to Martin.

Martin nodded.

Then Cath's desk phone rang and after she took the call she said, 'I'll make the meet with Jay the bouncer for a bit later, as that was DI Palmer on the phone, they want to interview me now. Apparently, I'm the only witness they have thus far to the killer.'

Martin said, 'Can you remember much?'

'Not a lot, I only glanced at him as I thought he was just going to the cinema. He was average height and well-built, dressed all in black.'

Martin knew that often witnesses to dramatic events had better recall the day or so afterwards, once their brain had started to edge away from the shock of it all. As it did, it created space for recollection and thought. Saying stuff out loud was also an excellent jogger of memory. 'What about his face?'

'He had a brown baseball cap pulled low. I remember it was brown as it stood out on top of his all-black apparel.'

This was a good start. 'Anything on the cap?' he pushed.

Cath paused in thought and then answered, 'Red squiggly writing - which also stood out - but I can't remember what it said.'

Martin let her go; she'd be getting all these type of questions by the bucketful from Vinnie Palmer's team. And she'd be shown any number of branded baseball caps until she was sick of the sight of them.

'They always slip up,' Colin threw in.

Martin knew what he meant; the killer prepares himself by dressing in nondescript black and then uses a branded baseball cap to hide his face. 'Probably his favourite cap,' Martin added.

Chapter Forty-seven

A few hours later, Martin was driving him and Cath towards Liverpool down the A59. She'd given her statement and told Martin she was amazed at how long it was. Considering, the actual event was over in seconds, and she'd not been able to remember any more about the assailant than she'd voiced in their office, the deposition still ran to over twenty pages of A4.

Martin knew how thorough homicide witness statements were, every detail could be important. The blue car parked opposite could lead to a further witness who had a bird's eye view, but had not come forward, for example. You could never put enough in, even if most of it ended up on the cutting room floor at any future proceedings as being redacted as not evidential, though the defence would always get a full copy.

What he had noticed since setting off, was that Cath seemed a bit more like herself; the few hours she had spent going over things had clearly had a cathartic effect. Plus, she was buzzing ahead of their meeting with the bouncer Jay and what it might lead to.

'I just hope he doesn't feed us a pile of rubbish just to get a grand out of us.' she said.

'I guess we'll soon find out.' Martin had expected the meeting to be back in the boozer where Cath had previously met him. But she said he was bothered about being seen again in there with her, plus, they might be overheard. On the latter point, Martin said, 'If he was bothered about eavesdroppers, why meet you there in the first place?'

'Because he knew he wasn't going to tell me anything, then.'

She made a valid point.

'Which is why I'm excited he might give us something good this time.'

Another fair point. 'How did he react when you said you were bringing "your editor" with you?'

'Surprisingly OK. I just said you had to be there to witness that he actually got the cash, which he seemed to readily accept.'

It was a bit like a handler taking her DS with her to witness a cash payment to a snout, Martin thought, and wondered if Jay had readily accepted it as he had once been one. But they needed to know who they were dealing with, and Martin said he would push for Jay's full details and get him to sign a receipt which he had mocked up while she'd been making her statement. Apart from that, he would stay quiet, it was Cath's gig.

Forty minutes later they arrived at a closed down cash and carry place on the outskirts of Skelmesdale, between Kirkby and Huyton, north of Liverpool. Skelmersdale's old village - known locally as 'Old Skem' - was typically West Lancashire, rural and as inviting as its name suggested. That was until the social planners of the sixties started work. Skelmersdale, or just Skem, was a now a huge concrete conurbation built as a massive council housing overspill for Liverpool. It was the North West's answer to Milton Keynes down south.

The car park adjacent to the cash and carry was vast and therefore a great meeting place. Martin realised they would know they were alone, and be able to spot anyone approaching which would suit both parties. The car park went down one side of the building but was mainly at the rear. There were several entrances and exits and they had driven on from one at the back. Ahead, behind the building, was a row of rubbish skips and large commercial bins which had up and over lids. Next to the row was a tatty red saloon car. The paint had oxidised in the way it did on Royal Mail vans. It had not seen much love. 'That must be his motor.'

'I guess,' Cath said.

'And we are supposed to follow him, is that right?' Martin asked. It was the part of the plan that he wasn't too happy with. He didn't like unknowns.

'Yes, he said he knew where Lucy stayed when she was in the UK, but it would be easier to show us as he didn't actually know the address, but had dropped her off in the past. He also said she was back in the UK at the mo. Imagine if Tommy is there, too.'

'That would be nice, and I have to admit, Skem would be the perfect place to hide out. There is not a single street here which doesn't have a lookout, paid for by local drug dealers.' Martin had asked Cath why Jay couldn't just do his own reconnaissance and then give them the address.

'He'd actually said that he could, but would only have time to do it tonight as he was busy all day tomorrow,' she'd answered.

Colin had rang while they were en route to warn them that Merseyside Police were now doing their press conference at 9 p.m. tonight, and would reveal the full facts about the car crash in the hope it might bring, otherwise unwilling, witnesses forward. Phil Devers had said he wasn't able to delay it, and Colin was worried that their press cover would be blown. And Martin had been to the club, as a cop, and the manager knew his name.

As they drove nearer, the tatty red car flashed its lights and started to move. Martin could see the driver was alone. He'd have thought Jay would have had the courtesy to say hello and explain more before taking them on a mystery tour. He didn't like that. And how could he be sure that it was them approaching. He must have had binoculars with him, he didn't like that either. He didn't say anything to Cath but this was starting to smell wrong; and he had no idea why it should. But as it was, he'd no choice but to follow Jay, if indeed it was Jay in the car, off the car park by the front of the premises. 'Perhaps ring him, just to confirm it is him in the red car,' Martin suggested.

'Good idea,' Cath said.

But before she could, her phone beeped an incoming call. She listened intently and ended the call, and then said, 'That was Colin, not Jay, and he says the cops in Wales have got a proper result. The witness has identified a known Liverpool villain as the speeding car driver near the viaduct who is now a person of interest. If they can't get hold of him straight away, the Welsh have asked that Merseyside name him in tonight's press conference while they have the media present, as an aside to the Tommy's murder news release. If he was just passing through at the wrong time, the Welsh reckon he'll come forward quick sticks, and they can rule him in, or out; as the case may be.'

'And if he doesn't come forward?'

'Exactly.'

'Who is it, anyone we know?'

'He didn't say, but said he'd text me the details with a photo as soon as he receives it from Phil.'

'Fair, enough. Now let's see where this idiot of a bouncer is taking us.'

Chapter Forty-eight

Lucy demanded that Broadbent let her in on the stooge interviews. He was resistant. He had picked the candidates, and he liked to keep some things to himself; it was a control issue. That was why she had insisted. Then she could interact with them, as and when required, with or without Broadbent. It made perfect sense to her. The first one Broadbent had lined up was with regard to Happy Jack from Preston. The stooge was a drug user and part-time dealer in crack. Part-time, as he'd only ever dealt to earn enough to support his own habit, and was therefore not considered a 'dealer' as such, by the filth. His current habit was the first thing Broadbent had asked him about over the phone. He'd then said he might have the best earner the guy had ever been offered; but it was dependent on him being clean. The guy had more than proved it; naming his rehab mentors etc. etc. but one look in the flesh would easily confirm or deny it.

The beauty of this guy was that he actually knew Happy Jack. Broadbent had established, by other means, that he'd shared a cell in Strangeways Prison with him a couple of years ago.

'When the cops check his antecedents and clock that, all reason will go flying out the window. They'll think all their meagre pay days have come at once,' Broadbent said.

'What's his real name? I'm sick of all these stupid nicknames.' Lucy asked.

'John Donnelly, but he does prefer Joe Doe. He's due here in half an hour.'

They had moved to another hotel just to be on the safe side, a downbeat place in Longsight a couple of miles out of Manchester's city centre. Lucy had no plans to spend the night there.

The second interviewee was Chris Wood, and thankfully, he had no nickname. He was a different class of villain. A grifter, as Broadbent called him; who reckoned he could con the crown jewels from the King if he could only be granted five minutes with him. A so called 'white-collar criminal'. Broadbent thought they were the most untrustworthy. 'Give me an honest robber, any day', he'd said. But they were where they were, and he would be a perfect fit for Sid the fraudster from Cheshire. She'd done some research online and it certainly appeared that Cheshire was being battered with grifters from Liverpool, and subsequently, Cheshire cops had set up a special unit to counter the threat. It was called Operation David, after King David; as they had poetically described fraud in their county as a Goliath problem. Whoever thought up these operational names, and the rationale behind them, obviously went to the same school that came up with criminal's monikers.

Lucy was interested to meet Chris as she had a good knowledge of fraud. Some of the best scammers in the world came from her native Nigeria. Broadbent called her brethren "The Scousers out of Africa". Cheeky bastard.

Her own brother, Paul, had already agreed to carry on in his stooge role, and he would slip in his knowledge of Mad Micky Moffatt to his handlers as soon as they were back on the job. It would all come down to tomorrow's 'sales meeting'.

There was a knock at the door, and Broadbent let John Donnelly in. A guy in his 40s, slim, with short dark hair. He had the look of a man who had seen a lot of things and not all of them good. But he looked healthy. It was abundantly clear that he was clean. A good start. She let Broadbent take the lead; he did the introductions and sat Joe Doe down with a beer.

'This will be the weirdest, but best job interview you have ever had.'

'Must admit, what little you told me over the phone sounded well-intriguing.'

'First thing; I can see you are clean, how long?'

'Six months, no sweat, ain't going back on that shit, no way.'

'Good. Secondly, are you active at the mo?'

'No, can't go near the stuff to deal it, I'd be straight back on it.'

'Excellent.'

'This is why I'm looking for a new line of graft.'

'I can't tell you the exact details, like names yet, but we've done our research and you are exactly what we need for a certain task, which will be a piece of piss, and long term.'

Nice of Broadbent to discuss it with her, Lucy thought, before virtually offering him the job.

'Last question, have you ever been a police informant?'

Joe Doe shot to his feet and Lucy thought he was going to punch Broadbent, which would have been amusing. The idiot could have phrased things better. Broadbent was quickly on his feet, too, but with his hands in the air, palms open and outward facing.

'It's not meant to be an insult, hear me out.'

'OK; but it better be good, and for the record, no.'

Both men sat down and Broadbent explained, after first having obtained Joe Doe's word - whatever that was worth - Lucy thought, that if he wasn't interested, what was said in the room stayed in the room. Broadbent had told her that he trusted the guy, so she had no option but to go along with it. But fortunately, he loved it and said he was in. Lucy gave him five grand as a signing on fee and they said they'd be in touch.

As soon as he had left, Broadbent said, 'One down, one to go.'

The next guy would be slyer by definition, but Broadbent said that of all the grifters he knew, he just about trusted this one. She hoped his judgement was right.

They had time for wee and a drink before a further knock at the door announced Chris Wood's arrival. He was a wiry guy in his 40s, greying hair and looked more like a vicar than a villain; which in his line of work was a great look. It was soon apparent that he could charm a Scotsman into tattooing 'I Love England' on his forehead. That was one reason why Lucy watched him closely as Broadbent went through his questions; just to ensure the guy wasn't rubber-dicking them. She came from a family of scammers and was confident she could judge him. Some folk say you 'can't scam a scammer', but she knew that was bollocks.

But by the end, she had warmed to him, Broadbent had told her before the guy arrived that they had grown up on the same street, which she knew counted for a lot. And it was clear that he was good at his job; he would put an insurance or car salesman to shame. And with his sickly eel-like persona, she was sure he could con the thick cops into believed he was bone fide. She caught Broadbent's eye and nodded her approval. Chris was clearly up for it, so he was in. She paid him his retainer and he left smiling. She just hoped he hadn't just grifted them; but she would be the judge of that going forward, not Broadbent.

Chapter Forty-nine

Ten minutes after leaving the cash and carry, Martin passed a sign for Digmoor. They were entering an estate which looked much like others they had passed; all white and box-like, and obviously designed to house giant rabbits. Cath had tried ringing Jay but it had rang out with no answer machine facility attached; a burner phone. She'd also texted him, but had received no response. But as he was driving, if it was him driving, Martin could understand that bit. But he was feeling less and less comfortable. The whole of Skem seemed to be one huge network of urban dual carriageways linking all the estates accessed by an inordinate number of roundabouts. And he'd noticed at the last three roundabouts numbers of youths in small groups, but the last group looked different. Two of them seemed to be watching the traffic go by and had taken particular interest as they had started to enter Digmoor. But what had freaked Martin more, was that they paid no heed to the tatty red car they were following, only them; even though it was clear that both cars were in convoy.

Then at the next roundabout, which was smaller and seemed to be part of the estate itself, rather than a highway to it, two more youths were stood. Both watching both cars, but both paying their car most attention; then one pulled out a mobile phone. That was it. Time to abort. Instead of following the red car farther into the estate, Martin kept going around the roundabout and drove the reverse route.

'What's going on?' Cath asked.

Martin quickly told her. He was only too aware of the trauma she had been through in Preston and he wasn't taking any risks. 'Text him, tell him to carry on without us; tell him we've clocked the watchers. Tell him to carry on and get the address, he doesn't need us with him to do that. Even I can tell him he's on the Digmoor estate. Then tell him to meet us back at the cash and carry. If he's not there in twenty minutes, the deal is off, and so are we.'

Cath didn't argue; she just got busy with the phone. Martin knew that the watchers might just be there anyway, and know Jay and his car. But he and Cath didn't need to follow him right into the estate. Jay could get the address and they could do their own recognisance on their own terms, at their own time. It changed nothing, and Martin would be far happier on the cash and carry's huge car park with its several exits and panoramic view. If it was all legit, Jay would meet them there presently. If he wanted his money he would be. He could still give them a micky mouse address, but Martin had no control over that. He was just glad to be away from Digmoor. He put his foot down and six or seven minutes later they were back at the car park which was still empty. This time Martin parked by the bins, with their boot towards the building.

A minute after that, Cath's phone pinged an incoming message, she glanced at it and then looked at Martin.

'He says there is no drama and no need to feel spooked, but to stay where we are, he's on his way to meet us.'

'Did he confirm that he's got the address?'

'He didn't say, but he must have.'

***

Kinsella noticed that the car behind had suddenly disappeared from view, and then his phone announced an incoming text. He pulled over to read it; it was from the press woman, Jill. He read it. 'Shit, shit, shit,' he said, before realising he had no Plan B. He waited a few minutes while he considered his next move, and then sent a quick reply. He turned his motor around and gunned the accelerator, back towards the cash and carry. He'd initially been thrilled when he clocked her driver through his binos when they'd first arrived, he couldn't believe his luck. He was as sure as he could be that the bloke was the same geezer who had been driving the motor that fateful day in Birkenhead, when he'd popped old Tommy in their back seat. Now he could take two stumps out with one ball, and then that would be that. All outstanding business sorted. That would put a smile on Lucy's face, and he always liked to do that. That was until they had bottled it.

He knew he had about five minutes before he arrived to fine tune a reserve plan. Or should he just plough in full on. He was good at that, and it didn't take too much thinking about. In fact, he could plough in at full speed; literally, the motor he was in was a knock-off from a scrap yard, so he could leave it and leg it, no dramas. As he neared the car park he decided to approach from one of the rearmost entrances, it might give him an extra few seconds of surprise. They'd be surely watching the front exit, and hopefully, be in the same spot as before; people were usually creatures of habit.

He arrived minutes later onto the car park and immediately saw that they had moved. They had parked pretty much where he had been earlier. Did that mean anything. He wasn't sure, so he decided to drive towards them at normal speed, so as not to alarm them, and then go for it. He patted the left side of his jacket to feel the reassuring presence of his handgun slung to his body in a shoulder holster.

***

Martin heard the tatty motor approaching the car park from the opposite direction before he saw it. It entered the vast space and was about 100 metres away when he heard Cath's phone ping.

'Incoming from Colin,' she said, as she picked up her phone and attended to it.

Martin kept his eyes front, concentrating 100 percent on the approaching vehicle. All was OK. Then it wasn't. Cath screamed.

'What?' Martin said, as he instinctively turned to face her.

'The guy in the speeding car near the Viaduct. He's called Jason Kinsella,' she said.

'So?'

'So he's the bouncer, Jay. The guy approaching us now.'

'Oh my God.'

'Look,' Cath said, and then held her phone up to show Martin the screen.

There was a full size mugshot of Jason Kinsella on it, and Martin immediately recognised him as the gunman who had shot Tommy Broadbent nee Dorchester. He'd only seen him for a

228

second before his gun had gone off, but that glimpse, albeit brief, would be indelibly inked onto his memory forever. Then he heard the engine note of the approaching car increase significantly, and looked up to see that it was now fifty metres away and heading straight towards them, at speed.

He didn't have time to explain anything to Cath, he just screamed at her to get out of their car fast, and take refuge behind the row of bins. 'Now,' he screamed at her when she hesitated for a millisecond.

He didn't have to tell her again. They both alighted from the car at the same time, and he saw Cath run past the bins towards the corner of the building. He must admit, the bins might be nearer, but they were on wheels; not that safe. She was making for the side of the building, which would take her to the front, and to safety. Hopefully, the driver of the approaching car, Kinsella, if it was him, would not see her. He would keep on towards their motor.

To try and ensure this and give Cath cover, Martin rushed to the front of their car and stood proud staring at the tatty red car which was now only thirty metres away and nearing very fast. It wouldn't be able to stop in time now even if the driver wanted to, which confirmed it as an attack.

He was about to dive to one side, when to Martin's horror, the car started to veer off, away from Martin and towards the side of the building; towards Cath. He knew he only had seconds to act.

Martin screamed after Cath to get out of the way in case she hadn't noticed the oncoming vehicle's course correction, and at the same time he drew his Glock pistol and took up a firing stance. The car was still in front of him, but only by several meters. It was now to one side, and would soon be level, and then past him in an instant. He would only have one crack at this.

In the next moment he fired several rounds in quick succession; all aimed, at the front grill of the car. Then he lifted his aim slightly and fired a double tap at the driver's side of the windscreen.

As the last flash of muzzle discharge flew out the end of his gun, Martin knew he had hit home as he heard the car's tyres screech and the engine note died as the car changed course once more, back towards Martin's car.

He saw directly into the face of the driver as he was struggling to haul the vehicle away from Martin's car, now trying to avoid a collision. Martin looked straight into the man's eyes. It was Kinsella alright. He also saw a mixture of hatred and fear. Martin raised his gun again, not sure how many rounds he had fired, and as he did so he could tell that Kinsella was desperately trying to steer away from him, now the hunter had become the hunted.

The car clearly wasn't responding properly, Martin must have done some damage to it, but Kinsella still managed to get it side on in an arc, which actually put it on two wheels momentarily. But all four tyres dropped back onto the tarmac as the driver's side skimmed off the front of Martin's car like a flat stone off a mill pond. The windscreen was shattered, and Martin couldn't tell if he had hit Kinsella or not. But if he had, he couldn't have done much damage as he was still wrestling with his vehicle.

The car then careered across the car park along the rear of the building, and Martin was tempted to fire after it, but didn't. It would pointless now, and probably illegal.

Cath rushed back around the corner towards him and threw her arms around him. She was clearly OK, and she could clearly see that he was. They both stood and watched as the tatty red car snaked and twisted across the car park at a reducing speed before it came to a halt near a perimeter hedge eighty or ninety metres away. The driver's door flew open; much to Martin's displeasure, and Kinsella jumped out and ran through the perimeter hedge. He'd got away. But he had failed, and now that they knew who he was, it would only be a matter of time before he was scooped up. On the plus side, Martin noticed that Kinsella was holding his left arm with his right hand as he disappeared through the privet.

After catching their breath, Martin double checked that Cath was OK, and she said that she was. But he knew it had been close, there was nowhere to hide down the side of the building. It was like a bowling alley and Cath was the skittle. Thank God Colin's message came through when it did.

'Kinsella?' Cath asked.

'Hundred percent. Got a real close look at him as his motor veered towards me. I had the gun, so I guess I became the threat.'

She nodded.

Martin added, 'You really have got nine lives.'

'I know.'

'And there is one other thing.'

'What?' she asked.

'He was wearing a brown baseball cap with red squiggly writing on it,' Martin said, and saw the shock on Cath's face as the realisation hit her.

Chapter Fifty

Three days later, Martin, Cath and Colin were at their Liverpool office having just finished an early evening meeting with Paul Harding. Jason Kinsella was on his toes, but being sought by Merseyside, North Wales and Lancashire's finest for the murders of Tommy Dorchester, Micky Mann, and Bobby Broadbent. And for the attempted murders of Martin and Cath; times two. They had managed to recover the brown baseball cap which Kinsella had left in the hedge as he fled - which Cath ID-ed - and the lab had already said was covered in gunshot residue and DNA from the sweat from Kinsella's fingers. Martin was sure that the forensics would get even tighter once further analyses were completed.

Cath kept thanking him for smelling a rat as they had entered Digmoor, and he kept thanking Colin for his timely text re Kinsella; allowing him to turn the ambush into one of their own.

Harding had also told them that ACC Sue Claire was lifting the ban on undercover and informant led operations as they had come to the conclusion that they had not been infiltrated, apart from fake Tommy. They reckoned the Clayton Rigby leak was probably down to one bad apple in their own barrel and their professional standards department were looking into that. They now considered the fake Tommy thing an isolated incident, engineered purely to keep tabs on police interest in the real Tommy. That decision had caused two further problems: one, that they still didn't know what Broadbent and Lucy were up to; though they suspected they were planning to get into forced prostitution, and why they had gone to such lengths to hide the real Tommy. Though the alleged murder of his mother would be reason enough for the latter; they just couldn't prove it. This was putting huge pressure on Colin to close down their investigations. Martin accepted that they would have to do so. The next issue they did not discuss until Paul Harding left.

'So where does that leave us with regard to Gilly, the UC?' Cath asked first.

'It means she will have to sack her deployments in the club and go back to what she was doing before.'

'A shame, but she hasn't seen anything of interest over the last few nights, and certainly no sign of Broadbent, Lucy, or Kinsella.'

Before Martin could answer he received an incoming from Gilly confirming the worst. He thanked her, and her sidekick - whoever he was - for their time, and she thanked him for paying for her to get pissed and for paying her overtime whilst she did so. He ended the call and then told the others.

'So she's not giving it one last go tonight?' Colin asked.

'She reckons not, she is en route now to meet the SIO of the job she was previously on, to discuss her re-introduction strategy, which she expects to start straight away.'

'At least Harding said that they would keep an eye on the place in case they do start to use it as a brothel for trafficked women.'

That was something, Martin thought, but he couldn't help feeling flat, and he knew the other two were the same. In fact, he felt responsible that they had not been able to keep Tommy safe, and all of them felt sorry that their interactions with Bobby had led to his death, too. Not that they could have known so in advance. The nurse's tragic death had been born about by her own addiction-driven actions and summary justice had been served on Micky Mann for killing her.

Colin suggested they grab some food from the canteen before it closed, and then they could all head home. His comments broke the void, but Martin knew it would only be a temporary reprieve.

***

Lucy had insisted that Broadbent get to the club early, so as not to put his face on offer, and she would follow up with their clients. Kinsella would drive the minibus from the arranged pickup point and she would entertain the three men in the rear. She'd noticed that something was wrong with Kinsella; he'd clearly injured his left arm, and was moody. Just before they left the pickup she gripped him by his dodgy arm and he yelped. 'The fuck's going on?' she asked.

'I'll tell you later.'

'You'll tell me now.'

'The loose ends.'

'Go on.'

'It got tasty.'

'So I see,' she said, nodding at his arm. 'Tied up though.'

'Not exactly.'

'For fuck's sake, Jason, you are becoming a liability.'

'I'll sort it, I promise. Soon as tonight is done.'

'You'd better.'

'The fuck's the hold up?' Happy Jack shouted from the back of the minibus.

'Come on,' Lucy said, and handed Kinsella her baseball cap. 'Grumpy bollocks is becoming impatient.

Lucy then spent thirty minutes in the back cajoling and sweet taking their guests. Sid from Cheshire seemed happy enough, though it was hard to tell through his leer, Happy Jack was starting to look slightly happy and Mad Mickey Moffatt hardly said a word, he just looked permanently annoyed.

They pulled into the carpark at the rear and Lucy told Jason to stay with the motor, keep his eyes open and to stay out of the shit. He just grunted. She then led Jack, Micky and Sid through the fire door and straight up the staircase to the main room on the first floor.

Inside was a large conference style table with three chairs at one side and four opposite. Sat on the far side was Broadbent, with her brother Paul to his left and Clayton Rigby to his right. On the table was a mixture of alcoholic drinks and nibbles. She asked her guests to take a seat and help themselves.

Mad Micky was the first to sit down. He nodded at Broadbent and said, 'Who are these two fuckers?'

''bout to ask the same question,' Happy Jack said, as he joined him.

Lucy said, 'This is my brother Paul, and I think you all know, or know of Clayton,' as she took the remaining chair.

Then Broadbent launched into their prearranged sales pitch with all the details and when he had finished the first phase, a moment's quiet descended.

Then Happy Jack said, 'I get by with giving the odd bent cop the odd bung. This idea of yours will never work. If I didn't know you Tommy, I'd think it was a scam.'

'And a top scam,' Sid added, 'and I know a good grift when I see one.'

'It's not a scam and it will work. In fact, it already has. Paul here was our pilot scheme,' Broadbent said, before handing over to Paul.

He had the undivided attention of all three clients as he explained how he was on the police books as a registered informant.

Lucy could clearly see the look of surprise on their faces.

'How do we know it'll actually work?' Mad Mickey asked.

Then Clayton stood up and said, 'But for these three, I'd be banged up now.' He then started to deliver his prearranged script explaining his near miss and extolling the merits of what was being offered.

Chapter Fifty-one

Martin, Cath and Colin were all sat around a table in the canteen at the NWROCU's Liverpool Branch Office when Martin's phone started to dance around the table. He picked it up, it was Gilly, and she sounded excited.

'Listen, I decided to have an hour in Banging Sounds after my meeting which didn't take long, and although the club is empty I've just seen a beautiful black woman, and three ugly looking blokes enter from the fire door and shoot upstairs.'

'Lucy?' Martin asked.

'I reckon so as one of the bar staff nodded obsequiously to her as she entered. And she entered like she owned the place.'

'Ted?'

'No, he's apparently got the night off.'

'We'll be with you ASAP, and cover you from outside until we can establish more. Perhaps the bar staff can confirm its Lucy, if you can find a way of asking surreptitiously.'

'On it.'

'Can you describe the geezers?'

'I can do better than that; I was dancing when they came in so started taking a selfie of myself prancing around, caught them all in the background. I'll send it to you.'

'That's excellent work, but can you sent it to Cath's mobile?'

'No probs.'

'And don't forget the texts if you need help.'

'No probs. In a bit,' Gilly said, and then ended the call.

Martin briefed the other two and added, 'Cath, can you grab a laptop and run an intel cell from a motor outside the club?'

'Yep, on it,' she said, as she sprang to her feet and headed towards the door. Martin could hear her phone pinging as she did.

Colin said he'd link in with Harding to arrange a van full of cops to be RV-ed nearby, and Martin said he would park near the front, and added, 'If she needs covert back up I can go in; Ted's the only one who's seen me as a cop.'

'That's a piece of luck for a change.'

Martin nodded.

'But we need to confirm that the woman is Lucy, and who is with her before we consider any action.'

Martin nodded again.

'And on what grounds we have to arrest her?'

Martin didn't nod. That was a tricky one; they did have the tenuous link to Broadbent's mother's death; but no evidence to back it up. He'd give it some thought en route.

He left Colin working his phone and grabbed a car from the garage and floored it into the city centre. Traffic was light as it was nearing eight o'clock, and he was soon parked on Dale Street, 100 metres back from the club. He could see the long-haired doorman stood alone outside, he paid Martin no attention. He was parked far enough away not to be related to the club. He rang Cath for any update.

'Gilly's done a great job with the selfie video clip, and I'm checking our databases now; oh, hang on, we have a hit on one,' she said, and then it went quiet and he could hear her tapping away. Then she came back on the line, 'Two are still being searched but one has come back and he's a drug dealer from Preston called Derek "Jack"/"Happy Jack" Jackson.'

'That name is familiar.'

'It should be, he's a target to our office; still shown as under active investigation; all sightings to be noted but no other action to be taken. I have the SIO's contact number if we need it.'

'Great work Cath, hang loose for the moment, and let's see how it develops. We still don't know what's going on, or who else we are dealing with.' Martin said, and then ended the call.

Next, he texted Gilly to make sure she was OK and told her to call him in if needed as Ted was not there. She acknowledged him and said she was going to try and find out what was happening and get back to him. He told her to take care. He would much rather be in there with her, but she was the expert, he had to defer to her advice. For now.

Then Colin rang to say he had arranged a van full of Merseyside's finest led by a uniform sergeant who was now parked around the corner and primed. Martin passed on the updates from Gilly and Cath.

'Happy Jack Jackson: that's a County Lines operation, I know the DI running it, I'll bell him and see what he wants us to do,' Colin said, and then ended the call. For the moment all they could do was to sit tight and see what develops. It might be even more prudent to do nothing and follow Lucy away when she leaves. If Broadbent left with her, great, they could consider striking, but if not, a covert follow of her might lead them to him.

***

Lucy kept quiet until Clayton finished talking, she was impressed. He'd earned his freebie; if what he'd said hadn't impressed them, then nothing would.

'And you reckon you have three stooges ready to go?' Happy Jack asked.

'Handpicked,' Broadbent said.

'And yours actually knows you, Jack,' Lucy added, stealing some of Broadbent's thunder. He glared at her, but she ignored him.

'Who is it?' Happy Jack asked.

'John Donnelly,' Broadbent quickly said.

'I was banged up with him, I'm impressed, and he's a top geezer. Are you sure he's in?'

'I've already paid him his retainer,' Lucy said, emphasising 'I've'.

Then Broadbent addressed Sid, and told him all about his stooge. Lucy let him; she'd have the last say introducing her brother Paul as Mad Mickey's man on the inside.

Chapter Fifty-two

The waiting was killing Martin so he decided to walk around the corner and introduce himself to the sergeant leading the arrest team. He told Cath, who was parked across from the club on some waste land; she said she'd keep a watching brief while he was away.

Whilst having a quick word with the sergeant he showed him a photo on his phone of Gilly and explained who she was, and to leave her alone if they went in loud and proud. He'd make sure he got her out of the way safely. The sergeant, a guy called Bill nodded his understanding. He seemed switched on, a career sergeant with over twenty years' service who'd seen most things.

Then he received a text from Gilly, she'd been chatting to the bar staff who had acknowledged the arrivals, and she has confirmed the female is indeed Lucy. There was some sort of meeting going on, she was going to try and find out more. Martin acknowledged and set off back towards his motor. He had a growing sense of unease. Then Cath rang him.

'Bingo, absolute fucking bingo,' she started with.

'We've certainly got a full house in there, but go on.'

'Second hit: Mad Mickey Moffatt, a nasty career robber from Manchester.'

'He sounds tasty.'

'He is, and get this; he's wanted by GMP for murder. He killed his girlfriend sometime last year. Been on his toes ever since. We going in?'

'Stay vigilant while I ring Colin, he might want us to wait until they leave. Might be less of a fuss. But do me a favour, ring Bill, the arrest team sergeant, and get him revved up.'

'On it,' then the line went dead.

***

After Lucy introduced Paul, Mickey Moffatt asked how it would pan out for him, exactly.

'Now I have earned their trust, it'll be easy; I'll just throw in that I know you with a bit of backstory which only you can give me. When I feed that into plod, the daft twats will eat it up for breakfast,' Paul answered.

Happy Jack laughed first, and then everyone joined in. Lucy waited until the mirth died down and then addressed all three clients. 'So unless you have any further questions; I have one for each of you, and it's the same for all three of you; 'Are you in?' She first looked at Mickey Moffatt hoping to bounce in on the back of Paul's performance.

'How much?' he asked.

'A hundred grand a year, renegotiable every twelve months,' she said, as she felt Broadbent's stare on her. She ignored it, again.

'I'll give it a go for a year,' Mickey Moffatt said.

'Me too,' Happy Jack added.

Lucy turned to face Sid, but he looked distracted. He put his right index finger over his mouth, and immediately the whole room fell silent. She watched as he quietly and slowly got to his feet and tiptoed to the door. He beckoned Mickey Moffatt to join him, which he did. Then Sid opened the door quickly to reveal a young skinny woman in her 30s, stood there. She nearly fell in the room as the door was opened.

'What the fuck are you doing?' Lucy asked.

'Just looking for the ladies,' the woman said.

Lucy recognised her; she'd been prancing around taking photos of herself when they had first entered the club. Moffatt grabbed her by an arm and pulled her into the room while Sid shut the door. The woman looked dazed and was probably drugged up, pissed, or both. 'This is a private meeting in a private area of the club,' she said.

'Sorry, just want a wee,' the woman said, and then started mincing about on the spot.

'Why didn't you use the downstairs loo?' Lucy asked.

'Couldn't, two girls were squaring up, soz, look; I've really got to wee.'

'Get her out before she pisses on the carpet,' Broadbent said.

Moffatt started to lead her back towards the door, when Lucy shouted for them to stop. 'Shown me your phone, first.'

'Why?'

'Because I saw you fannying around with it when we came in.'

Sid grabbed the woman's phone from her hand and threw it to Lucy. She couldn't open it as it was fingerprint code locked, and she was just about to demand the woman open it, when she saw an incoming message which part showed up on the home screen. It was from someone called Martin and it read: *"I'm on my way in to join you as backup."*

Chapter Fifty-three

Martin had a good view of the entire ground floor as he entered, but couldn't see Gilly anywhere. He'd sent her a quick text as he'd approached the club, but she hadn't answered. Then he realised he had forgotten about the ladies, she was probably in there. But as he approached the bar he heard a noise, like a scrapping of heels on a wooden floor and looked back and upwards towards the sound. He was horrified to see the back of Gilly disappear into the larger of the two admin rooms on the first floor. And was even more horrified to see a man's hand on her arm as she did so. He managed to get a glimpse of the side profile of the man's face: recognition forced a wild terror through his veins as he grappled for his phone in his pocket. He brought up the photos Cath had just sent him: and there he was; Mad Mickey Moffatt, wanted for murder.

As quickly as his fingers could type, Martin sent a group text to Cath, Bill and Colin with just three words, "S*trike, strike, strike.*"

He considered turning his police personal radio on, but didn't want to lose the element of surprise. The arrest plan was to send two officers to the front door to block it while the rest entered via the rear. Gilly was to ensure that the fire door was open. That was now Martin's job. He started across the dance floor towards the rear of the club when he heard more noises upstairs and instinctively looked.

The door Gilly had disappeared through flew open and a succession of people ran out and made to the rear staircase. They were led by Mad Mickey Moffatt, closely followed by a slim weasel of a man. Then the NWROCU target, Happy Jack, followed, with a face he knew well, right behind him. It was a shock to see the real Tommy in the flesh for the first time. Martin was stunned at the resemblance to their Tommy; Tommy Dorchester. Then another shock followed in the form of Clayton Rigby; things were getting very interesting. Next out was a stunningly attractive black woman - must be Lucy - and a black man; they each had a hold of Gilly who was being dragged along with them.

Martin started running as the first two or three went through the fire door; he just hoped Bill's team were already outside. But Martin's concern was Gilly. He just might be able to intercept before she was dragged out. He picked up speed, and thankfully, what few people were in his way stood back as they watched the spectacle unfold.

Gilly's abductors cleared the bottom stair and were making the short distance to the back door when Martin struck. He saw the man turn to look at him, but he was too late. He'd been too focused on his own egress to notice in time. Martin barrelled into the guy who immediately let go of Gilly.

The woman paused momentarily to look, as Martin felt a heavy fist connect with his face as the man ricocheted off the back wall and into him. The woman turned and continued to drag a struggling Gilly. She'd been slowed down by the loss of her co-abductor, but she was still going to get away. Martin had his hands full as a second blow nearly dislodged his footing. He turned towards his attacker, but as he did so, he saw a clenched fist fly over his shoulder and connect with the side of Lucy's face. The fist had painted nails, and he heard two women yelp in unison. The first, Lucy, who let go of Gilly, but continued running free through the rear door, and the second was from a voice he recognised; Cath.

Martin instinctively turned to see Cath shaking her right fist in discomfort. Gilly then ran across the dancefloor into the approaching arms of Colin, and then Martin realised he had lost his man as he saw him follow Lucy through the fire door.

Seconds later, Martin ran into the dimly lit rear yard. On the floor was a Tastered Mad Micky Moffatt, with Bill the sergeant sat on his back endeavouring to handcuff him. Two other constables were fighting with Happy Jack, and then Martin heard the electrical crackle of a further Taster discharge and saw a very unhappy Jack hit the deck. Already cuffed, against the front of a parked car, was Clayton Rigby; his long run had finally ended. Martin couldn't see the scally guy, nor could he see Lucy,

Broadbent or the other guy. He spun around and noticed a minibus which had been backed to the side wall, facing the exit, suddenly roar into life and speed across the yard. Bill's team only just managed to drag their prisoners out of the way: or else Jack would have been even less happy, Micky would have been madder, and Clayton would have never run away again.

It was all Martin could do but watch as the vehicle flew past him. It was big twelve seater; Lucy and Broadbent were climbing over the rear seats towards the front of the passenger compartment, as one of the rear doors swung open to and fro. He saw the man he'd fought with also in the front of the passenger compartment, now shutting the side slide door. The driver was Kinsella.

Then an idea hit him; he fished his mobile phone out and threw it at the open rear door space. He only had one go at it with no time to aim, hoping to miss the swinging rear door.

He watched as the phone flew through the air and bounced off the back of the rearmost seats and disappeared from view. The van turned towards Dale Street, and its rear door slammed shut as it did so. It was then gone from view.

Martin raced across the yard and out the entrance scanning the floor as he did; there was no trace of his phone. It prayed it was still in the vehicle.

He quickly wrote the minibus's registered number on the back of his hand as he was joined by Colin.

Chapter Fifty-four

Lucy glared at Broadbent in the back of the minibus as he asked, 'How the fuck did that happen?'

'I told you the club was too dangerous to use as a meeting place, but oh no, you knew best, as always; but know jack shit.'

'But, but how?' Broadbent said, weakly as all three of them were being bounced around the back as Kinsella drove like Lewis Hamilton's lesser known, but faster brother.

'That dipsy bird was obviously filth, keeping an eye on the place,' Paul offered.

Broadbent threw his arms up in surrender and then said, 'OK, Luce, but the main thing is we got away.'

'Just,' Paul said, rubbing the side of his head where the cop had punched him.

'But our clients didn't. And after all this work finally came good. They were all up for it, and now they're nicked. The job's fucked,' she said.

'I didn't notice Sid as we left,' Broadbent said.

'Forget him, he's well burnt,' She replied.

'We can always start up elsewhere; the system's good, it'll work anywhere,' Broadbent said.

Lucy didn't answer him, but turned her attention to Kinsella and asked where he was taking them.

'This is hired on a bent driving licence from a bent lender, so no probs there. We can dump it and grab a motor from my mate's car lot. I've still got the yard keys from yesterday when I was supposed to take a trade-in back. The one I left in Skem.'

'Will your mate be at the yard?' she asked.

'No, not at this time. No one will see us.'

Lucy settled down in her seat as Kinsella slowed the speed down to normal. They were safely away from the club now. And as annoyed as she was with Broadbent, what he'd said was true. They could set up again, as arduous as it would be to do so. The cops still had no idea what was going on, they'd just got lucky with Mickey and Clayton; wanted men. Poor Jack just got swept up, but as he'd done nothing wrong, as such, she was confident he would be out inside 24 hours, and the police would be happy with what they had.

Ten minutes later, they pulled up outside a backstreet car lot in Bootle. Kinsella opened the gates and drove in. Ahead of them was a portacabin which was obviously the office. Above it was a sign saying, "Dave's Bumper Car Lot". But looking at the state of the motors which lined both sides of the yard, she mused that the sign should read "Dodgy Dave's Dodgems Car Lot". They all got out of the back of the minibus and gathered in a circle in the dimly lit yard. Kinsella used the same bunch of keys he'd opened the gate with and accessed the cabin. The lights came on and gave better illumination into the yard; it made the motors surrounding them looked worse.

Lucy was mulling over what her next move should be as they waited for Kinsella. Paul was still rubbing his head and Broadbent was contritely quiet. Then the cabin lights went out, and it seemed even darker than before as Lucy's eyes adjusted. Kinsella walked over to them and joined the circle with a set of car keys in his hand.

'Where to, Luce?' Kinsella asked.

Broadbent frowned and turned to face Kinsella, and said, 'Luce, who the fuck are you calling Luce?'

'Well, Lucy, obviously,' he replied.

'You don't get to call her, Luce. Remember your place, Kinsella.'

'My place. I've just saved your ungrateful neck,' Kinsella said, before he turned to Lucy and added, 'He's a liability, Luce. I've told you that before.'

Broadbent then turned to face Lucy and asked, 'What's going on?'

'Nothing's going on,' she said to Broadbent, and then turned to face Kinsella. 'This puppy dog thinks I've got plans for him.'

'What?' Broadbent shouted.

'But I soon realised if I kept patting him on his head and tickling his tummy, he would do all our dirty work.'

'What?' Kinsella shouted.

Truth be known, Lucy hadn't been too sure which way to swing. Broadbent got on her tits most of the time, but he always brought something to the party that she couldn't. And what he'd done to his own brother appalled even her; Broadbent had been the one who was the product of an affair, not Bobby. That was why his mother never corrected him and put Bobby's mind at rest; to do so would have entailed her admitting to the affair, though her stopping Bobby speaking to his dad have effectively done that anyway. But how Broadbent had allowed Bobby to be tortured by the mistruth all these years was bad. But it also added to her attraction to him, in a perverse way.

It was why he had always sponged off his folks so much and in particular his mum. Lucy knew he would probably never have gone to her funeral, even if he could have. And as for his dad; well, he only had eyes for Bobby. Then she realised that she'd not told Broadbent about Bobby, yet. She could lay it all on Kinsella; Broadbent would believe her over him.

As for Kinsella, as much fun as he was in bed - the odd time when a tickle on the tum had not been enough - he was dead in the head. A thug. And in truth, he was the one who had in recent days become the liability. She was still head of the firm, it was just that Broadbent had never realised it. So no change.

She knew she had to close the conversation down before Kinsella said anything else. She reached into her handbag and pulled out a small automatic pistol; aimed it, and shot Kinsella in the face.

Both Broadbent and Paul just looked on, stunned, but Lucy knew that all the loose ends were now firmly tied.

Then she saw a red dot appear on Broadbent's chest. Paul had one as well. She looked down as a third red dot appeared on her own chest. Then a voice amplified itself all around the yard, *"Armed police, drop your weapons, put your hands on your heads and kneel down."*

Lucy instinctively spun around, her arm outstretched with her pistol still in her hand.

The metallic voice boomed, *"Female: drop your weapon now, or you will be shot."*

Lucy now had three red dots on her chest; she dropped the gun.

Chapter Fifty-five

The next two days were frenetic as the murder crime scene at the car lot was examined, and the prisoners were dealt with. Martin, Cath and Colin had been busy making their statements and the murder detectives from the North West Regional Homicide Unit got involved with Phil Devers and his team. Moffatt was handed over to the NWRHU for the killing of his girlfriend, and Clayton Rigby was handed over to a grateful Greater Manchester Police to be indicted for his robbery offences. Happy Jack was released from custody with no charges; he just thought he'd been in the wrong place at the wrong time. This allowed the North West Regional Organised Crime Unit to continue their covert investigations into him, he being none the wiser.

The lovely Lucy had to be dragged from her cell to the custody office to be charged with Kinsella's murder, and Phil Devers manged to obtain a remand to local custody from Liverpool City Magistrates while her other activities were further investigated. But for her shooting Kinsella at the end, Martin knew that they had little to hold her on and she would have probably made police bail while enquires continued.

Cath had shot off to Manchester to see what the search teams had found at the hotel room that Lucy and Tommy had used. They needed a breakthrough as they had nothing to charge Tommy with. They had put the murder of his mother to him, which he'd denied - as had Lucy. And as it became obvious to him, that they did not have Bobby's alleged smoking gun, Broadbent started to grin; he knew they couldn't prove anything. They had successfully obtained an extension to his custody from the magistrates, but the clock was counting down.

On the plus side, Lucy's brother hadn't stopped talking since he'd seen the inside of a police cell; probably for the first time. The whole fake snout scam thing had been a real eye-opener and Paul Harding nearly fainted when he was told all the details. Perversely, they had nothing to charge Paul with until he opened up, and then they threatened him with the offence of Assisting an

Offender when he'd helped Clayton Rigby evade justice. That had proved to be a tipping point as he now wanted to be signed up as a real informant if the charge was dropped. That was one irony for Paul Harding to consider; but at least they now knew what the whole thing had been about. And Harding could put safeguards in place to prevent such an audacious plan to infiltrate the police ever being tried again.

Martin and Colin had just arrived back at their Preston office when Cath came running in.

'You look excited.' Martin said, as he took a seat.

She held up a police evidence bag which contained what looked like a plain white plastic credit card.

'What's that?' Martin asked.

'It was found in Tommy Broadbent's real passport, which was in the hotel room. It has both Lucy's and the real Tommy's fingerprints on it,' Cath answered.

'Looks like a hotel room key,' Colin said.

'That's what I thought, at first.'

'So what is it?' Martin asked.

'One of the search team said they had seen a similar card before; it had been a key card to a storage facility. They are often plain in case the hirer loses it, so any thief finding it doesn't think all their giro days have come at once.'

'Go on,' Martin said.

'I took the search team leader's advice and made enquires of local storage firms, and bingo. If you look at the card closely there is a star in one corner which is hard to see. The second firm I rang, one in Liverpool - thought I'd try there, first - said it was one of theirs.'

'Now that is interesting,' Martin said.

'I've just left there. With the search team cop as a witness, we carefully swiped it over their electric card reader, with the exhibit still in its evidence bag, and it worked.'

'Where?' Colin asked.

'Liverpool City Star Storage; walking distance from the club. Phil Devers was sorting out a search warrant as I left. I said I'd stay away, as I'd been to the scene in the Manchester hotel, to protect against cross contamination should they find anything interesting.'

'First class work, Cath, as always,' Martin said, which Colin echoed.

The next hour was a long one, but eventually Phil Devers rang Cath and as she took the call, and mainly listened, Martin could see a smile grow across her face.

'Double bingo', she said, as she put her phone down. 'It looks like our Tommy wasn't as computer illiterate as Ted thought.'

'How do you mean?' Martin asked.

'The storage box is little more than a safety deposit box, and in it are a number of pen drives, each clearly marked. The exhibits officer has made working copies, and the first ones have been opened to reveal spreadsheets, times, dates etc. Early analysis suggests that large amounts of money have been laundered through the club by Lucy. And there are documents and emails from Tommy and Lucy. There is a lot to go through, but it seems all their nefarious and illegal practices, both here, and in Holland, are painstakingly documented. I'm going to head back over there; there is a lot to look at.'

'Looks like our Tommy had taken out an insurance policy.'

'Lucy or Tommy must have collected it from the club,' Colin said.

'Why didn't Tommy pick it up when he popped in after we'd collected him?' Cath asked.

'Perhaps it had already gone,' Martin said.

'Or Ted was there and stopped him,' Colin added.

Martin got to his feet and said, 'We can ask Ted that; as soon as we've nicked him.'

'I'll come with you,' Colin said.

***

If the first two days after the arrests had been busy, the next two were even more so. The amount of evidence on the pen drives was vast, and would take time to go through and follow up. But they soon had enough to charge both Lucy, and in some ways more importantly, Tommy, with money laundering offences. Colin had requested help from their asset recovery